ATTEND the DEAD

AUGUSTA OWENS
DOUAE BARGHOUT

To our moms.

PROLOGUE

October, 1978

Pepperback Press, Inc.

G eorgia Peterson was already dead by the time she got home.

Her daughter was the only one who saw her.

It had been a muggy night, the kind of night that made everything, every thought, every movement, fall into silence. Thunder beat at the windows, rain pattered over the roof—weak enough as it was.

Ophelia was seven years old. She was rarely on her own, and so although the rain was common, it unsettled her still. The small house had turned dark, more ominous than before with its emptiness. Every corner seemed as if it held something expectant, something waiting.

Finally, after hours of that terrible silence, that unnerving shudder of the ceiling above, the young girl heard the front door open with the click of a key, releasing the lock and her heart.

She ran faster than she ever had to the door, and there she found her mother. She had the urge to run into her arms, but for some reason, she didn't. Perhaps she sensed that something was wrong. Perhaps the realization had already set in. And yet joy still engulfed her.

Georgia leaned down, raven black hair cascading over her shoulders like tar. Her skin was tan and creamy like the autumn haze, her eyes gleaming like diamonds. There had always been such a warm energy to her, a mist of sun that seemed to surround her. Maybe it was simply how Ophelia—in all her seven-year-old awe—saw her. She worshiped her mother, and how could she not? All daughters did, at first.

Ophelia spoke, but Georgia did not respond. She continued looking down at her with those diamond eyes, always so knowing.

"Ma?"

Nothing changed. She hardly moved.

The door opened again, but this time it was her father who opened it. He stepped forward, towering over the girl. There was a shadow over him, and it seemed that his face had been sucked of all color.

And then he broke apart, his knees slamming against the floor. He shuddered with grief. "She's gone," he sobbed. "She's gone."

She's gone, she's gone, she's gone.

But where had she gone? Ophelia asked her father this, but he, too, was unable to respond. He must have been confused, she thought, for her mother was right there in the room with them.

And yet, when Ophelia turned, no one was there.

PART 1

February, 1989

Pepperback Press, Inc.

CHAPTER ONE

T he rabbit emerged from a pile of trash, timid and unsure. It had been a while since I'd seen something so beautiful, and I was gentle as I reached down, blowing a whistle between my teeth to call it near.

I was surprised when it began to answer my call, coming closer with every nervous step. Surely the smell of food was what encouraged it, emanating from the pile of cilantro leaves I'd placed there.

That's it, I thought as the creature's small fuzzy paw hit the ground.

The string beneath its feet twitched on contact. Without warning, the animal was snatched up off the ground and into the air by its neck. A quiet *snap* sounded, and in less than a moment, it was dead.

I smiled.

With care, I removed the string from its carcass. I didn't bother to set my trap once more, for it would be such a tedious task now. I was eager to leave this house, which was about as lively as the rabbit in my hands. The house had been abandoned long ago, and with time had turned into nothing more than an empty shell, the walls rotting at the edges beneath the spray-painted graffiti, broken glass on the floors, gaps in the ceiling revealing the dim sunlight above. There was some furniture inside, but that, too, was ruined. Behind me, there was a couch that was more wire than cushion. Beside me, there was a mirror covered in web-like cracks.

It was a terrible place, and I loved it.

I had always liked the quiet. I was about a mile from any semblance of civilization, and so I was at peace.

I left with haste, the rabbit tied to my side. My bicycle was by the door. Though the gears squealed with every movement, it was functional enough for me to ride home. The path was bumpy, but I was used to it. Cold air licked at my face as I rode.

Even as I neared Hinton, the silence remained. It was a quiet town, and I supposed it always would be. The sights were all too familiar to me. I whizzed past the supermarket, littered with men smoking, spitting on the concrete. I sailed across the rickety bridge, avoiding the rats feasting on a dead bird. There was a new couple in town, I'd heard, and I passed them as well. Why they would come to Hinton, I didn't know.

I slowed, my breath heavy. Beads of sweat had formed on my forehead despite the chill of winter. There hadn't been any snow for a few weeks, but the cold gloom lingered over the entire town.

My grandmother's house was covered in vines. I hadn't watered her garden for months, and all the flowers had turned brown. It was the least of our worries.

I circled around the house, and left my rabbit on the backyard table. I came in through the back door, which I'd left unlocked.

"Morning," I called, but I didn't wait for a response. There was no telling if Nan was awake yet. I made my way to the kitchen, which still smelled of burnt chicken from the night before. I was many things, but a skillful cook was not one of them.

As I washed my hands, I heard footsteps approach me from behind. I turned.

"Morning, Nan," I told her. "What're you doing out of bed?"

"I have legs, dearie," my grandmother cooed. "I'd be silly not to use them."

Even before she'd fallen ill, she'd been petite. Her thin fingers grappled clumsily with the head of her cane as she moved forward, and I helped her arrange her various pill bottles.

"How did you sleep?" I asked, if only to be polite.

"I slept well," she lied. "And you?" She smiled in a way that seemed to bring all her wrinkles together, revealing her graying teeth. Perhaps to others she may not have been model-worthy, but me, I thought she was almost beautiful.

"Me? Sleep? I've never heard of such a thing." I leaned in and kissed her forehead. She smelled like buckwheat and baby powder. I fought the urge to wrinkle my nose. "The fridge is empty, so you'll have to wait for breakfast, but I caught a rabbit for lunch."

"Rabbit. Oh, I don't know if I can stomach such a thing."

Red-hot rage spread across my vision. I slammed the pill bottle on the countertop with a *BANG* and the whole kitchen seemed to shake with the impact. I paused for a moment, collecting myself.

"Oh, dear," Nan seemed to realize her bluntness. "Rabbit is just f—"

"It's alright," I spoke smoothly, retrieving the pills that had fallen. "It's alright," I repeated. "I'll go to the store later."

I left the kitchen and found myself in my bedroom. It was smaller than Nan's, decorated only with the twin bed and pictures cut out from magazines taped to the wall. The peeling paint, despite its crude mark of time, held memories of my childhood. I still kept some old drawings in the drawers of my nightstand, though I'd taken them off the walls long ago.

Changing my clothes, I threw the old ones into my laundry basket where I could wash the dirt and grime out of them later. When I re-entered the kitchen, Nan sat at the worn table, fingers tracing the grooves etched into its surface from years of shared meals.

There was money in the kitchen drawer, hidden beneath a hand towel. "I'll be back." I leaned down to kiss her cheek again, but she reached up and ran her hand through my hair.

"My, you need a haircut, don't you?" she remarked.

I looked down at my grease-ridden hair streaming through her fingers, black as night and straight as straw. "Guess I do."

Nan looked up at me, her eyes warm as always, a certain naivety there. "Be a good girl, won't you? I'd love to see your manner match that handsome face of yours."

"Sure," I humored her.

I made my way to the door.

"Ophelia."

I turned again.

"I'd hate to see you in trouble," she said.

I opened the front door. "Sure, Nan."

***

I missed solid food. The canned shit that I always got for Nan reminded me of hospitals or baby food. As I walked down the aisle of the supermarket, grainy pop music playing above my head, I fantasized about the rabbit from earlier. I wondered if it would be worth it to cook it just for myself.

I approached the till mindlessly, waiting as the woman in front of me finished paying for her groceries. The cashier scanned one item after another. *Beep, beep, beep.*

I was next. The cashier rang up my items.

"That'll be twenty-five."

I looked up. "As in dollars?"

"No, as in rupees, obviously," he replied, a teenage boy of about my age. "Yeah, I mean dollars."

I ground my teeth as I began counting my quarters.

"Hey, don't I know you from somewhere?" the boy asked suddenly.

"No." I continued counting.

"You go to Hinton?"

"No." *Eight, ten, twelve, fourteen....*

"How old are you?"

"Eighteen," I replied. *Nineteen, twenty-one, twenty—wait.* I realized that I'd lost my count. I shoved the quarters to the side and began again.

"I should have seen you last year then," the boy continued. "What class were you in?"

"I wasn't there last year. Now, will you give me a second?"

11

"Nah, man. I know you, I'm telling you."

The coins fell off the table, clattering loudly on the floor. My ears were ringing. I looked back up at him. "*Give me a fucking second.*"

His gaze turned cold. I bent down to pick the quarters up off the floor, but I could feel his eyes still on me. After several painful seconds, I had my change returned to me and my groceries split into two plastic bags.

He looked me in the eyes.

"Don't you think you're a bit too poor to be such a fucking bitch?"

I felt my skin go hot. As much from the humiliation as the fury. Something inside me was begging to wrap my hands around this boy's neck. To wipe the satisfied look off of his repulsive, pubescent face.

Just as I felt myself begin to reach my limit, my emotions bubbling to the surface, my gaze caught something behind the cashier. A woman in the reflection of one blank TV screen.

The woman had soft yet sculpted features that I could have reproduced from memory alone. Long raven hair trailed over her shoulder, pulled into a single braid. There were creases around her eyes, made from decades of smiles. But she didn't smile now. Through the reflection, I could see her expression clearly.

She shook her head gently.

I glanced behind me, where the woman would have stood, and the spot was empty.

Slowly, I took in a breath. I turned back to the boy. "Have a nice day." I took my receipt from his hand and separated myself from him.

I barely made it out the door.

"Shit!" I heard him cry. I spun around. "Shit, I know you! I do! You're Ophelia. The junior who dropped out. I fucking knew it." He laughed, pointing in my direction as he approached. "Hold on." He reached for my arm.

This time, I simply could not help myself. I saw another glimpse of the woman in the reflection of the store window before I shoved him against the wall.

He had no chance to cry out. My bags had already fallen onto the concrete when he hit the brick wall. I brought him down off his feet, and struck him in the neck. I didn't know what I was doing at first. I only knew I had to hurt him. Guys like him, they didn't learn lessons easily. So I swung. And I kicked.

I got three hits in before a fist met my face.

I staggered back, a hand over my eye. I saw another guy there, slightly older, his fists in the air. "*Back up,*" he shouted at me, his voice gravely and cold. "Get the hell out of here before I call the police." The cashier was on the ground still, coughing.

I didn't hesitate. I grabbed my bags off the ground and ran.

***

I couldn't shake the image of the woman in the reflection. Her disapproving gaze. It wasn't the first time I'd seen her, of course, but today felt different.

My body ached as I walked through the door. I emptied the groceries into the kitchen, paying little mind to where Nan could be now.

I was alerted to her presence with the sound of her wet cough. I found her sitting on the sofa, spreading germs onto her sleeve. Another item of clothing that I would have to wash. I brought her a cloth to wipe her face with, which she accepted, her hands trembling.

She finally looked up at me, the wrinkles around her eyes deepening with surprise. "What's all this?" she asked, sticking a finger at my eye, where I could feel the warm tingling of blood drawing into a bruise.

"I fell."

The side of her lip curled into a less-than-pleasant smirk. "I'm not as quick as I used to be, but I'm still not quite as stupid as you think I am."

"Why would I think that?"

She gave me a harsh look before returning her face to the cloth and coughing up a ball of phlegm.

I sank beside her on the sofa, which creaked beneath my weight. I thought of how frail Nan must be now, how little effect her own weight would have on the small sofa. Her bones were brittle, her skin like paper. The television was still playing, the colorful lights reflecting off her dark blue eyes. After a while, I began to think that she had decided to drop the whole thing altogether, but she spoke again.

"You're a brave girl, Ophelia," she muttered, almost offhandedly. "Too brave sometimes."

I stayed quiet, my gaze on the TV.

"You have that in common with your mother."

Her words hung in the air, a delicate thread connecting the past and present. The mention of my mother always held that power, that suffocating shadow of grief. One might think that the years would turn to comfort with her loss. And yet.

Cheerful banter sounded from the television set.

When I glanced to my side, there was a hand on the arm of the sofa that was not my own, a silver ring on one finger. It wasn't Nan's.

I looked away, pretending I did not notice the presence of the figure beside me.

My studied ignorance had become routine over the years. There was an art to not giving a shit. As far as I was concerned, the fact that I occasionally saw people who were not there was little more than a personal inconvenience, and as long as I kept it to myself, nothing bad could come of it. Anyway, nothing good would ever come of telling people that I could see my dead mother. I detested the idea of being institutionalized—not that anyone would really care enough to put me in an institution.

I had my responsibilities in this house, and that was enough. I glanced again at Nan. How could she stomach it, I wondered, speaking so casually of her own late daughter? How could she sit there in her own sick beside me and be as she was? I always had a feeling that I would become her when I was older, that it was inevitable. I wasn't sure if that was still true.

You're a brave girl, the words echoed dimly, though this time they seemed to emanate from the figure beside me.

Leave me be, I thought as loudly as I could. *If you cannot help me, leave me.*

The figure dissipated.

It had been years since I'd missed my mother.

Chapter Two

T he day began with a sparkly pink pen. The strange choice of stationery was what Janie used to write down her orders. The ink itself wasn't even pink. The outside was only for show.

I watched her from across the room as she jotted things down for the mid-twenties couple in front of her. *Veggie burger (no onions), curly fries, small latte, medium banana milkshake, two straws.* Her handwriting was messy, but legible, all round scribbles with hearts over every "i". Perhaps one might think it was part of her charm. I didn't.

She made her way around the corner where I was leaning on an empty plastic bin. I'd taken my boots off and left them on the floor, but none of the customers could see, so Janie didn't scold me. Not verbally, at least. She did shoot me a sharp look before ripping a paper out of her notepad and handing it to the boy in an apron passing by.

"You're up at table five," she informed me as she fluffed up her dishwater blonde hair in the reflection of the metal register. "Fix your apron before you go out. You look like a mess." She took out a comb and teased at her mane a bit more.

"Tell me what you really think," I muttered, but she didn't seem to hear me. I tightened my charcoal gray apron as she suggested, slipped my boots back on, and proceeded out to table five. When I returned, she was gone again.

My eyes scanned around the diner. I liked to observe the customers sometimes, to make stories in my head about what they were doing and why they were here. It wasn't difficult, since I knew the majority of them by name. That's how it was in Hinton, when this diner was one of few. The place wasn't much, but in *this* town, one might even say it was luxurious. I, on the other hand, was too familiar with it now to like it. My one-year anniversary of working in this place had passed a few weeks ago. One year of pathetic paychecks and enduring my coworkers, most of whom would apply for and quit the job as they pleased.

The interior of the diner was less than elegant. The tables were covered with red and white checkered cloth. The room was surrounded by decorations placed in poor taste; empty alcohol bottles lined up on the shelf, an old, decorative shotgun hung up below them. Posters were pasted onto the wall, containing images of coffee beans and steaming waffles, everything tinted brown. That was what happened when you had a place like this run for thirty years with teenagers as your only cleaning staff.

Not all teenagers, I thought as Pam came trudging past, a bucket in one hand and a graying rag in the other. She grunted loudly as she leaned over an empty table, her wet rag making a *splosh* as she smacked it over the surface, wiping it clean. Pam was well into her sixties, but

I'd honestly thought she was older before Janie had told me. None of us were sure just how many decades she'd worked at the diner. She was short and rather round, with thinning gray hair that she kept chin-length. I didn't think I'd ever seen her without her bright, frosty lipstick. Interestingly, I often saw Janie smothering her mouth with a remarkably similar shade.

Janie wasn't a teen anymore, either. She'd turned twenty a while ago. The assistant chef scrambling through the back closets was a year older than me, and the other server with whom I often shared a shift—I didn't remember his name and he never mentioned his age—his voice would often crack when he spoke, and he had exactly five black hairs sticking out from his upper lip.

I hated all of them.

It was the manager, John, who I loathed the most. If shitty pay and even shittier hours wasn't enough, it seemed that he was constantly determined to make my life a living hell. He was as wide as he was tall, and he had the voice of a smoker—the breath of one, too. He had to have been about forty, though I'd witnessed him throw strange looks at Janie more than once. Every now and then, I wondered if he'd ever given her more than glances. I tried not to let my mind wander.

Janie and I began cleaning, wiping down tables, and arranging ketchup bottles. The sky was dark, and when I let my headphones fall to my shoulders, I could hear the crickets outside the windows. As we worked, each of us on opposite sides of the room, something shattered. With a start, I turned to see Janie racing for the dustpan and broom, a broken plate scattered over the floor.

The night wore on, and I began to catch onto the other girl's nerves, her occasional fidgeting. At this time of the day, she'd normally be relieved and exhausted. But she stayed tense. I watched her more closely.

"Gotta piss," I called over to her before making my way to the toilets, hidden around the corner.

I approached the girls' bathroom and opened the door, only to let it fall closed again without entering. I then carefully stepped back towards the main room, peeking around the corner.

I caught sight of shaking hands behind the register.

So, that was her angle. I supposed I should have seen it coming, but I was unimpressed as the ever-so-innocent Janie slipped a few bills into her pockets, before closing the register once more. She made her way hurriedly back towards the tables, taking the broom in her hands again as if nothing was wrong. I could not help but feel embarrassed for her.

I soundlessly stepped back into the bathroom and flushed the toilet before entering the main room again.

"Forget to wash your hands?" asked Janie, her voice forcedly smooth. She had one hand in her pocket. Her attempt to mask her nerves was practically nauseating.

"Nah. I just wiped them on your sweater back there."

She frowned at me, then rolled her eyes with a scoff. She probably told herself she was too good to dignify my words with a response, but in truth, she simply wasn't clever enough to quip back.

"Remember to lock this up?" I asked her as I approached the register.

I took joy in her discomfort. "Mhmm. It's all locked." She slouched a bit. Overcompensation.

She clocked out soon after our interaction, and didn't bother saying goodbye. Not that I wanted her to. Before she left, I caught her eyeing her sweater on the hanger.

In my solitude, I finished the last few tasks before closing. I changed the water filter and sprayed down the countertop. When I passed by the register for the last time, however, something pink caught my attention.

What a child, I thought, looking at the pink sparkly pen next to the register. How dull could she be to have left such a thing that only *she* used next to money that only *she*—or I—could have stolen? I studied the pen for a moment, contemplating. I thought of every snide comment she'd made to me over the last year, every disgusted look when I spoke, her subtle determination to make me feel as small as possible.

You know that sense you get that you're being watched? I had it often.

I slipped the pen into my pocket.

***

It wasn't long before I returned to the empty house. Not my grandmother's house. While that one may have been just as lifeless, it was far from empty. Most days, I found it noisy and cluttered. With Nan coughing and hacking every two minutes, it was far from silent, and I needed the silence of the abandoned house in the woods. I'd been that way for most of my life, craving solitude. It was out of choice, not necessity; Janie and the others from work had always offered for me to accompany them on days when they went partying and whatnot, but after my first dozen-or-so rejections they'd stopped asking.

I simply did not like people. Most people were stupid and mean and lacking self-awareness. It wasn't a spiteful notion—it was just true.

I rode to the old, abandoned house on my bicycle once more, always taking the bumpier path to avoid the busier roads and side-eyeing loiterers. Here's where Nan would call me an *antisocial teenybopper*. Technically, I was more likely to get kidnapped along this route, but nothing so exciting would ever happen in Hinton.

A blanket of calm came over me when I stepped into the house, floorboards groaning beneath my boots. The place smelled like ash and dead things, and the lightbulbs above probably hadn't shone for a decade. In my head, this place was how things should be. This place was honest, the only true reflection of the world within a bike ride's distance.

I retrieved a sandwich from my backpack, then sat against a pillar and ate it slowly, savoring the expired sour cream and cucumber. I crunched the aluminum in my fist and let it fall to the ground where it would stay. The wind hummed distantly outside like an ode to my sinful littering.

With my stomach half satisfied, I lay on the cold, dusty floor, lungs expanding and deflating with musty air. I became conscious of every inch of my skin, the tips of my fingers at my sides, the space between my toes, the back of my head. I closed my eyes and allowed myself to relax. Memories, once buried and forgotten deep inside my mind, clawed their way to the surface.

I'd never been exceptionally talented when it came to self-control, but in the right environment, I could force myself to relax. Meditation was one of the things I remembered my mother teaching me—one of the few things. It was funny to imagine a little kid practicing mindfulness, but nevertheless, it helped me now.

But every now and then I would lose myself in my thoughts as I tried to quiet them. Like swimming through a current and being swept off course.

I remembered the day I found out that Nan was ill. It was a moment etched in the crevices of my consciousness. The fear, the helplessness, and the realization that life was about to change. Even then, the weight of my decisions pressed down on me. My burden of responsibility had already begun to close in before I'd reached my junior year of high school.

I couldn't envision the face of the doctor who had told us the news. When this memory came back to me, his face always seemed smudged out. I remembered his voice, though, something gruff and dire.

"There are a number of treatments that can work us through this issue," he said. He smiled then, as if this was a great solution. I had the impression that he cared more about our feelings than Nan's health, that he was willing to embellish his words for the sake of preventing panic.

Soon after that, we'd moved Nan into Mom's old room, which had more sunlight and was free of dust that would clog her lungs. After the switch, it seemed for a while that she was beginning to get better. She was happier, talking more in the early mornings, and she didn't need my assistance to get out of bed. It only took another month for things to go downhill again. Things became worse than before, her mood always dark and her weight dropping dramatically. It felt that I had to be with her for every waking second, and so I missed more and more days of school. It became impossible to juggle my education and her needs.

I didn't waste any time. The day I turned sixteen, just at the beginning of junior year, I dropped out of school. Nan hated the idea, but it was my choice. And what was she going to do? She could hardly take a step without my help, much less control *my* actions. I'd never much liked school anyway. Not the social aspect, at least. The learning part hadn't been so bad. I enjoyed reading and studying, but I had no time. That was a sacrifice I *was* willing to make.

"It's not worth it," my nan told me one night before my birthday. Behind her words, I heard only *I'm not worth it.*

"We've been over this," I reminded her.

"I still think you're being silly."

Silly. How dare she call me names when I had done so much for her?

"Ophelia," she began again. "Don't you want something else? Something...aspirations?"

"And what are you, a psychologist?" I snapped at her. I knew that was far from true. Nan herself had never gone to college, but I knew it was something she'd always wanted for me. She'd spent her years as a housewife with my late grandfather, and though she'd never said it, it was clear that she had wanted more.

As time went on, I tired of the repetitiveness of it all, as I knew I would. Anger became my constant companion. Nowadays, I rarely had a conversation without having the dull urge to throttle the other person. It hardly mattered if that person was a stranger or my sick grandmother. It wasn't to say that I wasn't sympathetic to her. I was.

My emotions resurfaced then, as I laid on the floor. The hair on my arms stood up on end.

When I opened my eyes, I was no longer alone.

I was surrounded by dozens of misty figures in the once-empty room. People who I didn't recognize; a woman in a sun hat, an old weathered man with a walking stick, a police officer, a child in pigtails wearing roller skates. None of them seemed to notice me, only wandering around the small space as if searching for something. The dead were always searching, waiting, but not quite wanting.

I rose to stand, making my way through the small crowd. I was careful to avoid them, for it was never pleasant to touch one of them. I stopped in front of a small boy with smatterings of freckles across his cheeks, his hair drowning in gel. He wore a band T-shirt, stained with bleach.

I waved a hand in front of his face. Sometimes I could get their attention, but sometimes they were too preoccupied. His eyes ventured to the side, focused on something that I could not see.

The edges of his silhouette began to blur, losing all sense and definition. He turned, and his body faded to mist, lost to me once more.

I focused my attention on the woman in the police uniform, her hair pulled into a tight bun at the nape of her neck. I spoke, trying to grab her attention as I had with a boy, but she, too, vanished after a moment. Soon, I felt myself losing focus. As much as I attempted to calm myself and find that serenity that I'd acquired before, I could not stabilize them.

After a minute, I was alone in the room again.

I looked around, searching for remaining traces of the people I'd seen, the ghosts.

25

I saw people like them often, strangers who would come and go that nobody else could see. They always had a different air about them, a distinct aura. As I saw it, there were only two reasonable explanations for what I saw. One: I was a paranoid schizophrenic and everything I saw was purely hallucination. Or, two: I saw ghosts. Real ghosts. Like, supernatural, horror-film, dead people *ghosts*. Personally, I felt more comfortable with the second option.

No matter which of the two possibilities was true, one fact remained the same. This was not something I could share or confess to anyone.

It was far from difficult, anyway, for I had no issue with being private. Besides, whether it was schizophrenia or ghost-vision, I'd never be short of company.

I knelt to the floor and brushed a hand over the dusty floorboards, dust that hadn't been disturbed for years. I'd seen the ghosts walk over these boards one after the other, and yet, no footprints.

I left the house and began my return to Hinton, thoughts of ghosts and spirits pushed to the back of my mind.

CHAPTER THREE

The day began with a letter. Usually, I received letters from my father once every few weeks. They tended to be short and flavorless, which suited him well. In one letter, he'd written exactly one paragraph in which he described what he had eaten for breakfast that day, and notified me that he would not be visiting Nan and me anytime soon. It had been the first time we'd heard from him in a month, but with the check attached, I couldn't really complain.

I felt the letter before opening it, squishing the white envelope to test the thickness. It was certainly too thick to be just a letter. I tore it open and my fingers groped around the slivers of paper, but I cut myself on the edge. Sucking the blood from my finger, I began to empty the envelope onto the table.

I checked every sheet, every single one. There were copies of my official documents; social security card, birth certificate, and every other important piece of paper that I never would have been able to find myself. I couldn't remember the last time I'd seen any of these.

"There's no money," I whispered below my breath.

Finally, I reached the last wretched sheet, addressed by my father on the front, folded neatly. Trembling, I opened it.

Dear Ophelia,

I trust this letter finds you well. Your grandmother, too. I'm writing to let you know that the time has come for you to return to school. I know you'll be averse to this, but it's not a suggestion.

My financial support will continue once you're enrolled. Until then, I'm withholding the money. For the sake of keeping this letter short, I will tell you that I may have found new opportunities for you, should you choose to pursue them. Furthermore, I refuse to keep enabling a high-school dropout.

Do not disappoint me.

Sincerely,
Your father.

My muscles seemed to lock in place, my blood boiling with rage. Never had I felt so much hatred, so much loathing. The *nerve,* I thought. Everything I had done, every sacrifice I had made up to today, and my horrid ancestor believed it appropriate to withhold the already pathetic support that he had managed to send over the years.

I slammed my hands against the wall, which shuddered with the impact. I nearly ripped the letter right there and then.

"What is it?" Nan asked with a start. As if she could do anything to help.

"It's him," I replied, the words passing through my teeth like venom. "It's that no-good, ignorant, fat-headed little weasel of a man."

She coughed. "Otherwise known as your father?"

I shot her a look, but her expression remained serene, unbothered. I wanted to scream at her, too. I wanted to grab her and shake some sense into her. Was she too obtuse to realize what he had done, or did she just not care? Either way, it made me burn even more.

"He's not going to send anymore money," I told her, making an effort to keep my words even. What I really meant, though, was that he would not send *her* anymore. None of the money he sent benefited me, none of it was intended *for* me. It barely covered the life-saving medicine which my grandmother needed, much less three meals a day. It was so little, and now nothing.

"Unless," I began, scratching my fingernails along the wooden table. "Unless I go back to school." I looked to her, expecting that she would share my same incredulous reaction.

But once again, she was unaffected. She raised a trembling hand, the other gripping her cane. "Maybe it would be good for you."

"*Good* for me?" I guffawed. "Have you forgotten why I left in the first place?"

"Oh, I know it's difficult—"

"I left for *you*, Nan. To take care of you." What could I do to get it through her head? Was there truly no one who could understand me?

Nan sighed and picked the letter off the table. She slid her glasses down her nose and read the words carefully. "'An opportunity'," she muttered. "Whatever could he be talking about?"

"You're asking me to explain my father?" I ripped the letter from her hands.

I would not be a puppet, that man would not be my puppeteer. My senses were clear, my intentions decided as I gathered up the documents and shoved them into a drawer like trash.

"Don't be a child," Nan scolded.

I ignored her, fighting the urges that threatened to bubble to the surface.

Over the following days, despite all my decisiveness and my cold resolve, a debate raged within me. My thoughts were riddled with pros and cons. (*Pros: Education! Learning and worldly experience, a high-school diploma to hang on my wall. Cons: Human interaction. And I can't kill myself.*)

Work seemed more gloomy than before, more pointless. The extra money that I made for slaving away at that place wasn't enough to cover our expenses without the checks from my father. I tripped over myself with trays in my hand, breaking two glasses and one plate in the span of a week, and I was rude to customers without meaning to be. One day, I let the word *cunt* slip from my lips while attempting to explain that I could not serve a vegetarian steak.

"You've gotta get your act together, girlie," another one of the servers remarked during one of my shifts. We called him Dee, but I couldn't remember his real name. He was a skinny guy who looked younger than he was. He seemed to saunter wherever he went, his spine rarely straight, and I wondered just where he had found such confidence in that ugly orange hat he wore. "What's up with you?" It seemed he could not contain his curiosity.

"Nothing's up with me," I reassured. "Just tired."

"Tell me about it." He wiped a bead of sweat from his brow.

I glanced at him and wondered when he had last showered. While looking, I stumbled over the threshold into the kitchen. He only chuckled as he passed me by.

The letter had put me on edge, and I could not fight the effect it had on me. I spent every waking moment either internally cursing my father or cursing myself for depending on him. When it came to actually complying with his demands, I couldn't bear to consider it. The thought made my skin crawl.

But what other option did I have?

***

Nan's condition worsened and within days to the point that she couldn't leave her bed. We'd both seen it coming, and yet it still felt too sudden. With the arrival of the letter and my grandmother's new bedridden state, tension in the house was at a breaking point.

The days passed slowly. The hands of the clock seemed to move reluctantly, lazily. I was always either at work or caring for Nan, waiting patiently at her bedside for anything she needed. I couldn't return to the abandoned house, but I discovered other ways to pass the time. I found some old books of my mother's, stored in dusty plastic bins beneath her bed. They were classic, poorly-bound novels that had somehow survived over the years. Each one had her messy handwriting scrawled in the margins, her name on each front page. There, in my mother's old room, I would read to myself, listening to the sounds of Nan's breathing in the background. I began with *The Outsiders,* and then *The Bell Jar.* I read them hungrily, consuming each word. It was the first time in a while that I'd been left to wait, to pass the time with few responsibilities other than making sure that Nan didn't choke on her own vomit. I began to bring the books with me to work, breathing in Sylvia Plath beneath the counter.

As I read one afternoon on the stool beside the cash register, my boots thrown aside, Janie approached.

"You haven't seen my pen, have ya?"

"The pink one?" I asked absentmindedly, turning another page.

"Yeah. With sparkles."

"As if I'd come anywhere near your girly-ass pen."

My mood had not improved since Nan's new state. I hadn't slept for days, and I kept having to pick up new shifts at the restaurant. Any time I could take to work, I took it. I convinced myself that the toll it had taken was all in my head. A discipline thing. And I could be disciplined.

I tried writing to my father more times that I could count, but didn't receive so much as a peep from him. Not even a phone call.

I am all alone. And not in a good way this time. No one would come to help me, and I was far from capable of producing the amount of money we needed for Nan's medications as well as the house bills. I couldn't fight the tightness in my chest.

The idea that I had a choice in all this began to fade away. I could feel that something was going to change soon, most likely for the worse. It was the first time in a while that I felt real fear.

The hospital was not a pleasant place to return to, but Nan and I found ourselves there anyway. I sat idly beside Nan's bed, as always. I thought that maybe, at this point, I should have been wearing a name tag that described me as the official *sitter that sits next to the bed*.

The hospital seemed so clean and so dirty at the same time. I couldn't escape the harsh glow of the white lights, each flicker only intensifying the sterile atmosphere.

In the corner of the room stood a ghost. At least, I was fairly sure it was a ghost. He was a tall, thin man wearing a light blue hospital gown that draped over his frail bones, and while nothing about him looked particularly ghostly, the fact that none of the nurses who had been in and out of the room had acknowledged him—that had clued me in. Unlike most of the figures I saw in my day-to-day, his image was clear, no blurred lines around him, no ominous glow in his skin. I supposed the reason for his clarity was obvious. So much death in this place. For all I knew, he could have died in this very room.

The air reeked of rubbing alcohol and illness, a nauseating combination that seeped into my very being. If I could have asked to be sedated with Nan, I would have.

Her eyes, dark blue and opaque like mine, were now closed. She looked calmer this way. I held her fragile hand, which was cool and damp, blue veins popping up out of her papery skin. The machines around us beeped and whirred, providing a techno soundtrack to the emotional turbulence within me.

Should I go back? Should I give my pride away? I found it hard to believe that my father would really care either way.

I felt emptier than before. I hadn't caught a glimpse of my mother for days, and I began to wonder if perhaps the ghost had finally left me in peace.

The door clicked open behind me.

"Have you made a decision, dear?" This was the doctor, a small man with close-cropped hair and round glasses. The logical part of me knew that this man was not the one who had given Nan her first diagnosis, but whenever I looked at him, it was all I could think of, as if I was seeing the monster of my nightmares. "Have you thought about the surgery?" he inquired again.

Surgery.

The spinal stenosis that Nan had been diagnosed with had gotten severe enough that the doctor had concluded the meds weren't enough to treat it. Nerve damage, when left without proper treatment, could have disastrous consequences. The surgery in question that the doctor had suggested was a spinal fusion. It sounded like something out of a bad sci-fi movie to me, but he'd assured me that it was, in fact, a real procedure.

"How long can she go without it?" I asked him without raising my head, my voice low and tired. Still, I tried to protect my pride.

I could feel his piercing, educated eyes on me, pity emanating off of his clean, white coat. "A little while," he answered finally. "A couple months, if you're lucky, but the sooner it's done, the better results we'll see."

"And how much will it cost us?

The doctor hesitated. Maybe he could tell just by looking at me how hard his next words would hit.

"About twenty thousand. More or less." But by the look on his face, I could tell he'd given me the low end of his estimate.

I felt sick to my stomach.

I looked down at her again, her chest rising and falling shakily with shallow breath. It seemed that if I moved too quickly, she would fall apart. One wrong decision, and she would be gone.

Now was the time.

I had to decide what I was willing to sacrifice.

Come on, Ophelia.

I raised my head to meet the doctor's eyes.

CHAPTER FOUR

I couldn't remember the last time I'd taken an exam.

Memories of scratching pencils and the smell of anxiety filled my mind. I could recall the nervousness that used to fill me in the days before, the importance that it had all held then. It was my future, my worth, my intelligence defined down to one letter. Back then, it had been *A for Acceptable, B for Bad, C for...* well, C was never an option.

Now, something had changed. I was calm, my hands steady, my heart rhythmic. My chair was comfortable, and I didn't care enough to correct my posture.

I swept my pencil against the smooth, white paper, question after question. Part of it was exhilarating, like a game or a puzzle in the newspaper. I no longer despised the sound of the buzzing radiator, but rather it soothed me.

Beside me, I spotted the guidance counselor out of the corner of my eye. She sat at her own desk, a little bird-shaped decoration near her wooden name plate. I could feel her eyes on me, and I guessed that she was probably waiting for my own gaze to wander, maybe to a hidden cheat-sheet beneath my sleeve—which she'd already checked before the timer started. As I rolled them up to my elbow, I wanted to ask, *Does the cavity search come now, or later?* but I had restrained myself.

The answers came to me easily. I hardly had to think before my pencil filled in each little black circle on the page. When I finished, I slid it across the desk. The name plate rattled a bit with the force of how I did it.

The counselor glanced up at me over her cat-eye glasses, her pearl neck chord swaying with her movement.

I'd had plenty of run-ins with the school counselor in my first two years at this same school. But this woman wasn't familiar to me, so she must have come in this year or last. Her skin was caked with makeup, piling in the crevices of her aged face. She wore a bright pink sweater with synthetic fur lining the edges around her neck. Her appearance reminded me of something I'd seen in a zoological documentary, a bird covered in bright colors and dramatic silhouettes in an evolutionary attempt to scare off predators. I wondered distantly if she thought of herself as prey.

"Done already?" asked the woman. Her name plate read *Dorothy Quirk*. I enjoyed imagining just how much she'd been bullied in her own highschool years for that name.

"Mhmm," I replied wordlessly.

She watched me closely. "What was that, Miss Peterson?"

I think I felt my eye twitch just then. "Yes."

"Yes, ma'am," she corrected.

I fantasized about stabbing her with her own desk decoration. "Yes, ma'am."

The rest of orientation went well; absolutely no violence involved outside of my own imagination. After a couple more arbitrary questions, she led me out of the office, which was decorated like the inside of a hyper-feminine serial killer's mind. She took me down the white-washed hallway, where I could hear the chaos of the classrooms at our sides. Chairs scraping against floors, erasers banging on walls, teenagers screaming like toddlers. I envisioned myself walking the gauntlet, ducking against thrown fruit as my jailer led me along.

We paused before one of the classrooms, this one quieter than the rest. Quirk knocked gently before entering, and I caught a glimpse of the inside. It looked like an English classroom, book covers lined up on the walls, a small woman with a short bob above her shoulders sitting at the teacher's desk. Each student was wordlessly scribbling away in notebooks, glued to their own desks.

While I remained standing out in the hall behind her, Mrs. Quirk stuck her bird-like neck into the classroom and motioned to one of the students, a honey blond kid seemingly very absorbed in his work. He did not seem surprised by the acknowledgement, and quickly closed up his materials before rising out of his seat. The rest of the class watched him closely as he weaved between tables and made his way to the guidance counselor.

The door shut loudly after him. I was face to face with mister honey blond.

Upon closer examination, he seemed a lot older than I'd thought at first. He had the classic, fuckboy fluffy fringe resting above his eyebrows, thick and darker than the rest of his hair. He was sharp lines all around, chiseled like the statue of an ancient Greek hero. His eyes, though. They didn't quite match the rest of his face. They were brown and deep, a bit rounder. They made him look nicer, and smarter than I'd originally pegged him to be. However, I knew better than to judge by looks.

I expected him to greet me. He didn't. Maybe he expected *me* to greet *him*. I didn't either.

Quirk seemed to sense the tension in the air. I didn't mind, but she bristled instantly. Without another moment's wait, she spoke. "Ophelia, this is Connor. Top student, really. He's volunteered to help you around in these first few days. Isn't that nice?"

The boy flinched.

"Really nice," I agreed, my words a bit too sharp to sound genuine. Connor glanced at me again, possibly catching onto my falseness.

"Mhmm," Quirk hummed. "Anyhoo, Connor is a year ahead of you, but I trust he'll be able to help you out nonetheless."

"A year ahead of me?" I asked.

"Yes, he's a senior," Quirk informed me.

I studied her for a moment, trying to read her properly. "I thought the point of my exam was to see which year I'd be in." It was true that I had dropped out in the first months of my junior year, but at this point I was two years older than those kids. When I'd been given the exam and made aware of the possibility that I could join the seniors, I had thought it was at the very least *that*. A possibility.

Quirk pursed her lips, once again uncomfortable. She flipped her graying hair over her shoulders, the fur on her collar shuddering as if she really was one of those strange birds, trying to make herself seem bigger. "Well, you were a junior when you left, weren't you? When you never complete the year, dear, you don't get to simply skip over it." An ugly grin spread across her face. "I'm sure it's been a while since

40

your time in the education system, but we have certain rules here. No shortcuts, sweetheart."

Sweetheart. Oh, how I'd like to hurt her.

I played out every possible scenario in my head, everything I could say to her. It would have been so easy to submit to my urges then, so simple.

But Connor spoke before I could respond. He smiled kindly, those brown eyes gleaming like a well-intentioned kitten. That smile was almost sickeningly sweet. "I, for one, admire your cavalierness, Mrs. Quirk."

The woman blinked stupidly, then rustled with satisfaction. "Why, thank you."

A smile pulled at the corner of my lips, an involuntary reaction. A kind I hadn't had for a while. Connor's gaze fell on me again, and for a moment, I thought there was an amused understanding there. I thought I saw something underneath. Something I liked.

My smile fell. A cold chill ran up my spine.

After Mrs. Quirk left—which was the most helpful thing she'd done for me thus far—Connor led me through the labyrinthine corridors of the school, moving in confident strides. He pointed out various classrooms, the cafeteria, and the small library. It was all too familiar to me, but I did not tell the boy that it wasn't my first time in the school. No need to tarnish my reputation so quickly.

I glanced at him from the corner of my eye, trying to gauge his mood. He seemed focused, his brow furrowed in concentration as he navigated the familiar paths of the school.

It had been a while since I'd spoken to anyone in a non-hostile context, so I was careful with my tone. I knew the off-putting effect I could have. "So, you volunteered for this?"

He didn't look at me. "Not exactly."

I couldn't tell if he was just naturally reserved or it was me that he didn't like. But then again, I wasn't exactly in the mood for small talk either. I was only here for the money, after all.

As we reached the end of the school, Connor stopped in front of a nondescript classroom door and turned to me. His expression remained impassive.

"Your class," he stated.

Before I could say anything—not that I planned to—he turned his back and left.

*Ophelia: **0***

*Strangely literate boy who I didn't immediately loathe: **1***

*Guidance counselor who's never picked up a book in her life: **0***

I entered the classroom, hoping for a moment of peace after the tension-filled encounter with Mrs. Quirk and the silent tour with Connor. But my hopes were quickly dashed as I realized that the classroom was filled with a cacophony of noise. My attention drifted to the front of the room where the teacher's desk sat. It was cluttered with papers, textbooks, and various knick-knacks, giving the impression of disorganization. At least I wouldn't stand out in that sense. The surface of the desk was marred with coffee cup rings and ink stains, a testament to the lack of care it had suffered. As for the students' desks, there wasn't one that wasn't covered in scribbles and scratches. *Did he lead me into a middle school classroom?* I wondered to myself.

The teacher herself was leaning against the front desk, her posture slouched and her gaze unfocused. She appeared to be completing the crossword in the newspaper, a chewed-up pen in her hand. There was no lesson in progress that I could tell.

The classroom had an air of neglect about it, as if it had been forgotten by time. The walls were lined with faded posters and cracked paint, peeling away in places to reveal the dull concrete beneath. The windows were frosted with a layer of grime, blocking out the weak sunlight and casting the room into shadow. A chill hung in the air, seeping into my bones and sending shivers down my spine. Despite the feeble attempts of the ancient radiator in the corner, the room remained stubbornly cold, the temperature barely rising above freezing. The floors in the back of the room were littered with tiny puddles and haphazardly strewn buckets, evidence of a leaky roof that had plagued the classroom for years. I thought I could hear the faint *drip—drip—drip* of water hitting the floor.

Strangely, I felt at home.

If it wasn't for the students.

While each of them remained in their respective seats, it didn't stop them from throwing paper planes, gum, and spit wads across the room. Some of the chairs were missing legs, forcing students to balance on the remaining three. The kids in the room were a motley crew. They huddled together in their coats and scarves. I almost expected their breath to form clouds in the air. As for the few that weren't trying to raise a ruckus, their faces were pale and drawn, dark bags beneath their eyes.

As I observed the new faces in my class, a wave of amusement washed over me despite the grim atmosphere. They looked like a cast

43

of characters straight out of a low-budget horror movie—each one more bizarre than the last.

There was the girl with the frizzy hair that resembled a bird's nest, her glasses perched precariously on the end of her nose. Then there was a boy with an oversized jacket that swallowed him whole, making him look like a child playing dress-up in his father's clothes. He fidgeted awkwardly in his seat, his eyes darting nervously around the room as if he expected to be attacked by a swarm of angry bees at any moment.

Looking around at this ridiculous group, I suddenly came to a startling realization.

That bitch put me in the dumb kids' class.

Amidst the sea of strange faces, I spotted someone familiar—a sort of rat-faced boy with a curious look about him. It took me a moment to process where I'd seen his face before when he wasn't wearing the bright green apron of a supermarket cashier, but then it hit me. It was the boy from the supermarket who hadn't left me alone.

I felt a surge of anger rise up within me at the sight of him, memories of our altercation in the supermarket coming back like a flood. I remembered the way his arrogance had pushed me over the edge. While I knew that some people simply lacked the instinctual knowledge of when to shut up, that didn't settle my distaste for him. Regardless, he either hadn't noticed me yet or was purposely avoiding eye contact.

As the teacher finally looked up from her crossword puzzle, her brow furrowed in irritation at being interrupted. She seemed to look through me, her gaze distant and unfocused. It was as if I were a mere nuisance, an inconvenience disturbing her from her solitary world of puzzles and pens.

"Can you tell us your name, please?" she asked, her voice lacking any real interest or warmth.

"Ophelia Peterson." I matched her dry tone.

"Yes?" she pushed, her attention already drifting back to the newspaper in her hand.

"I'm...supposed to be in this class." I wondered if her ignoring me, letting the rest of the class simply stare at me as I stood at the front of the room, was some sort of humiliation ritual. I wondered how many recognized me from two years ago—if any of them did.

"Right. Welcome, Ophelia. Please find a seat," dismissed the teacher.

As I made my way to the back of the classroom, I found a desk tucked away in the corner, its surface littered with stray papers and half-broken pencils. With a heavy sigh, I dropped my bag onto the floor and settled into the chair, trying to ignore the wobble beneath me. I waited for the *lesson* to start.

Instead, the teacher, her attention momentarily diverted from her crossword puzzle, had propped her feet up on the desk in front of her, crossing them casually at the ankles. The action caused a stack of papers to teeter on the edge of the desk, threatening to spill onto the floor. I held my breath, expecting her to reach out and steady the papers before they fell. But to my surprise, she simply watched with detached indifference as they tumbled to the ground in a flutter of white.

As time went on, it became apparent that this woman had absolutely no intention of teaching any of the heathens in the classroom. (Was I now part of the heathen category? That seemed fitting.)

One thought continued to rage on in my mind while I gritted my teeth hard enough to give myself a headache: I had to get out of this hellhole as soon as possible, despite what my father said.

***

The cafeteria wasn't any less disgusting than the rest of the school. Filled with chaotic teenagers who left a hormonal stench in every room I entered, every surface seemed to be suspiciously sticky and generally unclean. A wave of revulsion washed over me as I took in the sight, doing my best to avoid every student that nearly bumped into me—they all seemed intent on doing so, not a single one of them aware of their surroundings. My history teacher passed me by as I lingered at the threshold and the smell of cigarettes emanating off of him hit me in the face like a slap.

Then, a wonderful idea came to me. I recalled the double doors that I had passed on the way here, and one word echoed in my mind; *library*.

***

Lunch ended too quickly. Even after the bell blared through the speakers above me, I remained in the library for a while, running my fingers across the delicate spines of old books, taking in the musty smell of them. Pacing there, I had an odd feeling that I wasn't quite alone. Though I listened hard for signs of another presence, I heard nothing. Still, there was a mysterious air about the place, as if every corner held secrets waiting to be uncovered.

I made my way into the dimly lit hallways, the flickering fluorescent lights casting eerie shadows that danced along the walls. The air thick and cold, as if the building itself were holding its breath, waiting for something to happen.

It was in this unsettling environment that I first caught sight of the boy. It began on my way to class, my nose stuck in the little map that a teacher had scribbled out for me. Even in my distraction, my attention was drawn his way.

He stood alone in a pool of shadow, away from the crowds around the lockers where students chatted and giggled. His brownish hair was a tangled mess, his figure hunched and forlorn. His clothes were worn and faded, as if he'd been wearing them for days. They hung loosely on his frame, emphasizing his gaunt and lanky appearance. But it was his eyes that drew me in. From afar, he could have been fifteen, but there was a harshness to his expression, a seriousness that made him look to be at least my age. If not older.

As our gazes met, a chill ran down my spine as if I were staring into the abyss. There was something undeniably otherworldly about him which made me pause. I couldn't put my finger on it.

But even as I struggled to make sense of what I was seeing, the boy's expression remained unchanged with fixed intensity. It was as if he were trying to convey some silent message, some unspoken truth that hovered just beyond my grasp.

Instinctually, I stepped forward. The familiarity was overwhelming. "Hey, don't I—"

And then, in the blink of an eye, he was gone, my view obscured by a frail girl in front of me. She blinked inquisitively. "Who are you talking to?"

I looked up at her face. She was slightly taller than me, with eagle-like features and a tattoo peeking through her sleeve. Thinking back, I recognized her as one of the hoodlums in class who had been eyeing me before.

"Not you," I snapped at her.

When I looked over her shoulder, ignoring her offended scoff, the boy I'd seen was nowhere to be found.

Chapter Five

A s the evening descended and the last of the customers trickled
out of the diner, I found myself once again immersed in the
familiar routine of cleaning and closing up shop. With each wipe of
the cloth and each sweep of the broom, I allowed myself to slip into
a state of quiet reflection, the rhythmic motions providing a welcome
respite from the chaos of the day.

The diner was bathed in the warm glow of the overhead lights,
casting long shadows across the worn linoleum floor. The air was filled
with the scent of coffee and baked goods, that is, once I blocked out
the greasy hamburger odor from the kitchen.

My coworkers—Janie and the other guys who I liked to pretend
were nameless—were dealt the job of kitchen cleanup. I could hear
them clanging pots and pans together along to the sound of faint
music from the radio. They liked to make a game out of things, either
by dancing to music as they cleaned dishes, making a competition out
of who would make the most tips, or making bets on which customers

would complain about the state of their meals. I supposed that made it easier for them; to find distraction in each other.

I looked at the register as I recalled the incident with Janie, the stolen bills. I wondered if the girl had even realized what had happened that day. I imagined her reaching into her breast pocket the morning after she'd stolen the money, feeling it was empty, and taking a pause. I could see the confusion that would overtake her, maybe she would even retrace her steps. But never in a million years would her thoughts lead back to me, to the pen now resting in *my* pocket.

The weight of the sparkly pink pen inside my pocket became heavier. Had I done the right thing by keeping silent? Or had I become complicit?

As I made my way around the restaurant, tidying up tables and wiping down countertops, I noticed the wall where the aprons were hung, each one neatly folded and waiting to be used. Among them was Janie's apron, marked by her little name tag, its fabric worn and faded with coffee stains from years of use.

After taking stock of my surroundings again, I slipped the pink pen inside Janie's apron pocket. *That's that,* I thought.

With no one's help, I finished all my tasks and locked the front door of the diner, the outside light flickering above me. I turned that off, too. Whether the others finished their own jobs was not my responsibility, and so I felt no guilt as I mounted my bike and drove away from the diner. The town was different at night, quieter. It might have made someone else nervous, but for me, the route was so familiar and I was so accustomed to it all that it was the perfect time to lose myself in my thoughts. Music hummed comfortingly through my headphones.

I soon arrived at the hospital, and as I settled into the wobbly, rusty seat next to my grandmother's bed, unease washed over me. After so many visits, I'd nearly gotten used to the sterile smell of antiseptic and the constant hum of machines. But despite the routine, the sight of my grandmother lying there, connected to a tangle of wires and tubes, never failed to tug at my heart.

With my new schedule, I could only visit her twice a week. Tuesdays and Sundays were my days off, but any other time I was either working or at school. I hadn't blown off any classes yet, but it was growing more and more tempting with each spitball that flew across the classroom.

The bright lights overhead cast harsh shadows across Nan's pale face, making the lines and wrinkles stand out in stark relief. Her frail hand clasped gently in mine and a small smile graced her lips.

"How was your day, dear?" Her voice was barely more than a whisper in the quiet room—despite the loud machines that gave me a headache.

"Fine."

"Hmm?"

"It was alright. School. You know."

Even in all her sickness, the woman still found the strength to roll her eyes at me. "It's like pulling teeth with you, sweetheart," she muttered.

I paused. I knew that Nan hated my tendency to omit details, my constant need for privacy. After a moment, I relaxed my shoulders and tried to be normal for a moment. "The other kids are all nice. My teachers don't pay much attention to me, so I can lay low. It could be a lot worse."

Again, Nan eyed me. "Just because I'm bedridden doesn't mean you can't tell me about your own problems. Lord knows how bored I am here. Tell me something. Complain. Entertain me!"

I scoffed at her. "There really is nothing to tell." A beat passed and I realized that she wasn't going to let up. I sighed. "Fine. I think they're all annoying. Everyone is younger than me, and a lot dumber, obviously. They throw things and pick their noses and yet somehow, they all look at me like I'm the inferior one. It sucks. Whatever."

"And?"

"And I haven't hurt anyone yet." I wanted to add *you ungrateful wench, you,* but I refrained. Was it not enough that I was making such an effort?

Her wrinkles deepened with distaste, but even the smallest movements seemed to suck the strength out of her. I did pity her sometimes—when she wasn't weaponizing her weakness—and I did believe this to be something that she did. I had a suspicion it was something *all* people did after reaching a certain age. She liked to pretend that her physical incapacity and the fact that she had spent decades of her life contributing as a functioning member of society were all excuses for her to be as judgemental as possible towards the younger generation. Nan didn't abuse this excuse quite as much as she could have, but I knew she'd fallen victim to it. I knew that, despite her pretending, she tired of me easily and found herself constantly disappointed by my *waste of potential.* In that sense, she was right. I saw it, too. But it was the fact that *she* thought it, the way I could see it in her expression. That bothered me whether I wanted it to or not.

"I suppose that's all we can ask for, isn't it?" sighed Nan, laying back. Slowly, she glanced back over to me, speaking hesitantly with a conspiratorial smirk. "Any boys, then?"

My mind went to the boy that I'd seen that day in the hall. The strange, dark-haired one. He was like no ghost nor human I'd seen before and I couldn't shake the image of him from my mind.

And then I thought of Connor, the softer, blond boy that had shown me to class and taken a jab at Mrs. Quirk. He'd caught my attention, too. But in a much different way.

I smiled. "No, Nan. No boys."

***

As the dull drone of the teacher's voice echoed through the classroom, I found solace in the worn pages of the book I had rescued from the forgotten shelves of the school library.

The books—the *free* books that the library held, available to all students—were the only reason that I hadn't jumped from the window to my left just yet. The blissful literature in which I buried my nose turned everything to white noise, the commotion all the more reason for me to let the words absorb me.

After enduring yet another morning of tedious classes that seemed to blend together in a haze of boredom, I found myself seeking refuge in the dimly lit cafeteria, the smell of overcooked food assaulting my senses as I navigated the crowded tables in search of a place to sit.

I began to recall the days I'd spent here in this very school, an anxiety-ridden, self-important fifteen-year-old. I wouldn't have dreamed of setting foot in the library back then, opting to stick myself at the end of tables so everyone could see how much I *didn't* care. In the end, I think it had the opposite effect.

Coming here, I'd hoped that I wouldn't be remembered from those days. Despite how much I may have changed in the last two years, I knew I was bound to be recognized by someone. Nevertheless, there were more important things to worry about in Hinton than *that weird chick, Ophelia.* (A direct quote I'd heard muttered in the hallways.)

I'd spent the whole day looking for that *strange* guy I'd seen in the hall, the image of his odd, slouched figure still fresh in my mind. I took the long route to class every time, trying to cover as much area as possible. I had already run into him one time, and if he was a student here, I had to see him again at least once. His image lingered in the back of my mind like a persistent shadow. His sad—yet empty eyes seemed to follow me, haunting me with their silent plea.

Lost in my thoughts, I barely noticed the two figures approaching me from across the cafeteria. Two girls, the same height, with the same nose, same eyes and same light beige skin, and yet strikingly different comportments. And the hair. One had bright dyed pink hair, cut short to her shoulders, whereas the other one sported a natural blonde. As they approached, their identical faces twisted into identical smiles that sent a shiver down my spine.

"Ophelia, right?" The pink-haired one said softly, her voice surprisingly gentle compared to the coldness I had expected.

"Yeah?"

"I'm Agnes," she continued, her smile widening as she gestured to the girl beside her. "This is Laura."

I watched them expectantly.

Laura tucked her hip-length hair behind her ears, blinking at me like a broken doll.

The twins, Laura and Agnes, were a sight to behold, their bright colors and contrasting styles standing out like beacons in the sea of drabness that surrounded them. As for Laura, the clothes she wore were the same I'd seen hung up in storefront windows, and yet none of them seemed to fit her quite right, hanging off her bones like a poorly-sized mannequin.

Beside her, Agnes gleamed in a different way, her shorter, bright pink hair standing out in stark contrast to her sister's more subdued appearance. Despite their identical features, there was something about Agnes that seemed softer, more approachable, as if she were the yin to her sister's yang. Despite her softness, something about the way she stood out from the rest seemed almost comical, disingenuous. Every last decision down to the color of her shoe laces seemed like a desperate attempt to be different.

"We couldn't help but notice you sitting here all alone," Agnes remarked.

"Mind if we join you?" the other continued.

I weighed my decisions carefully.

"Sure, go ahead."

As Agnes and Laura settled into the seats across from me, I couldn't help but feel a twinge of satisfaction at the thought of finally having someone I might be able to benefit from. I'd had enough of feeling like a pawn myself, and I knew a thing or two about these girls already. I knew they were seniors in the advanced class ahead of me. If there was one thing I wanted, one thing that could make the experience at this school bearable, it was to get into that class. Day after day, I would see them all walking together in a pack, giggling to each other conspiratorially. There were about ten of them that I saw together often, and when I did see them, there was never just one. The twins were glued at the hips, obviously, but the others travelled in pairs, too.

The boy who had walked me to class, Connor, was always with them, too. He interested me as well, though I couldn't quite put my finger on why. When I saw their group moving through the halls like an organized army, each movement they made calculated and artificial, my eyes found him first.

If there was any group I would consider giving my time to here, it was them. I'd never mastered the art of cliques, mostly because I had a reputation as a heinous bitch, but I believed the time had come to try.

However, given the apparent exclusivity of their group, I wondered why the twins bothered to sit with me now. I studied the girls in front of me closely, and then looked back down to my own muddied boots and pilling sweater. Perhaps they thought that conspiring with a charity case like me would up their popularity points. I doubted there was no ulterior motive there.

The twins—they may have seemed friendly enough, but I wasn't about to let my guard down just yet. They fell into a pattern of gossip almost immediately after they sat down, speaking naturally as if my presence made no difference at all.

"Then she fell. Like, actually fell," said Agnes. "And her jeans *ripped.*"

Laura cried out in shock. "On the knees or the crotch?"

Agnes smirked. "Johnny said he spotted *Hello Kitty* panties."

I studied the way they spoke, imagining that I was some kind of zoologist with two new specimens to observe.

"Why does it smell funny?" I asked, Perhaps I could change the subject. The subject of Andrea's jeans was far from interesting to me. While I had no idea who the girl even was, I doubted I would have been quite as engrossed in the topic as the twins even if I did.

"Oh, that's because it's Friday," chimed the pink-haired one. "Pizza day. It's not real pizza though, since they use some sort of yellow powder for the cheese, and the tomato sauce isn't made of tomatoes."

I blinked. "What's it made of, then?"

She shrugged, taking a sip from her soda.

As the conversation drifted to the peculiarities of the school, I couldn't resist the urge to ask the question that had been gnawing at me since the moment I stepped foot inside its walls.

"You know, you two are the only ones who haven't been cold to me," I pointed out. "Why is that?"

Best to get it all out in the open now.

Laura and Agnes exchanged a glance, a silent communication passing between them before Agnes spoke up, her voice tinged with sadness. *This should be good,* I thought.

"Well, you see," she began. "You came in at the worst possible time." Her words hung heavily in the air.

Laura spoke up. "A few days ago, a student was killed here, on school property."

My heart skipped a beat at her words, a chill running down my spine as I struggled to comprehend the gravity of what she was saying.

"*Killed?*" I repeated, my voice barely above a whisper. I waited for the punchline, but they both remained serious.

Agnes nodded solemnly. "Yeah. And the police couldn't find anything. No clues, no weapon, no suspects."

"His body was found in one of the hallways," Laura explained. "Literally, inside the school. Everything was supposed to be closed down afterwards because of the investigation. We're not even supposed to be here, but...well, here we are."

A heavy silence settled over us. How was this the first time I had heard anything about it? All this time I had been attributing my classmates' coldness towards me as disdain, but could it really have been an external issue? Was it *mourning* I had been sensing?

I let my gaze wander away from the twins in front of me, studying the students that crowded the cafeteria. Beside me, a girl picked at her food with a fork, looking at nothing in particular. Another table over and a group of friends sat in awkward silence, seemingly not able to find any interesting topic to chat about. On the other end of the table, it was the same story, with most kids staring off into the distance, making half-hearted attempts at conversation, or sneering at the bland cafeteria food in front of them. The place was utterly miserable.

As Agnes's words sank in, my mind raced, connecting the dots between her story and the *ghostly figure* I had encountered earlier. The boy in the hall. *The boy in the hall.*

Was it possible that the boy she spoke of was the same one I had seen wandering the halls, his ghost haunting the building where his life had ended?

A chill ran down my spine as the pieces of the puzzle began to fall into place. The sad, empty eyes of the ghostly apparition flashed before my mind's eye, his silent plea for understanding echoing dimly within me. *He* could be the victim Agnes spoke of, the clue calling out to me all along. It seemed too much of a coincidence to be mere chance.

When I looked back up, the twins were both looking down solemnly.

"That—" I coughed. "That sucks."

They exchanged a look.

"A lot," I continued.

If I was going to try and use these girls to my benefit, I was probably going to have to work on my social skills.

I bit into the pizza and felt a wash of regret.

Chapter Six

The letter came early in the morning while I fried bacon in a pan, the house empty and quiet aside from the dull sizzling of the meat before me. My pockets were filled with crumpled bills, the measly salary the boss had handed me at the diner an hour before.

I was trying to fix my hair, putting it in a braid so I could move freely while washing the dishes, when a sharp knock came from the front door. I wiped my sudsy hands on a towel before making my way to the door, where I found the mailman waiting.

"Morning, Miss Peterson." He smiled, flashing a row of uneven, discolored teeth at me. I had told him before that it seemed strange for him to call me that, and I was perfectly comfortable with him using my first name, but he never listened.

He was in his mid-40s, and I called him Mr. Smith. I'd forgotten *his* first name at this point. All I knew about him was the stories he would tell me about his wife and son, most often accompanied by jokes that the son would make a good husband for me. *I was talking with my son this morning about you, Miss Peterson...* he'd begin each time. Over the years, I'd perfected my repetitive, friendly refusal.

Mr. Smith wore his postal uniform with a sense of pride, the navy blue fabric stretched over his broad shoulders and cinched at the waist with a thick leather belt. A cap adorned with the emblem of the postal service sat atop his head, shielding his graying hair from the morning sun.

"Got something for you this morning," he said as he reached his blue bag, sifting through envelopes. The one he grabbed was slightly crumpled, with my name scrawled across the front in my father's unmistakable handwriting.

"Here you are," the mailman said, handing it to me with a knowing look. "Looks like you've got a letter from dad." No talks of his son this time, it seemed.

I took the letter without a word, thanked him, and closed the door.

> *My dearest Ophelia,*
>
> *I hope this letter finds you well. I know it's been a while since we last spoke, but please know that you are always in my thoughts, no matter how far apart we may be.*

Ew. Affection didn't suit my father.

> *I wanted to take a moment to tell you how proud I am of you. Life has been harsh on both of us, but through it all, you've shown me again that you never disappoint*

my expectations.

I know it hasn't been easy taking care of your grand-mother, but hold up there, I'm hoping that I'll be able to visit soon.

With all my love
Your father

P.S. The extra money is for the operation. Spend it wise-ly.

As I removed the signed check from within the folds of the letter, I could already feel the weight lifting off my shoulders. The number written there was enough to make me fall against the wall in relief.

***

As I stepped into the hallway, the contrast between the damp, musty air of the classroom and the crisp, clean scent of the corridor was stark. Mrs. Quirk led me down the hall, her footsteps echoing in the empty space as we made our way to her office, her pink high-heels like an ominous drum counting down the seconds leading up to my demise.

While following her steps, I couldn't help but notice her expressions were more controlled than usual. While her wide, fish-like eyes were usually darting over me, inspecting me as if I were a ticking time bomb to be monitored, now, she couldn't seem to meet my gaze. Something was different, and it put me on edge.

The questions swirled in my mind, leaving me feeling increasingly anxious as we approached the door with *Counselor's Office* written front and center. She walked inside and I lingered at the threshold.

"Come in," Quirk called, offering me one of the seats that was facing her desk. She quickly glanced up from the floor, meeting my eyes at last, and I caught a glimpse of something strange in her expression. Was that...embarrassment?

As I sat, facing her, waiting for her to say something, she began shuffling through files and things across her desk, though she had no real objective or purpose in mind. After a moment, she gave up and clasped her hands together on the desk. She met my gaze over her cat-eye glasses.

"Well, Ophelia," she began heavily. I could tell this was about to be a difficult conversation. Difficult for *whom*, I wasn't sure.

"Yes?"

The interaction sparked a vague memory for me. Something about her mannerisms reminded me distinctly of the time a skinny, acne-ridden boy had confessed his love for me in the school hallway when we were twelve. That conversation hadn't ended well, either.

"We've received your exam results back from the county," Quirk informed me. "You remember. The exam you took on your first day?"

Go on, I thought.

"Well, Mr. Williams and I are impressed by the results. To say the least." That phrase seemed to hold more depth than she let on. "It's safe to say you did—" she coughed— "*far* better than expected.

I blinked. "Oh."

I could have jumped out of my chair and begun to dance. I could have squealed with joy at the validation. I wanted to point and laugh in that woman's face. *Far better than expected, my ass.* I was absolutely giddy, and yet I kept my composure, folding my hands neatly over my lap.

"Mr. Williams recommended changing you to a higher class," Quirk went on, as if it physically pained her to do so.

"I wasn't as dumb as I look, then," I said before I could reconsider the words.

Quirk glared at me, her gaze digging knives into my flesh. After a moment, I smiled softly, easing the tension a bit. She straightened out a stack of papers. "Your exam scores were exceptional. In fact, they were some of the highest we've seen in years." She grinned artificially. "At least, that's what the principal thinks. Congratulations, Miss Peterson."

Exceptional.

Exceptional.

Not bad, Ophelia. Not bad.

They were moving me up. After these sickening days among the younger, clueless juniors. It was laughable, absurd even. Without thinking, and because I couldn't help myself with the ridiculousness of it all, a barking laugh escaped my lips.

"I'm not certain this is a laughing matter." Quirk's tone became colder—if that was possible.

"Sorry," I said, and added before I forgot, "Ma'am".

After that, I found myself listening to Mrs. Quirk outline my new classes and schedule on a chart in front of me. She gave me a list of the new books I'd need to pick up from the library. Finally, she handed me my timetable. I took it eagerly, scanning the list of classes and their corresponding times.

English Literature with Mrs. Johnson,

History with Mr. Roberts,

Mathematics with Mrs. Whitlock...

The names blurred together as I tried to make sense of it all.

"I'm going to accompany you to your new class, if you don't mind, Ophelia."

It was clear it wasn't up for discussion, and so I went with her willingly.

Hell, yeah.

***

I stood at the front of the class waiting for Mrs. Quirk and the new English teacher—a small-framed woman with a choppy brown bob and a polka-dot dress—to finish their talk. At first, I assumed that the two of them were discussing my transfer, or something else more relevant to my current situation. When I tried to listen in, however, I discovered that they were actually chatting about the social studies teacher who had cheated on her husband the week before. I had the distinct feeling that I was simply being left to the wolves.

The wolves in question, a large group of teenagers sitting at desks in rows before me, did not seem quite so vicious at first glance. It seemed that the majority of them had at least developed basic hygiene. Contrary to the junior class, I had gotten no whiff of animal cadaver or something similar when I stepped into the room. Rather than staring at me as if I was part of the new zoo exhibit, they entertained themselves with their own conversations, giggling and chatting similar to how the teachers were doing. I was the only one left silent.

When Mrs. Quirk made her way to the door, she paused and turned back to me. "Oh, sweetheart. I almost forgot. Mrs. Johnson, our new student, Ophelia," She said, gesturing towards me, and then left.

"Well, welcome, Ophelia. Why don't you introduce yourself to the rest of the class?" Mrs. Johnson spoke. She gave me a bright smile, apparently trying to make me feel less awkward before my peers. It wasn't working.

Good God, I thought. It was the painful start of any corny coming-of-age movie.

"My name is Ophelia Peterson," I began, keeping my voice steady and avoiding eye contact. "And I'm new here." *Technically*, I thought.

One of the girls in the back of the class leaned sideways and whispered something to a friend. Thankfully, I couldn't hear what she'd said from where I stood.

Agnes was smiling at me, I tried to return the gesture.

Some of the faces seemed vaguely familiar, but one of the nice things about having been so reserved in my first years at this school was that few had cared enough to recognize my face now. Regardless, I knew I had changed since then. And not just in appearance.

"You can go and have a seat next to Connor at the end," Mrs. Johnson said, pointing to the blond boy a couple paces away. I recognized him instantly, one of the few people whose face had stuck in my mind. He wasn't smiling.

I was about to make my way to where she'd pointed, but I paused. "There's no seat."

The teacher blinked quizzically at me, holding her hands clasped together. "I'm not sure what you mean."

I looked over at Connor again, not one free seat around him. "Where am I supposed to sit?"

The woman's eye twitched before she moved across the room and gestured plainly to the desk in front of her. With a certain aggression, she grabbed the chair where a boy was already sitting and pulled it out across the floor. "Right here, dear."

The boy in question, who had been sitting comfortably in the chair, didn't show any sign of being bothered by this, his face completely impassive. Then, suddenly, I wondered why I hadn't recognized him before.

It was the figure I'd seen in the hall. The dead student. What was his name? I couldn't remember. Just like everyone else, his eyes did not leave me as I moved towards his chair. He had an intent look on his face, almost pleading. Now that I was closer, I could see the fear in his expression. Or maybe it was simply my interpretation from what I'd been told about him. I could imagine him now, wide eyed and lifeless lying on the hallway floor. I wondered how exactly the killer had done it. Stabbing? Beating? A gun?

My thoughts were interrupted.

"Well?" the teacher pressed.

I glanced between her and the ghost. Slowly, his figure began to dissipate, and the chair was soon empty. I took that as my cue to finally sit, painfully aware of all the eyes on me. I thought I heard someone snicker over my shoulder, and I spotted Agnes whispering to her sister. When I turned my head to see Connor, however, his expression had remained completely blank.

***

When the last bell of the day rang and Mr. Robert's class had finally ended, I made my way from school to the diner. I had some extra time in between to go home first and rest, but those few minutes weren't worth the trouble. I unlocked my bike at the front of the school and whizzed past the groups of teens walking back to their own homes. When I arrived, my back ached with the weight of my bookbag. The teachers had already stocked me up on far more textbooks than I probably needed, and my spine was paying the price.

I found Janie in the back room, and dropped my things beside her with a grunt.

"Watch it," she spat, closing up her bottle of nail polish. She began blowing at her fingernails.

I ignored her and turned around, stripping off my worn jacket before wrapping my apron around myself. I straightened the name tag on my breast pocket.

"Ooooh," Janie hummed behind me. "Someone's got a crush, I see."

I turned around. "What?"

She was sitting there, one of my textbooks open in her lap as she continued waving around her hands like a bird doing some sort of mating dance to dry her nails. "He's cute, isn't he? Someone from school?"

I stepped forward and snatched the book out of her hands, only to look down and see the page she had opened was covered with sketches.

At first, I couldn't quite tell what the endless scribbles were supposed to be. I looked closer.

"What the hell?" I muttered. "Did you do this?" But I knew she couldn't possibly have, since she'd only had the book open for a moment. And anyway, Janie never really struck me as much of the artistic type.

I flipped the page. There were more pencil scribbles, erratic and senseless markings scrawled across text. The same faint image hidden withing them.

Janie raised an eyebrow at the image. "Maybe 'stalker' is a better word," she muttered under her breath, still taking on that sort of teasing older sister attitude that she liked to use on me.

I slammed the book shut, "Do not touch my stuff again," I ordered. When Janie opened her mouth to protest, I was already gone.

My skin felt cold as I shut the bathroom door behind me.

What the actual fuck.

On the page Janie had opened to, there was one image that stood out among the meaningless scribbles. One distinct face.

Connor, the clever blond boy from the school. It was his face that I found there. I wished it hadn't been so clear, but it was. I recognized his features from the moment I saw it.

I had the sudden and startlingly clear feeling that I was no longer alone in the bathroom stall where I sat.

I shut the book and rose to my feet.

CHAPTER SEVEN

Growing up, I carried a weight of curiosity that often led me astray. I had the constant and unrelenting need to know absolutely everything there was to know. In some ways, it was a good thing. It was the reason why I could do well in school when I wanted to, why I'd never really had to study a day in my life. But it was also one of the many causes for the never-ending problems between my parents, the constant fights, the anxious worry, the over-protectiveness in my early years that was nothing but detrimental to me now. It was part of the emptiness I felt after dropping out of school that I always tried to ignore.

My father called me impulsive. My mother called me curious. I supposed the truth was somewhere in the middle. But what I did know was that I had a fundamental inability to accept things without understanding the reason behind them. The *why*.

Connor's drawings in my textbook didn't make any sense at all. Not to me, anyway. I racked my brain to try and figure out who it could have been, who could have possibly had the time and opportunity to leave such sketches in *my* book, of all places.

I had three questions whirling through my mind.

Who?

Why?

And how?

"Ophelia." The teacher's voice broke through my reverie, pulling me back to the classroom in which I sat.

"Could you share your thoughts on the passage we just read?" he asked.

I could feel the scrutinizing gazes bore on me. At that moment, everyone in the room, including myself, realized that I didn't have a clue what was happening.

A glanced around. "It was good."

"Page thirty five." The whisper echoed softly in the air beside me, unmistakably Connor's voice. Something fluttered in my chest.

Without looking at him, my gaze fell down to my book, scanning the only text that was on that page, and then answered.

I didn't meet his eyes for the rest of the hour.

As the bell rang, and students started to leave the room heading to the cafeteria, I began to gather my things into my bag when Connor's voice cut through the classroom chaos.

"You alright?"

The question stopped me in my tracks, my hand resting over my notebook. The urge to pretend that I hadn't heard him at all, take my things, and run was stronger than ever. But rather than succumb to it, I slowly looked up. He was standing there, watching me expectantly.

"I'm fine," I told him cautiously. *Why do you ask?*

For a moment, it seemed like he was still waiting for more. But when I didn't deliver, he nodded and carried his bag away. "I'll see you around."

I could not tear my attention away from him as he turned his back to me and walked away. Further and further from me before he disappeared out the door, where I caught another flash of his face and slight, natural smile. It looked as if he had been smiling all his life, as if he had been born to smile at people.

Why you?

***

In the end, Nan's operation went well. Although I was aware that I'd have to start caring for her at home again, I was still glad she would return. The house was beginning to feel too spacious, the woods surrounding it too dark and eerie. The relief of no longer being responsible for her had been overpowered by the strange loneliness I felt in the quiet shell of a house.

It's not that I hated my nan. In fact, I knew I'd been overly harsh towards her at times. After all, without her, I would have been sent to a foster home when I was seven. (Unless, of course, my father would have taken the responsibility of raising me—which he never would.)

As I slowly flipped through the pages of the book, Connor's face stared back at me, frozen in time. It was uncanny the way his features came together within the manic scribbles. It was drawn in a way that the image actually became clearer the farther away I stood. It made the image of his face on the page feel like a secret, like something I wasn't meant to see.

I slipped the textbook into my bag and left the quiet library, the large door falling closed behind me. As I walked through the hallways, making my way to the cafeteria, Laura approached me.

"WHAT THE HELL IS WRONG WITH YOU, OPHELIA PETERSON?"

I stumbled back, taking in the image of the slight girl and her bared teeth, screaming down at me in rage.

"Excuse me?" I asked, incredulous. Her eyes were filled with a rabid anger, and now that she was closer, I got the feeling that maybe I *should* be a bit afraid. I smiled a bit, attempting to ease the tension. "Laura, what's wrong?"

"You tell me, you *hussy.*"

I blinked at her.

"What did you say to Connor?" she demanded. "I saw you talking to him earlier. I know you did something, because everything was going so well, and now he'll barely look at me!" I could see a glint of tears in her eyes, but she was still shaking with pure anger.

Agnes came up behind her and placed a hand on her shoulder, her expression stony. "You know, we really trusted you."

"That's what this is about?" I scoffed. "A boy?" I inconspicuously slid my textbook back into my bag. It would do nothing for my case.

"You think this is just about a boy?" Laura's voice cracked as her hand's grip tightened. "It's not just Connor. It's everything. It's the way that you always act like you're better than us, the way you think you can just—"

She looked around at the gathering crowd, their curious eyes fixed on her like we were some sort of zoo attraction.

"We know you told him something," spat Agnes.

"You stole my boyfriend, you *whore*!" Laura cried.

Just then I had an oddly validating realization. I'd had a bad feeling about the girl from the start, with the serene smile she always wore, her tendency to stay quiet, contrary to pink-haired Agnes' lively conversation. It was that same feeling of discomfort that I found when faced with things unknown or incomprehensible to me. She had been a mystery, and she'd finally let herself be solved. There was the real Laura I'd been waiting for. Fuming, screeching, accusatory Laura who screamed in hallways and jumped to assumptions. And I'd clocked her insincerity before, but to claim that she was Connor's girlfriend? That was another level.

Murmurs began to flutter through the air around us and a wave of fear rippled through me. It wasn't Laura that I was afraid of, but the effect she would have. We were surrounded by the onlookers, the prepubescent students watching us wide-eyed as if they'd never seen anything more interesting than two screaming teenage girls.

"Don't you have anything to say for yourself?" asked Agnes, practically glued to her twin's shoulder.

"I haven't said a word to him," I stated.

Laura shook her head. "You're a liar. You're lying through your teeth. I mean, *god*. Everything we did for you! *We* were the only ones actually willing to even *speak* to you when you first came here. We gave you the benefit of the doubt!" She was dripping tears now. "I just wanted to do something...something nice," she said, trembling.

"Do you feel nice now?" I muttered. However, she clearly heard me, and heaved a sobbing breath in response.

"*We* were willing to be friends with you, you ugly..." She took another breath, seeming to collapse in on herself. "Even though...even though *everyone knows* that it was probably *you* who killed that guy!"

I flinched. "What?"

"It's a pretty good coincidence, huh?" She stepped forward, confidence swelling, but I spotted that disingenuous flicker in her eye. "That just when this whole *terrible*—" she glanced at the onlookers— "disaster happened, you just *happened* to turn up with your creepy black clothes and your dirty hair."

Agnes looked at me with disgust. "Well, it makes sense, doesn't it? I mean, she's such a dick. And just, like, *mean.* Cindy, don't you remember?" She pointed to someone watching us from the crowd. It was that girl with the tattoos that had questioned me in the hall when I'd spotted the boy's ghost for the first time. "You were telling me how she was bullying you."

"*Bullying*—?" I began, but the tattooed girl cut me off.

"I was just trying to talk to her, and she was all like *why would I talk to someone like you?*" the girl said, sticking out her lip with a twisted expression when imitating my voice.

It was so ridiculous I hardly knew how to respond, a nervous laugh forcing its way from my throat. "I never said that."

"So you think it's funny?" asked Agnes, looking down her nose at me.

"No, I—"

"Face it, Ophelia," Agnes went on. "You're a loser and you're weird." There was slight laughter from the crowd that was almost hesitant. Others murmured in agreement.

"I bet it's true," called out a boy from the crowd. "I bet she killed that kid."

"*That kid?*" I echoed, anger bubbling within. "Do you even know his name?" All around me, I saw anger and accusations. However, I saw no sympathy for the person who had really lost their life.

"Do *you*?" hissed Laura.

I paused, closing my mouth. "Laura, you know that's bullshit." I turned to face the onlookers, spreading my arms wide. "Can't you all see this is bullshit? I wasn't even *here* until after—"

"I've heard enough," Laura snapped, voice breaking. "All I hope is that you get what you deserve. But until then..." she leaned in close, venom lacing every syllable. "You stay away from me."

CHAPTER EIGHT

The following days were miserable. Granted, I had experienced worse moments throughout my school career, but very little could compare to the unwavering and laser-focused attention that remained glued to me each day as I strolled through the halls. Eyes followed me no matter where I went. Normally I would brush the feeling off as paranoia, a feeling also not unusual for me, but in this situation it simply could not be denied. When I walked into a room, heads would turn. When I rounded a corner, voices would quiet to a whisper. When I would cough or sniffle, worried glances would be thrown my way. And it wasn't just Laura's class. It seemed that our three-minute conversation in the halls had somehow spread across the entire school. Even the Freshmen were absorbed in the drama, gossiping like twittering birds.

The gossip itself, however, wasn't limited to one story. I overheard a few accusations strewn together; *homewrecker, murderer, accomplice, junkie.* The list went on, each one more outlandish than the next. The other students must be finding the classes just as boring as I was, if they were really that desperate to entertain themselves.

It got to the point where even my teachers seemed more uneasy around me. No matter how illogical the accusation was, no matter how little sense it would actually make, the grown adults in this god-forsaken school were seriously suspicious that *I* had killed a boy whose existence I was not aware of until *after* his death.

The only one who seemed unaffected by the drama was Connor himself. He remained distant as ever, despite all the chaos swirling around us.

Connor and I had found ourselves in this tough situation together. Despite rumors labeling me as the school murderer, I was also *the homewrecker*. People hurled insults at me, but they also condemned him for cheating on Laura for someone like me. Eyeing him in class day by day, I was wondering how *he* felt about that part, but his expression rarely gave anything away.

One thing that set him apart was that he didn't seem to care about the unwarranted stares and whispers. Really, I never saw him entertain it once. He remained so set in his resolve to ignore it all that I began to actually wonder if he could have had a hearing issue.

To my chagrin, it didn't come so easily for me. I could practically feel insecurity eating me from the inside out, and I had discovered a strange new feeling like a rock in my chest every time I left the house to make my way to school. I was constantly unfocused, treading through a fog. Small things would startle me, and I'd sometimes slip up by addressing figures that weren't really there. I generally had a certain talent for separating the ghosts from the real people, but now faces just seemed to blur together. And it didn't make it any better that there were more people around to notice when I mixed the two up.

Matters only got worse one day during physical education, one of the worst classes to ever be created. Really I hated it with a passion. Sweaty teens running, jumping, and hitting each other, stinking of puberty and hormones. There was also getting screamed at by teachers twice your size, having to listen to the horrid dance music they blared through the speakers, and of course, the changing rooms.

Anyone could have guessed based on looks alone that I probably wasn't the type to have taken her shirt off in front of very many people. I felt stiff and awkward as I removed it, my skinny arms contorting above my head. I did not look down at my own body nor did I look behind me to see if anyone was watching me. At this point, I was sure they were, but I was determined to ignore it.

As I reached inside my locker for my bland gray gym shirt, I brushed my fingers over the top of my arm, feeling the tattered bumpy skin there, covered in scars. I imagined what I must look like, all sharp bones sticking out through thin olive skin. On some days when I looked in the mirror, my skin looked almost gray, the color swallowed by the pool of black greasy hair and eyes the shade of tar. I knew my scars would get people talking, but I also knew that their assumptions and the rumors they spread would be untrue. I wasn't in a gang, or hiding from the police. I really tried not to fight often. The scars were from hunting animals, and the slashes running down my arms like lightning were from a fox. I remembered the day it had happened clearly, and the pain I'd felt when the blood streamed down my clothes. I think I'd been about fifteen, overly ambitious and with an ego the size of an elephant, but I learned my lesson quickly. I never went for anything bigger than a bunny with my knife again. Not for food, at least.

With my gym shirt and sweatpants on, I left the changing room as quickly as possible and walked into the large gymnasium, two years older than the last time I'd seen it. I noticed a new leak in the ceiling to my left, a bucket already set up beneath it.

The gym teacher walked into the middle of the room, a fat half-bald man wearing tennis shoes with a clipboard in hand. He blew his whistle and the class quieted.

"Today's game's played in partners," he announced.

With those words, the class was sent into a frenzy, friends clinging to each other frantically before anyone could become the unlucky one left out. I stayed where I was, waiting for another whistle blow, but to my surprise, I spotted pink hair nearing me out of the corner of my eye. I turned and locked eyes with Agnes. It immediately struck me as odd that she was without her twin, looking as incomplete as a puppy with a missing leg, until I noticed Laura hanging off of Connor's arm. I wondered for a fleeting moment if maybe the girl wasn't all that deluded when she said they were together, but that, too, passed when Connor gave the girl a sour look, carefully removing his arm from her grasp. When she gave an offended huff, he reluctantly returned his arm to her. I gagged a little.

Agnes, now partnerless, took a step in my direction, but before I could process the audacity of that girl, the teacher blew his whistle once more. "I'll choose," he grumbled, and a collective groan echoed through the gymnasium.

In the end, I was paired with a small, round-eyed, one that I recognized from the few classes that we shared. She wore a brown hijab that flowed over her shoulders and a fuzzy purple sweater.

"This should be fun," she said, which I at first interpreted as sarcasm, but soon realized it wasn't. She always smiled when she spoke, and held out the vowels of every other word in a funny, sing-songy way. Normally, I might find it annoying, but there was a certain authenticity to her that made her cheery mood almost bearable. "I'm Fouzia. I like your boots."

"Thanks." I couldn't help but glance at her own shoes. They were white with blue stitched details. I imagined her mother sitting at the dining table, meticulously running a needle through them over and over again beside a dim lamp. I imagined the girl being content when they were presented to her before leaving for school in the morning. Out of nowhere, I felt a pang of envy.

Fouzia's wide-eyed smile never faltered as we waited for the teacher to explain today's activity. My gaze, however, kept wandering across the gym, seeking out Connor. He stood a few feet away, talking to Laura, who was still clinging to his arm.

The thoughts swirling in my mind faded away as the teacher started to yell. "Let's play some tag!"

Tag? Seriously? I waited for the punchline but it never came. With a sigh, I looked to my partner, but her smile had only widened.

"They like to make it more complicated every year. So we don't get bored. Hence the partnering up," she explained.

The teacher spoke again, his voice echoing off the gym walls. "Cardio and agility training, amiright? Everyone, spread out!"

The students dispersed. The gym was an obstacle of mats, cones, and the buckets of collected water, making the game more challenging. A wave of misery spread over me. I hated running, I always had. And I especially hated being chased.

"Alright," the teacher continued. "We're starting with two taggers. Blondie and Laura, you're it." He gestured to Connor at the word *blondie.*

"Go!" The whistle blew and chaos erupted.

I bolted, darting between the buckets and mats that were placed randomly on the floor, my eyes scanning for an empty spot. Fouzia was right behind me. Her laughter loud as we zigzagged through the gym. I glanced over my shoulder to see Connor sprinting in our direction.

"He's coming this way," cried Fouzia, childlike joy lacing her words.

"Let's split up. He can't chase both of us," I said.

"That defeats the whole—"

"Whatever." I ran in the opposite direction. Glancing back, I saw her follow suit. Suddenly, I felt a hand against my shoulder. When I twisted, I expected to see Connor and my heart took a leap, but instead I saw Laura, her forehead damp with sweat.

"Gotcha!" she squealed, grinning. She nudged my shoulder as she let go of it, her face twisting into something smug and awful.

I bit the inside of my cheek and dug my nails into my palms. I would not hurt her. I would not give into the taunt.

I made my way to the sidelines, still catching my breath, watching the game unfold. My eyes followed Connor, who was now chasing a group of boys near the center of the gym. He moved with purpose, his eyes never leaving a target. He reminded me of myself when I was on the hunt, the unbreakable gaze and laser focus, the controlled lunges, ivory skin glistening with sweat, surprisingly muscular arms.... Normally, I would feel disgusted watching such a thing, but he was just...

Ugh. My stomach was doing somersaults.

A loud *bang* knocked me out of my trance. Connor had hit the floor, and the teacher was running to his aid. I stood instinctively. Lying there among the fallen cones, with the rest of the class looking down on him, he cradled his leg in his hands, knees pressed to his chest. His expression was contorted with agony.

"What happened? What hurts?" the teacher asked quickly. If I wasn't so preoccupied, I might have rolled my eyes.

After a moment, the boy was able to smooth his expression and slowly rise from the ground. He approached another boy who had his arms crossed, his mouth twisted into a sly grin.

"You knew I had a bad leg, you *dick.*" Connor shoved the smiling boy with both arms, but his look of contentment did not falter.

"Hey, hey. Break it up!" The teacher set himself between the boys. "Blondie, walk to the nurse's office. Patrick, hit the showers and keep your hands to yourself."

"*He* shoved *me!*" protested Patrick.

"Shut your mouth and go."

As I watched Connor walk away, I began to think that maybe gym class wouldn't be so bad after all.

***

The next afternoon, it took me longer than usual to make my way out of the school, caught within the crowded halls. I was beginning to worry about Nan, for she was supposed to have her next dose of medicine half an hour ago and I wasn't quite sure if she was smart enough to know to wait for me to administer it rather than do it herself. Feeling anxious, I opted for the faster route home. I didn't normally go this way because—though it was more efficient—it was riddled with hills and bumps, and I didn't need the extra sweat. I was more vigilant as I sped down this road, my headphones slipped off of one ear. The late afternoon sun cast long shadows across the path, and the wind whipped against my face, mak—

"Whoa!" The exclamation escaped my throat and I yanked one bike handle forward, swerving sharply around the figure in the middle of the road. I skidded to a stop and mud splattered over my boots.

"Watch where you're going, asshole!" I yelled, turning my head.

Connor stood there, his hands raised in surprise. "Sorry," he said, stunned.

My cheeks flushed with embarrassment and I tightened my grip on the handles. "I didn't see you there," I muttered.

"No worries," he spoke. "You were really going for it."

I looked him up and down. I wanted to know if his leg had gotten better, I wanted to ask if he lived around here. I didn't ask either thing, reminding myself that we weren't friends.

"Yeah, I was." I set my bike back on course. "See you." Then I sped away.

When I arrived home, I quickly propped my bike against the side of the house and hurried inside. The familiar scent of Nan's baby powder and the faint sound of her coughs greeted me as I made my way to the living room, where she was sitting idly on the sofa.

"I'm home." I dropped my bag and made my way to the kitchen, peeking at her around the fridge door.

Nan seemed to not realize I was there until about five seconds after I'd spoken, but her face lit up with a warm smile when she did. Her skin looked paler today, and her hands trembled slightly as she reached for her glasses. After the spinal fusion, her condition had gotten better, though you wouldn't know by looking at her now.

"Oh, hi, dear. How was school?" She managed to get her glasses placed evenly on her nose. It was almost comical how she still pretended like *she* was the one taking care of *me*.

"Good," I replied, walking over with a small medicine bottle and a syringe. "Time for drugs."

Nan bristled. "You make me sound like an abuser."

"Well, aren't you, ya junkie?" I motioned for her to roll up her sleeve, growing irritated.

Shaking her head good-humoredly, she held out her arm. As I administered the shot, crouching beside her chair, she gave me a searching look. Nosy as ever.

"You seem in a good mood today," she remarked.

"Do I?" I pressed down on the spot with cotton and she winced in response, but the knowing glint in her eye remained.

The image of Connor's shocked expression on the road flashed through my mind, recalling how his blue eyes studied me. I shook the image and stood. "Did you need anything else? How are you feeling?"

"I'm feeling alright, dear. Just a bit tired," she said, settling back into the sofa. "I'm lucky to have your company aren't I? Yes, it was lonely today, with you at school."

The next morning, I tried to brush off thoughts of Connor, but they kept creeping back. As I was brushing my teeth, as I showered, as I loaded my countless textbooks into my bag, only one thing occupied my mind. Images of his face seemed ingrained in the back of my vision, the sound of his voice when he'd spoken to me, that mischievous smile I'd seen so few times from him, the way his face seemed to transform whenever that grin appeared, brightening like a beacon. No matter how I tried to recall the chemistry formulas I'd learned the day before in class, or count as high as I could in French, everything came back to him.

When I left home that day, I had no intention of doing what I did, but I did it anyway.

I took the same route as yesterday—the one that I now knew crossed paths with his.

The air was crisp and cool, the route was quiet, with only occasional jogger or dog walker passing by. It was one of the reasons I liked living far from school—nobody came too close to my house. I pedaled quickly, the bumps and hills feeling less daunting today.

As I rounded the same sharp bend where I had almost collided with Connor the day before, my heart raced. When was the last time I had felt such excitement? But there he was, walking along the muddy path, hands in his pockets, looking like he didn't have a care in the world. His blonde curls waved to me in the breeze and my breath hitched in my chest.

I drove past without a word. I wanted so badly to look behind me, to see his reaction when he saw me, but I didn't.

At the end of the school day, I repeated the process and took the same hilly path towards my house and I saw him again. The morning after, again. Seeing him became part of my daily routine, a staple in my morning and afternoon. Even better than seeing him was knowing that he saw me. I got the strangest high every time I passed him, and if—god forbid—we made eye contact, my skin would be on fire until I arrived home.

Subconsciously, I knew that what I was doing was strange. That, combined with the drawings in my textbook, was enough to fuel the rumors of my doubtful sanity times ten. Still, it was such a small thing, and so harmless that I couldn't help myself. His face was burned into the backs of my eyelids. It filled my dreams while I slept.

The feeling that I associated with him, a warm and dull fluttering in my chest—something like fear—grew incessant. But I hid the feeling well, pushing it back each time into the recess of my mind.

Obsession was only that if you let it manifest outside yourself. And I was determined to keep every thought of him locked behind my eyes, our conversations limited to my imagination, the scenes I created while lying in my bed in the dark, pretending to sleep.

But the worst part wasn't my mind, it wasn't the pounding of my heart or the glances I stole in class. It was the fact that I still had absolutely no idea *why*.

CHAPTER NINE

Things felt off from the moment I walked through the school doors. I could feel eyes on me, whispers trailing in my wake. I tried to ignore it. It wouldn't be the first time now that that stupid rumor had begun permeating through the school walls. But as I was about to head to my first class, the PA system crackled.

"Ophelia Peterson, please report to the principal's office immediately."

Annoyance crept up my neck. *What now?* I made my way to the office, each step feeling heavier than the last.

When I came up to the office door, I found my mother waiting there for me, her spectral figure lingering in my path. She said nothing. She never did. But her eyes followed me closely as I approached. That was the first sign that I wouldn't like whatever was coming.

Inside, Principal Williams was sitting behind his desk, his expression a mix of concern and something else I couldn't quite place. "Have a seat, Peterson."

I hated when people called me by my last name. No one in my life who had ever had good intentions for me had ever referred to me by my last name. Police, paramedics, the over-excited mailman, principals.... It made me uneasy at once. I sat down, my heart racing. "What's the matter, sir?" I tried to keep my voice smooth and steady, the picture of innocence.

He leaned forward, steepling his fingers. "We've received some troubling reports, Ophelia."

This should be good.

"There are rumors about your involvement in the incident with that poor boy, Xavier. I'm sure you've heard about it, with the way kids are these days. Some students are saying you might have something to do with the...tragedy that occurred."

My stomach dropped. "What? That—" The idea that Williams, a grown man, would have bought into such a rumor was so utterly ridiculous I laughed, half in shock and the other half in discomfort.

"This is not a laughing matter." He smacked a hand on the surface of the desk. I flinched.

"Of course it's not." I cleared my throat. "It's just that you can't be serious. That's a rumor that Laura made up. *Obviously*—"

"Calm down," he ordered patronizingly. "I'm not accusing you, but we have to take things seriously." He sighed. "You need to understand the severity of these accusations. The police have taken weeks searching for a shred of evidence, and yet they've had no leads until now."

No evidence? I thought. *How is that possible?*

I gritted my teeth, wondering what it would take for just one person in this town to grow a brain. "That isn't a lead, it's a petty rumor thought up by a seventeen-year-old girl."

A muscle in his jaw twitched. "I implore you to keep your composure, Peterson."

I clenched my fists beneath the table. "What am I *supposed* to do?"

"If you have anything to do with all of this, I suggest you turn yourself in. You're not an adult yet, Miss Peterson, it ca—"

"I already told you, it's a goddamn rumor. I mean, what are you on? I wasn't even enrolled until two weeks ago. I have no idea who this kid was, it's just something Laura said to rile me up."

He blinked slowly before carefully adjusting the files on his desk. "And I see it's worked."

A beat of silence passed.

I wasn't sure if the man had heard a single word I'd said. Should I have been relieved or offended that my outburst hadn't elicited a reaction?

"Are you done, then?" he asked.

I stared at him. I was almost certain that he wouldn't look quite so smug if I had him on the ground, pinned by that delicate, veiny neck of his. If I was less smart, I would be using more than words to plead my case.

"Right," he continued, straightening his ugly, orange tie. "Like I said, if what you're telling me is true, then no harm, no foul. If *not*, then I promise you will be very, *very*, sorry. This is an incredibly serious matter, and absolutely not something to joke or gossip about, so I suggest you take a teensy weensy step *away* from teenage drama. I know it will be hard, but I do have quite high hopes for you."

I wanted to bang my hands on the table and force him to understand, to grab him by his thinning hair and beat some sense into him. Unfortunately—though it would do wonders for my suppressed rage—it would do nothing for my reputation nor my criminal record.

"You're dismissed," he chirped.

Slowly, I began to turn, using a great amount of will to make myself walk away.

But he spoke again, as if the information was an afterthought. "And of course, I've called the authorities about these concerns. I'm sure they'll come by sometime."

I looked back at him.

"Oh, don't look so worried, Ophelia," he chided. "After all, it's just a rumor. Like you said." His lips curved into a tight grin.

***

The energy around the gym felt heavier than usual, the air thick with the usual stink of sweat mixed with the added tension of the latest gossip. As I changed into my gym clothes, I tried to ignore everyone. Today, more than ever, I needed to keep my head down and stay focused.

Mr. Thompson, our gym teacher, blew his whistle to gather everyone in the center of the gym. "Alright, today we're doing circuit training! I'll be assigning pairs."

A groan rose from the class. But Mr. Thompson ignored it, scanning his clipboard. As I stood there I could already feel my muscles melting into the ground, devoid of any motivation.

"Connor with Sophia."

A pang of disappointment hit me square in the chest.

Laura's eyes followed Sophia as she made her way to Connor, smile fading. I found it funny how she made no attempt to hide her contempt for the girl.

"Laura with Agnes."

Laura rolled her eyes and nudged Agnes, whispering something in her ear.

He continued down the list, finally saying, "Ophelia with Fouzia."

I breathed a small sigh of relief. At least I was paired with someone I felt less...confrontational with. Fouzia gave me a quick smile as we moved to our station, ready to start the circuit.

As we began the exercises, I couldn't help but feel a mix of anger and anxiety bubbling under the surface. Each jump, each push-up, each sprint was a way to release some of the tension, but it wasn't enough. Fouzia noticed.

"Dude," she spoke as we moved to the next station. "You okay? You seem really...intense. More so than usual, I mean."

I took a breath and wiped the sweat from my forehead. "Can I ask you something?" I said as I started doing another set of push-ups.

"Sure, anything." Her tone was earnest, a trait that wasn't easy to find around this town.

I collapsed onto the floor, my damp shirt clinging to my back. I looked up at her. "Why are you nice to me?"

She blinked.

"Aren't you at all freaked out? Everyone else seems to think I'm some sort of psycho." I felt strange for asking, but there was something so suspicious about her kindness. I had to get to the bottom of it.

"Pfff, you?" She laughed. "Didn't you come to school like, two weeks ago?"

I suddenly felt lighter. *Finally, someone with a brain.*

Fouzia waved a dismissive hand in the air. "Besides, you don't seem like the type."

I couldn't have disagreed more, but I let it slide anyway. "Thanks." Even if it was a lie to make me feel better, I appreciated the sentiment.

Fouzia paused. "Does it bother you? The rumors?"

My initial instinct was to hit her with a smack of sarcasm. *No, I'm completely fine with the notion that everyone in this whole shithole school thinks I murdered a kid in cold blood. Just peachy, thanks!* However, I restrained myself, wiping more sweat from my lip and sitting up on my knees. "I got called to Mr. Williams' office today. He's heard about the rumor and is questioning me. As if he believes it."

"No way!" she gasped. "The *principal of the school* fell for that? What did he say?"

I recounted the events of the morning to her as she did the jump rope, and in those moments as I spoke, I finally felt some real release. Not the kind I got from running or hitting or digging my nails into my palms, but a true emotional weight lifting from my shoulders. With my words, out came all my ongoing anxieties and stress through my mouth like vomit.

Fouzia frowned, looking at the floor. "I really am sorry for the way they've treated you. It's not right."

I stared at her, keeping my expression stony. The last thing I wanted was her pity. However...it had been a while since anyone had spoken to me in such a way, and maybe it felt a bit *nice* to have someone understand.

My mother had always been the gentler type, even before she became a brooding, non-verbal apparition. I could still remember the way she would comfort me as a child when I cried, always grasping my hands in the same way. Her words were like honey, and her touch light like a breeze. I used to have a notion that I would someday end up like her when I was a grown-up. Wasn't it usually inevitable that daughters became like their mothers? It wasn't long before I came to understand that would not be the case.

Sometimes I thought it had something to do with the fact that I could see her ghost. Like I didn't need to keep a piece of her within my personality, because I hadn't ever really lost her completely. Rather than her spirit lingering in my voice or my mannerisms, like with most children, I was left with the looks and habits of my father and an occasional glimpse of my mother out of the corner of my eye. It wasn't exactly a fair trade-off if you asked me.

Watching Fouzia and the sympathetic furrow on her brow, I wondered what people would think if they could hear my thoughts. I wondered if it would make a difference.

After gym, matters only worsened. You would think that with their attention span, my fellow teenagers would have abandoned the rumor after a week or two, but in a town as small as this they didn't have much else to entertain themselves. And so the whispering persisted. But then the whispering turned to speaking, which turned to jeering, which turned to kids leaving rude notes and painted words on my locker. Each day there was something different written there for me to find. *Leave now. Murderer. Psycho. Freak. Out of our school.* And my favorite, the most creative: *bitch.*

I was beginning to wonder just who could possibly care this much about the matter that they would dedicate themselves to leave such notes every morning. It was one thing to believe the rumor, but it was another to believe it so firmly that they would commit to practicing vandalism on the poor kid's behalf.

Then there was the morning that I'd finally had enough. Not only had someone painted big red letters across my locker (this time it was *crazy cunt,* which I could at least appreciate the alliteration of), but they had also left nearly a dozen handwritten notes inside, probably slipped in through the grate. There, they detailed numerous threats and curses directed towards me. There was even a little red stain on one, which I supposed might have been meant to represent blood, but had most likely been from the paint on the locker.

I stood there in the middle of the hall, holding the notes in my paint-stained hands. The bell rang above my head and the students around me—who had no doubt been watching the events unfold, snickering at my reaction to the letters—quickly dispersed and made their way to their respective classes. I remained there, staring down at the damage done.

At first, I'd felt numb. The words had just felt like words, scribbled lead on lined paper and nothing more. The paint was just paint. That cold numbness was what I had let wash over me as I heard the snickering around me, it was what helped me not care about the constant gazes turned my way.

But the layer of ice on my skin began to melt away. My self-control was more than they deserved. Why was I the one not allowed to be angry? Not allowed to lash out? Why was it that the boy in my class, Patrick, got to push people around, got to kick Connor in his bad knee whenever he wanted to, and was still loved like all the rest of them? And yet when I did my best to keep my head down, this was what I got.

"Fuck it," I muttered under my breath. I wasn't going to let anyone break me. I wasn't going to let anyone win. If they wanted a *villain* to pin their stupid jokes on, I'd give them a villain. But I wouldn't give into a lie.

I caught a glimpse of myself in the reflection of a classroom window. My tattered hair, the purple shadow beneath my eyes, my stained clothes. These were the things they could write about. Rip me to shreds, I wouldn't care. But to spread such utter bullshit?

I looked back down at the words on the notes. *Murderer, Freddy Krueger bitch, serial killer psycho.* The list went on.

That was enough.

I was going to solve this shit myself.

I crumpled the notes in my hands, stuffing them into my backpack as I made my way to class.

PART 2

March, 1989

Pepperback Press, Inc.

CHAPTER TEN

When I entered Mrs. Johnson's class, my mind was still buzzing with rage and determination. As I took my seat, I glanced around the room, my eyes scanning each student, trying to read their faces, their expressions. But the more I looked, the more it seemed impossible. Some of them were chatting amongst themselves, others were glancing at me and whispering, and two boys in the corner were having a spitball war. None of them struck me as capable of something like murder. They were too wrapped up in their petty dramas and high school antics. Although I didn't have much faith in the justice system, I thought that the detectives may have at least been able to catch the killer if said killer was as stupid as any of the students in this classroom.

As I kept looking, searching for any clues that could help me find the *real* culprit, I spotted Fouzia, sitting on her seat while chatting with our classmates, Maria and a girl whose name may have started with P. They seemed to hang onto her every word, laughing at something she'd said. Watching her, I thought that the way she spoke made me think she was performing, putting on a show in a way. It wasn't that it struck me as disingenuous, her jokes and smiles, but I got the feeling that there was a certain art to what she did. Fouzia was one of those effortlessly social people, the kind who could blend into any group and make friends with everyone.

I thought back to the day before, when she had listened to me speak about my problems. I thought of the way I'd felt relaxed in her presence, and how the girls she was talking to now seemed to have a similar reaction. I wondered about people like her, about how much she must know about everyone. People were comfortable around her, and when people were comfortable, they tended to let a bit more spill out of them than intended. Just like I had done.

So then, just how much did Fouzia know?

Despite all this, I couldn't ask her for help. This was my problem, my issue to fix. I need to prove that I could clear my name without dragging anyone else into it.

It wasn't long enough before the PA system crackled again, feedback whining into my ears for a few seconds until it finally quieted and my pain subsided.

"Ophelia Peterson, please report to the principal's office immediately." The same words, the same voice, again and again. The school secretary, whose name I could not remember, was beginning to sound like a broken record.

Some students looked at me with disgust, and some with pity. Fouzia, I noticed, was on the pitying side. Connor looked impassive, and yet his eyes seemed to linger on me a little longer than the others. Or maybe that was my own delusion.

The principal's office was just as flat and gray as I remembered. Mr. Williams sat there, fiddling with his wooden name plate as I took my seat, which creaked ominously beneath my weight.

"I have to say, Miss Peterson, I am not at all convinced by you."

I blinked at him. "What've I done wrong?"

He set the name plate down and straightened it on the desk. "I had a student come to my office today to report that they believed you were stalking them."

My heart stuttered in my chest.

Williams leaned back in his pristine black chair. "Stalking is a very serious accusation, I'm sure I don't have to remind you."

"Who?" I forced the word out.

He looked me up and down with that judgemental gaze of his. "Michael Coats. He seemed very concerned this morning and says you were loitering around his locker."

A sigh of relief escaped me and I crumpled in my chair. "I don't even know who that is."

If Connor had come in and told the principal that I was stalking him, I don't know what I would have done. Not that I believed what I was doing was stalking. I didn't.

"Nevertheless," sighed the principal, "I think it's time for you to speak with the authorities."

"I have nothing to tell."

"Lovely. Then it should be no issue."

"There is most definitely an issue." I felt anger bubbling within me once more.

"You had better watch yourself, missy," snapped the principal. He banged his hand on the surface of the table which shook with impact.

"I really am warning you this time. You will speak to the authorities, and you will begin telling the *truth,* or else you will find yourself in very big trouble." He spat the last word out like a curse. I could tell he very much wanted to curse.

I stood up, my chair sliding out behind me. "Who do you—"

He cut me off. "*Dismissed.*"

***

Of course.

Of course, of course, of course, I thought. The answer couldn't have been more obvious. Weeks of police searches and detectives snooping around town, desperate for answers, and yet it seemed so clear.

I knew from the moment I had stepped inside that classroom that not one of the students inside had the capabilities nor the intelligence to pull off such a thing as murder. And the kicker? I was right.

The killer never could have been one of the students, and that's because it was an adult. The *principal.* Williams. The one man trying his absolute hardest to pin that very murder on *me.* I had originally assumed that his need to prove that I had done it was due to misogyny, as in most cases, but this possibility made much more sense.

However, I had to quickly remind myself that it would be reckless to jump to conclusions. There was no way in hell that I could make such an accusation with my reputation the way it was. Not to mention, I hardly knew anything about the murder itself yet. Suspicion would never be enough to get him off my back.

What I needed now was proof. And information. Clues, one could call them.

I began with the newspapers. At the front of the diner, there were a bunch of them always laid out, a new stack dropped off every week. I rarely touched them myself, for I cared little about Hinton, but I knew where the extras were normally thrown out at the end of the day to be used as recycling. Fortunately, Janie was in charge of the recycling, and she hadn't done the job for weeks. For once, I was actually thankful for what a flake that girl was.

Flipping through the papers, I found that I'd been correct, and the oldest one dated back over a month ago. I only had to skim through the headlines for a few minutes before I caught a glimpse of Xavier's name.

Just as I was looking closely at the papers, I heard footsteps behind me. I quickly folded the newspaper and hid it behind my back, trying to seem nonchalant. I turned around, it was Janie, looking a little bit more miserable as usual. She didn't seem to notice my suspicious behavior.

"Oh, Ophelia. Thank god you're here!" she groaned. "I need you to cover the front for me. Missy wants me to take over her shift tonight, and I already have plans." Her eyes widened like a sad puppy, her bottom lip jutting out.

My heart raced. This was perfect.

Janie continued. "I'm supposed to be meeting my little cousin to help her with her science project, and it's due tomorrow. Can you take my tables for me? Just this once? I already asked Pam but you know how that hag is." She chuckled awkwardly.

I looked her up and down. She had on a new lipstick which was significantly redder than the one she normally wore, her nails were freshly painted, and she must have gotten her hair bleached again. For a girl who made such a face at the mention of Pam—the older waitress who'd worked at the diner for who-knew-how-long—she did bear a striking resemblance to her sometimes.

"How's John?" I asked.

She blinked, fidgeting with the edge of her dress. "The manager? He's fine. Why do you ask?"

I didn't break my stare, wondering if she'd double down on her lie.

Janie sighed, accepting defeat. "I might be...meeting up with him after, too." She gave an awkward little smile and a shrug. "You know. Nothing serious."

I was sure then that she knew what I would say and what my opinion on it was, but I also knew that if I did vocalize it now, it wouldn't make much difference. She'd get defensive and I would feel like shit, and then she'd probably tell John to fire me.

Besides, I wasn't her mother.

"Sure, I can take the shift," I said. I reasoned with myself that at least I would now have time to continue rifling through the newspapers and do my research in peace on break. "You owe me one, though."

"Really? Oh, thank you!" She burst forward and wrapped her arms around me in a suffocating yet supposedly good-natured hug. When she pulled away I could still feel my skin crawl. "It's just one table right now. Number six." She pointed towards the back of the diner.

"Fine," I agreed, not bothering to really look. Whether it was a group of ditzy middle school girls or a lone perverted balding man, I didn't really care.

When I strolled over to the table, my mind was still racing, thinking of the newspaper. Xavier, that poor kid. Those articles and the dates attached to them could be the first step into cracking the case, the key to—

My gaze flitted up from my notepad. "What can I—"

The boy sitting there smiled up at me.

Connor.

Connor?

My heart skipped a beat. Why the hell was Connor here? I could have sworn I'd never seen him come in before, and it was only once in a blue moon that we had someone new come in. There was no way he could have known where I worked, so it had to have been a coincidence, but *some coincidence* it was.

I forced myself to stay composed, clearing my throat. It felt strange to look down on him, considering he was several inches taller than me most of the time. Something came alight inside me.

"Hey," I greeted him, feigning indifference. "What can I getcha?"

"Hey," he echoed, his mouth hung open in surprise. "Didn't expect to... Just a coffee. Black."

"Coming right up," I said, writing down the order. As I turned to leave, I couldn't help but notice how the late afternoon sun highlighted the sharp angles of his face and the intensity of his gaze.

He was undeniably hot. In Hinton you never saw boys like him. There was the occasional guy you would pass on the street, or help tutor you with math, and they were always too old for you, probably with a patchy beard and a girlfriend out of town. They were the kinds of guys who were disgustingly average but most likely played guitar or wrote poetry so it was easier to pretend that they were actually attractive. Connor wasn't like that. He had no bad angles, he had perfect teeth and always clean hair. Then there were his *arms.*

I'd peeked at his grades one or two times which left me unsure of whether he was a genius or whether all the female teachers were crushing on him. Either could have been true. He had perfect hand-writing, so good that he was constantly being asked to copy notes on the chalkboard in class. I'd never come close enough, but I always had the suspicion he must smell like cinnamon.

I absentmindedly poured the coffee, stealing glances at him when-ever I could. He was sitting at a corner table, absorbed in a book. An idiotic grin was pulling at my lips. He seemed different from the other boys at school, from anyone I have ever met... so much more thoughtful. The way he talked, the way he walked, even the way he looked at me, all were just so... As hard as I tried, I could not find a single thing I did not like about him.

As I tried to catch the name of the book he was reading, I thought of my textbook and the sketches it had. For a moment, I thought, *what would happen if I showed the book to Connor?* Would he love them the way I did? Could he help me find out who drew them?

I shook my head, bringing my consciousness back to reality. Of course he wouldn't. He would think I was a crazed stalker and gladly help the principal kick me out of school.

I spotted a place on the counter where I must have spilled, and went around the back to grab a clean towel. But when I returned, and leaned to steal another glance at his table, I had to pause.

He was gone. I scanned the room again, searching for where he could be.

That was when I saw him standing out in the parking lot through the window. Three boys were standing in front of him, arms crossed over their leather jackets. It was hard to make out exactly what was going on in the dark of night.

Alarm bells were sounding off in my head.

I recognized one of them immediately—Patrick, the same asshole who had pushed Connor in gym class. From here, I could barely see his face, but I could pinpoint that smug grin from a mile away. The other two, I wasn't sure about.

They were talking while Connor did most of the listening. His back faced me so I couldn't see his expression, but just shoulders were tense, his hands curled in nervous fists.

Suddenly, one of them shoved Connor, and then another went down on him with punches. Panic surged through me as I saw him hit the ground, now facing a three-on-one, clearly an unfair game.

I dropped the coffee back onto the counter where it splashed up onto my hand. It burned like hell, but I was already on the move. I leapt into action, climbing up onto the counter. I reached up to where the rifle was hanging on the wall, and pulled it down towards me. It was heavier than I expected, but it settled into my arms with ease. Adrenaline pumping, I burst out the door of the diner and lifted the rifle.

"Hey!" I bellowed.

The three boys stopped and looked up at me. When they caught sight of the gun, the blood seemed to drain straight from their faces. They looked ghostly with fear beneath the fluorescent diner lights.

I stepped forward, confidence swelling. "Get out of here before I blow your fucking faces off." I allowed a certain venom into my words, which wasn't difficult with the rage bubbling within me.

Patrick rose to stand. "You don't understand, girlie. This...this is our friend. Right, Connor? Connor, tell her."

Girlie. I wondered if he even remembered my name.

"Go home before I do something I'll regret," I spat.

With that, all three boys turned and scattered without another word, tails between their legs. I watched them run away to a black pick-up truck and drive swiftly out of the parking lot.

Connor slowly rose up off the ground and met my eyes.

I wasn't sure what to say at first. "You okay?"

"I'm fine." He furrowed his brow. "You mind pointing that away from me?"

I let the barrel of the rifle drop to my side and took a steady breath. "Sorry."

He let out an airy laugh. "Sorry? I should be thanking you." He paused. "Thank you."

There was a few feet of distance between us, mosquitoes illuminated by the buzzing light bulbs above us as they flew through the air. Somehow he looked even more beautiful out here. I thought I saw a bruise blooming on his cheek.

"You're welcome," I said.

He hesitantly lifted his hand to gesture at the rifle still in my arms. "That's not really loaded, is it?"

I shook my head. "No."

He smiled.

Without meaning to, I smiled back.

Chapter Eleven

I made Connor a new coffee and iced the burn on my hand. He was already back at the seat where I'd left him, staring down at his thumbs. He looked shaken and I felt sorry for him.

"Here." I set his drink down in front of him, watching his reflection wiggle in the black liquid.

"Thank you," he said again, wrapping his hands around the mug. His fingernails were short, yet neat. "Shit, I don't know what I would have done if you weren't here." He glanced up at the rifle, which I'd returned to its spot on the wall.

"Get the shit beaten out of you, I guess."

He laughed. The sound made my heart jump in my chest.

I glanced over at the door, thankful as hell that it was only me and him in the diner. Technically, we were supposed to close in three minutes, but I'd die before telling him that. I'd already flipped over the open/closed sign and I was pretty sure the cook had snuck out the back half an hour ago.

When my gaze returned to Connor, he was already looking at me. His eyes were exceptionally blue. Was that a fleck of gold in them towards the middle? I'd have to come closer to be sure.

I lingered for a moment as we held eye contact.

"Do you want to maybe...sit with me?" he asked.

I hesitated for a moment. The feeling I had then was similar to the adrenaline I'd felt when I'd come out of the diner earlier with the rifle. This, I thought, was why I didn't normally talk to boys.

"Yes," I said, and then took my seat down across from him.

"So, why'd you come to Hinton?" he asked.

That surprised me. Had he not heard the rumors? "I'm from here."

"Oh." I saw the gears in his head turn. "So why did you only start school now?"

"Just got out of juvie."

"Oh," he said again, probably sorry that he'd asked, and maybe even regretting having invited me to sit with him. But instead of awkwardly excusing himself, he studied me a moment longer with his curious blue eyes. "You're kidding, aren't you?"

I nodded.

He gave a little roll of his eyes, but an amused smile was pulling at his lips.

"I dropped out at sixteen," I told him, speaking carefully. "But not because I went to juvie. My nan got sick and I couldn't afford to be away from home all day when I had to take care of her. And I needed a job that would pay for food."

I wasn't sure what had prompted me to say it. Perhaps I couldn't handle him thinking poorly of me, and had to defend myself before he did. The words spilled out regardless like sick.

His expression had turned more serious. He seemed to hang onto my every word, and it made me a bit self-conscious. "I'm sorry."

I shrugged like it was no big deal. "It's old news."

"So what made you change your mind?" wondered Connor.

"It's my turn to ask a question," I informed him. "So, tell me. Why are you drinking black coffee at nine o'clock at night?"

"You're going to think I'm crazy," he said, "but it helps me sleep."

"That does sound crazy," I agreed unseriously.

He cocked his head to the side with a sly smile. "So you're fine with juvie, but drinking coffee at night is where you cross the line."

"Indeed."

"Noted." He took another sip.

"So," I began, "you read a lot."

"I thought it would be my turn to ask a question this time."

"That wasn't a question."

"*Touché.*" He began tracing his finger around the edge of his mug. I watched the movement carefully, imagining holding his hand in mine, those same fingers tracing against my skin.... "I do read. I wouldn't say 'a lot'."

"What do you read?" I asked.

He pointed a finger at me. "Now that was a question."

"*Touché,*" I echoed him. I was enjoying this game much more than I should have.

"Do *you* read?"

"When I can," I replied. "I just finished *The Bell Jar*. It was...compelling." I wondered for a moment if he would be put off by that one. Maybe I should have gone with the safer choice, something not as dark as the novel about a mentally ill woman.

"I love Sylvia Plath," he said, taking me by surprise.

"Really?" I asked, not quite convinced.

"Really," he confirmed. "There are a couple biographies in the school library. I can show you sometime. If you haven't already found them yourself."

"No, I haven't." I looked down at my hands. "That would be nice."

"Great." He took the last sip of his coffee, leaving behind only the scattered grounds at the bottom of the cup. "I should probably get home."

"Sure." I tried to pretend that I wasn't wishing he'd stay for longer. I thought that I could probably talk to him for hours without getting bored.

He stood. "It was, um." He paused, looking down at me, his arms hanging cautiously at his sides. "It was nice talking to you."

"You too."

With that, he picked up his coat and left. Once he was out of sight, I pulled his empty mug towards me and began running my fingertips along the edge just as he had, feeling the spot of warmth where his lips had been.

That boy was going to be mine.

***

The weather was getting warmer and my eyes no longer watered when I rode my bike to school in the mornings. The sun shone down on me like a warm hug as butterflies flitted in my stomach. I was so giddy I had to make a conscious effort not to begin jumping up and down, screaming my head off. There was only one thing on my mind.

Connor.

He hadn't stayed for long after being jumped outside the diner. I imagined he must have still been on edge from the attack. His image was vivid in my mind: his blue eyes, the way he looked at me...I couldn't get over the way he'd looked at me.

As I wheeled my bike into the school's bike rack, my thoughts still on Connor and his glamorous smile, I heard Fouzia's voice behind me.

"Morning, Ophelia!" she called out, a wide smile on her face as she approached.

"Morning," I replied, managing a small smile in return. It was hard not to feel lighter around Fouzia, especially since I was in a good mood already.

She fell into steps beside me as we walked towards the school entrance. "Nice day, right? It feels like summer's close."

"It does," I agreed. I hated small talk, but I could muster up the energy to talk about the weather today.

Fouzia chuckled. "Oh, by the way," she started. "How's it going with the principal and, you know, all of that mess?"

"Pretty much the same." I paused, glancing around the hall. "I mean, I have a theory, but it's pretty far-fetched."

Fouzia's eyebrows rose in curiosity. "Really? What is it?"

"He's been acting so eager to pin everything on me, it feels like..." I gave her a knowing look, "like he's hiding something."

Surprisingly, Fouzia's expression stayed the same. "The principal? Ophelia, that's... Well, it's a big accusation."

"I know," I said quickly. "But he's been acting so weird, and he's so determined that *I'm* the culprit. It doesn't make sense unless he has something to gain from it." I knew I was unlikeable and perhaps odd-looking, but his persistence was ridiculous nonetheless.

Fouzia chewed her lip thoughtfully, then shook her head. "I don't think it's him. I mean, do you even know they're related? Mr. Williams is Xavier's *uncle*."

The shock hit me like a slap. "What? How did I not know that?"

Fouzia shrugged. "You just got here. You don't know everything." She looked over at me, holding her books tighter. "I'm just saying you can't jump to conclusions like that. That's all."

The heat of embarrassment washed over me. It would have been nice for her to mention such a thing to me earlier, I thought.

"It makes sense why he'd be so involved," stated Fouzia, suddenly sounding less like a flaky teenage girl and more like a private investigator. I could imagine her smoking a pipe as she reasoned. "He's grieving his nephew's, maybe he's not thinking straight."

"He didn't seem like he was in a very grief-stricken mood when *I* talked to him."

"I would drop it."

I felt a sinking sensation in my stomach. "So, you're telling me that I'm back to square one? Nowhere?"

Fouzia nodded. "Pretty much. But that doesn't mean you're out of options. You just need to look at the situation from a different angle, y'know?"

"Like what?" I asked, feeling a mix of frustration and helplessness. I was not even close. The idea of having to start over was daunting—to say the least. I had been so sure I was onto something, and I had just needed a proof, but now...

Fouzia glanced at me with a quizzical look. "You're really deter-mined, aren't you?"

I hardened my resolve. "I'm going to solve this murder, even if the authorities can't. It's a small town. It can't be that difficult."

She scoffed lightly.

"Something you wanted to say?" I snapped.

"It's just that…" Fouzia leaned against my locker, "you don't know the first thing about this place. All things considered, you're still the 'new girl'," she said in air quotes. She then leaned in close. "Listen, I know you haven't made a really big deal out of it, and most of the class doesn't realize since you look so different, but I know you're not technically *new*."

I frowned.

"Don't give me that look," she said. "I don't care that you dropped out. I'm only saying that even though things might feel familiar—all the same faces and whatnot—things have changed since you were last at Hinton."

"I know that."

She went on. "You're never going to figure this thing out if you don't have all the information. And I'm not talking about the basic stuff, like the principal being Xavier's uncle. I'm talking about the gossip, the secrets, the *dirt*. You don't get that by sitting alone every day at lunch."

I was taken aback by her bluntness. "I'm not completely clueless, you know."

"Oh, really?" she challenged. "Go ahead, then. Tell me some gos-sip."

I opened my mouth, then closed it again. I began wracking my brain, recalling the endless conversations that I'd observed between Laura and Agnes, their incessant complaining about something new every day. "I heard that...Audrey fell in gym and ripped her jeans open. Hello Kitty underwear for the world to see."

Fouzia eyed me for a moment. "Her name's Andrea, but close enough."

I berated myself internally for a moment. All that I'd tried to learn this month, and I was still mixing up names within my grade. I had my own world mastered; take Nan to her hospital visits, give her the right number of pills, learn how to skin a rabbit, don't let the house get infested with termites or black mold, sneer at anyone who looks at me for too long, try to ignore the ghosts in the corner of my vision. But Fouzia's world? Teenager world? That was a different story.

The two of us ventured on through the halls, right past the spot where I'd seen Xavier for the first time. I paused there for a moment and Fouzia glanced back at me with a questioning look. "You alright?"

"This is where he was found, wasn't it?" I asked.

She shuffled her feet anxiously. "The custodian saw him first, and they tried to cancel school, but the kids on the bus were already arriving. I was with them as the kids came pooling out of the buses, about to start class like normal. Everything was *so* normal at first. But then they just shut all the doors that morning and sent everyone back home. And when we had that assembly it didn't feel real."

I stepped closer to her so that no one could overhear. "So no one actually saw the body?"

She shook her head. "No. Thank god." Her gaze was set downwards, and I thought I caught a glimpse of tears glistening in her eyes.

Her tone became quieter than before. "The next day, this whole hall was closed off, but a couple kids broke in during a free period to sneak a peek at the damage done. They said there was still some blood on the floors. And the...smell. I heard the smell was terrible."

I studied her for a moment, taking in her sudden sensitivity. "Did you know him? Personally, I mean."

I worried that I might have overstepped, but the question didn't seem to surprise Fouzia. "Yeah. I guess we were friends."

How could I not have realized? Fouzia knew *everyone*. Even walking with her for five minutes as I had been now, I'd seen her throw a smile to a dozen people already. Xavier, no matter how shy or reserved he may have been, could not have been the exception. It hadn't even crossed my mind that he could have been her *friend*. Had my question been insensitive?

She was about to turn into the classroom, but I touched her arm to make her pause. "What's it going to take for you to help me with this?" I asked her, hoping that my expression conveyed earnestness.

She held my eyes for a few moments and then sighed. "I don't see how you could do any better than a real detective. I wish you the best of luck, but..." she gave a half-hearted shrug. "But I don't want to get my hopes up. I'm sorry."

I watched her stroll into her classroom, her book bag covered in pins disappearing through the doorway. The door fell shut behind her.

Standing there in the silence as the rest of the students began to shuffle into their respective classes, the hallway emptying, I wondered hopelessly just what I could do to convince the girl. I had no money to bribe with, no social currency, and no charisma with which I could try and charm her. I was empty handed.

I was pulled away from my thoughts as something caught my eye.

Stopped in the middle of the hallway was a figure shrouded in shadow. Just the silhouette. Perhaps if the last three lights at the end of the hall weren't broken as they had been for the past month, I might have been able to make out something else, but from here, I couldn't even tell if it was a girl or a boy. They were unmoving, watching, as if waiting to attack.

I stalked towards the figure. Was it a ghost? A lost soul from nearby, maybe? Or Xavier?

With a start, the strange person spun around and ran off to the side, out of my line of sight. I increased my speed until I reached the spot where I'd seen them standing, but when I looked around the corner, the person was gone.

A ghost. It must have been a ghost.

Suddenly, something clicked in my mind. Maybe I was not so empty-handed after all.

***

I stepped into my first period class, and rather than Mrs. Whitlock standing there by the chalkboard to begin her lesson, I was met by two officials in suits, a man and a woman, who straightened at my arrival.

Well, at least Williams warned me.

"Ophelia Peterson?" the first one asked. He was a man with dark hair and a roundish figure. He must have been in his mid-forties, holding an authoritative air to him that let me know exactly what he and the woman beside him were. Detectives.

"Yes," I responded, avoidant the eyes of my classmates sitting below me, lingering at the threshold of the door.

The detective wordlessly motioned towards the hall. I hesitantly stepped out and they both followed, the female detective shutting the classroom door behind her gently.

"We'd like to ask you some questions, Ophelia," she said, clearly trying to make her voice softer than natural.

I looked around the hall. "Here?"

"No, not here," she replied. "If you'll follow us?"

They led me through the school, all the way down to the guidance counselor's office, which had become all too familiar. Mrs. Quirk gave me a curt look before stepping out of her office and allowing me and the detectives inside. I settled into the same chair as always, while the male detective took Mrs. Quirk's seat across the desk in front of me. The other detective remained standing, her warm, false smile looming over me.

If she didn't want to be here, I thought, why pretend that she did with the forced grin? Everyone in the room knew why I was here, and it was far from a light topic. I much rather would have preferred that she scowl at me or insult me directly than put on such a performance.

The man sitting before me, on the other hand, had no such mask. His face remained neutral, bordering on grave as he leaned forward and clasped his hands together on the table.

"I take it you know why you're here, Miss Peterson," he said.

"Enlighten me," I said. The more he talked, the better. I wasn't exactly upset over missing math, anyway.

The detective eyed me carefully, undoubtedly seeing through my act. Still, he went on. "My name is Detective Burke. This is my colleague, Detective Sanders. We're here because we've been called to investigate a murder from a couple weeks ago. Ring any bells?"

"I heard about it."

"What did you hear?"

I shrugged. "Not much. It happened before I enrolled, which..." I smiled, "I'm sure you know."

"Is that so?"

"Yes." I didn't waver.

Sanders chimed in from above. "So how come your fellow students are claiming you're involved?"

I shrugged.

"Answer the question please," pushed Burke.

"I don't know why anyone would say that," I stated simply.

"I hope you know that it's very important that you be a hundred percent honest with us, Ophelia." There it was again, that use of my first name as if we were friends. It was like the woman's fake smile. The false warmth was so much worse than the genuine coldness

The anger it triggered in me felt like a low, sweltering flame coming alight in the depths of me, rising slowly. I didn't fight it off, but I made an effort not to show it.

"I assure you, detective," I began, my tone as earnest and warm as I could make it, leaning into each syllable as if it were a poem. I leaned forward, feeling that flame flickering behind my eyes. "If I knew *anything*, I would tell you."

A shadowy figure faded into my line of sight, circling the detective in front of me with an ominous energy, dark tendrils creeping around him as if in warning. My gaze flickered to the ghost's face—losing a precious moment of eye contact with the detective, but I made the sacrifice. At least, I now had a name to match the face of the spirit before me.

Xavier. He stood over the detective, his head hung low so that his thick black hair hung over one eye, but the other was directed towards the detective below him. He was watching, waiting, judging. I couldn't tell what he was thinking. I wasn't sure if ghosts *could* think.

I looked back to the detective.

With a sudden movement, I reached forward, over the desk, and clasped the detective's hands in my own. He flinched, which almost made me smile, but I kept my expression grave.

"I promise you," I told him. "If I hear *anything*. You'll be the first one I'll tell. You detectives are doing God's work out there."

With a gulp, Burke dropped my hands and patted them lightly. "Yeah, alright, well..." He glanced nervously over to his colleague, who now had her lip curled in a confused sort of distaste. "We'll keep in touch, then."

With that, he rose and the two detectives led me out the door, both of them keeping more distance away from me than they had before. But before I stepped out of the office, I gave them one last look.

"Thank you for your service."

With a nod, Burke shut the door firmly behind me.

Fucking cops, I thought.

Chapter Twelve

The sun was beginning to set as I locked my bike up to a wooden post that connected to the front porch of the abandoned house. The conditions were perfect for what I wanted to do.

As I made my way inside the house, rotting floorboards groaning beneath my weight, I recalled the first time I had summoned a ghost.

When it came to seeking out the spirits that I saw so often, I normally leaned towards the method of meditation. It took a long time, and it usually called the most ghosts to me, but they would vanish quickly, and rarely spoke at all. I also wasn't very good at meditation when my nerves were already shot to hell as they had been the last month.

There was, however, another method.

The first time I had summoned a ghost, I was twelve. I was a naïve middle schooler, being constantly disciplined for acting out, cursing and hitting and more. I was no stranger to bullies. I had no friends and very little self-control. My class had gone on a camping trip and it was well past midnight when I'd been risen from my sleep.

"Cover her mouth in case she screams!" whispered a girl's voice.

I felt a hand clamp onto my mouth, and before I could react, I was being pulled out of my sleeping bag. It was dark and I couldn't make out the faces of my three attackers, but I soon realized who they were once I was already being manhandled out of my tent.

I couldn't remember the kids' names. They were older than me, one girl and two boys. If I recalled correctly, I had insulted the girl for one reason or another. I couldn't even remember what I'd said that had affected her so harshly. Whatever it had been, it had offended her sorely and she'd asked her older brothers to help enact revenge.

I could still remember the feeling of helplessness that had consumed me as they'd dragged me along through the dirt and into the dark woods. I clawed at the ground and kicked my legs desperately. I tried to bite any skin I could reach, and I hit my mark once when I bit the palm of the oldest boy, clamping down until I tasted blood, but he'd kneed me in the chest in return.

I saw a flash of blue as the air knocked out of me. I whipped my head around, looking at the spot where I'd seen it, but it was dark once more, and only getting darker. They dragged me further into the woods. I was skinny then, even skinnier than I was now, and my twig arms were no use against the burly pubescent boys.

They dropped me into a pile of leaves. It was fall and I could smell the mildew when I swallowed a mouthful of dirt.

Another flash of blue. This time, when I lifted my head, I caught a glimpse of it. It was a man, or a faded image of one, fluorescent blue light shining off of his figure. He vanished within the second before the sole of the girl's sneaker made contact with my skull.

Another kick landed onto my stomach and pain shot through me. With every blow, I saw more blue, more lights, more people. A woman in a police officer's uniform, a bearded man in weathered clothes, a child in a tiara, an old man in hospital scrubs. As the pain continued, they stopped disappearing. Soon, the woods were crowded, and my beating had an audience. I stopped fighting back, so mesmerized by the sight I was seeing that I couldn't focus anywhere else. The sounds of the ghosts chattering drowned out my tortured moans.

Finally, the girl and her brothers left me there in the woods, laying on my back, looking up at the moon. I was bruised heavily and every attempt at movement felt as if I was ripping my skin off the bone.

The ghosts did not leave. At that point, I had already come to terms with what they were, but I had never seen so many at once. When I craned my head to look past the crowd surrounding me, I saw that they went back farther than I could see. Most of them watched me silently as I writhed, and others muttered to themselves unintelligibly.

In the days following the incident, the ghosts continued following me. They were with me as I finally crawled back to my tent. They were with me when I spoke with the counselors and denied that I had been attacked at all, just because I was too proud to admit they'd gotten the best of me or to be called a snitch for the rest of the year. The ghosts watched me as I packed my things and took the next bus home, my body still aching terribly the whole way there.

The ghosts did not leave me until I arrived home and stole some of Nan's pain meds. With the pain, went the spectating ghosts. Within the hour, I experienced solitude for the first time in days. And the following afternoon, when the meds began to wear off and my bruises began to ache again, the ghosts returned.

My theory, after a few years of trial and error, was that some things took me closer to death—whether it be a complete state of calm or the sensation of pain. And this proximity allowed me to see the spirits more clearly. Or it lured them towards me. I wasn't really sure which.

I sat down on the floor in the middle of the room, brushing the dust away. It was now golden hour and the sun was painting orange hues across the wall in front of me, surrounding my dark silhouette. I crossed my denim clad legs and pulled a lighter out of my pocket.

I didn't smoke. It was an expensive hobby and I'd always hated the idea. My father smoked, and just the smell that permeated off of him on the days when he came home was enough to make me nauseated. I would smell it in my hair afterwards until the next time I washed it, scrubbing my scalp raw in my rusted shower.

I took off my jacket and rolled up my sleeve, ignoring the cold that bit at my skin. Spring had not yet arrived, but I preferred the cold anyway. I sparked the lighter with a flick of my thumb and it came alive. Slowly, I brought the flame to the underside of my arm, a spot already covered in faded scars where I'd done exactly what I was doing now at least a dozen times. I withstood the pain for as long as I could, my eyes watering, fist trembling. Finally, I released a breath and the flame went out.

I opened my eyes and saw my mother sitting in front of me, her legs crossed just like mine.

"Xavier," I choked out. "Where is he?"

My mother blinked.

"I know you know. I just—" I coughed. "I've got to speak with him."

Her face was too blurred for me to analyze the expression she made. She didn't move and didn't speak. In the nine years I had been seeing her ghost, she'd never spoken a word to me. Some ghosts did, but not her. I had yet to discover what it was about them that did or didn't allow them to form words, but I theorized that it had something to do with the personality of the ghost from when they were alive. My mother had never been a loud or exceptionally talkative woman. It got me wondering what sort of ghost I would be when the time came.

Her figure dissipated, and I was left sitting alone once more. I tried to summon another ghost using my trusted lighter, but it only brought me a confused middle-aged man who paced around the room as well as an old woman who seemed to be searching for her cat. Neither of them were responsive to me, so they failed to be of any help.

Tired and frustrated and with my arm still aching, I left the abandoned house and returned home on my bike. I took nothing for the pain, hoping that it would subside eventually, but when I laid down to sleep that night, every time I shifted in bed, I felt the skin twinge and I would meet a visitor at the foot of my bed.

The next morning, I sat idly through my class, fidgeting with pens and picking off my split ends. I waited as patiently as I could before lunch arrived. At the sound of the bell, I caught Fouzia in the corner of my eye, moving towards me. We had sat together at lunch the past few days, but I didn't have the time to explain to her why I couldn't today, so I pretended not to notice her and slipped into the hall.

When I stepped through the double doors, the librarian gestured to me with her pointer finger against her lips, a reminder to stay quiet. I nodded politely and continued into the library.

I retrieved my lighter once more, and there in the dark corner of the library, I tried to summon Xavier's ghost again.

Something hit the ground behind me and I spun around to see Xavier's shimmering figure standing before me, his back turned to me. Though I couldn't see his face, I could recognize the dull black color of his hair and the sad slouch of his shoulders anywhere. A book laid by his feet and he hung his head to look down at it. Had he knocked it over himself? Could his form be strong enough to do such a thing?

"Xavier," I whispered.

He turned and his eyes met mine. He did not open his mouth to speak. His expression seemed distant, but clear enough that I could see the downward curve of his mouth.

"Xavier," I repeated, stepping closer, "what happened to you?" I was hoping that he would speak, or at least motion somewhere. We were so close to the place he died, standing in the very building where he must have spent seven hours of his day for years. There had to be some connection here, something that would help me.

On the other side of the bookshelf, the door to the library creaked open. It was met with a sharp *shush* from the librarian, and the door fell closed again. I swore internally.

"I'm trying to help you," I said quickly, keeping my voice low. "If you can give me anything. Tell me anything."

His eyes remained blank, and before I could speak again, a flash of pink caught my eye.

Agnes stepped out from behind the corner, tucking her dyed hair self-consciously behind her ear. "Hey, Ophelia."

I was caught off guard. I got a sort of unsettled feeling at seeing the girl without her twin. They were together so often that I sometimes forgot they weren't conjoined. "Hey," I answered.

"I think I'm ready for us to have a conversation," she said with a small smile.

Weird, but okay.

"A conversation?" I prompted, trying my best not to make eye contact with the ghost still standing in front of me. I stealthily slipped my lighter into my back pocket.

"Yeah. Y'know I just felt really bad about what happened and about what Laura did to you in the hall that day. It was totally uncool." She paused. "Well, like, obviously she had a reason for what she did but what happened after was really uncool and you *so* didn't deserve that. I've just been feeling really guilty and thought that I could clear things up with you, make sure you're okay and stuff."

Though her words vaguely resembled an apology, I wasn't quite sure if it could be considered one. I weighed my options for a moment.

"So, like," Agnes continued, "I'm s—" She paused again. "I feel really bad."

Interesting, I thought. *She's discovered empathy.*

There was a long silence before I realized she was waiting for me to speak.

"Oh, um," I began. "Yeah, I—"

Xavier's ghost, which I had nearly forgotten about, suddenly turned and began walking away. I wasn't sure if the movement could be described as walking. His legs swung back and forth, but they didn't quite hit the ground. More like he…swam through the air purposeful-ly.

"Why don't we continue this conversation in the hall?" I blurted. "It's so quiet in here. I wouldn't want to get told off by Dewitt."

"Who?" Agnes cocked her head.

"The librarian."

"Oh."

I scooped my bag up off the floor and darted around the shelf, not bothering to see if Agnes was following me. Xavier passed through the solid door seconds before I opened it. I began speed walking through the hall, trying desperately to catch up with the ghost before he could leave my sights without alarming Agnes by running.

"Uhh, are we going to the cafeteria?" Agnes asked from behind me. She was shorter than I was, so it cost more effort to get her tiny legs matching my pace.

"Yup," I answered without thinking.

"Well, it's that way." She jutted her head in the opposite direction.

"Short cut," I explained, zipping around another corner. Xavier seemed to be going faster and faster by the second and I wasn't sure how much longer I could keep up with him.

"Ophelia," called Agnes, trying to hide the fact that she was pant-ing, "why are we running?"

I was too distracted to answer her now. Xavier had disappeared through a metal gray door at the end of the hall, and I would die before losing him now. I didn't hesitate before grabbing the handle and swinging the heavy door open to find a tiny closet-sized room with only a ladder leading upwards. I stepped in and looked up. There was no ghost inside, only a small hatch above the end of the ladder.

I looked back to Agnes. "Is this door usually unlocked?"

"Mhm." She put her hand on her hip, and I could tell she was getting fed up with my antics. "I heard it's a safety hazard, but whatever."

My gaze went upwards again. "Whatever, indeed."

With that, I began climbing the ladder.

Agnes was scandalized. "You're going to get us in trouble! Ophelia, get down!"

"*Shh!*" I continued climbing. "Just watch for teachers." I told myself then that if she could successfully get her shit together and keep me from getting suspended again, I would consider accepting her half-assed apology. But at this point I didn't really care either way.

When I reached the top of the ladder, I used one arm to hook myself in place so I wouldn't fall while I raised the other to unlatch the door above my head. It popped open with an easy *click* and sunlight poured in. As I pulled myself through the door, I felt the ladder shudder beneath me. I looked down.

"What are you doing?" I hissed to Agnes.

"I'm coming with you!"

"No, I told you to watch!"

"Here," she said, taking a step down. "I'll close the door so nobody comes in."

"*Agnes, don't—*"

The door slammed shut and Agnes began her ascent towards me. I pinched my nose, regretting every single life decision which had brought me to this point.

"*Great*," I muttered under my breath.

Agne's head popped up through the hatch, her eyes widened with fear. "I didn't mean to close it!" she whispered rapidly.

"You literally said—Nevermind. Forget it. Just stay close to the wall," I advised, "and try not to freak out. We're not that high up."

Her face told me she was indeed close to panicking. I tried to resist the urge to push her off the edge. I scanned the roof, searching for any sign of Xavier. The roof was mostly flat, with only a few air conditioning units and vents breaking up the monotony. Then I saw him, one solitary figure sitting on the edge, his back facing me.

I waited until I had put enough distance between me and Agnes before speaking. The last thing I needed was another rumor that I was a schizophrenic.

"Xavier," I called, inching forward. As I came closer, trying to keep my balance, Xavier's ghostly form became clearer. He sat hunched over, his knees drawn to his chest, staring blankly at the horizon.

I cautiously sat down beside him, close enough to see his downcast eyes but too far to reach out. We sat in silence for a moment, the only sound being Agnes's nervous voice calling for me to come back. As I glanced around, something caught my eye on the roof's surface—a carving, an old one. I leaned closer, squinting to read the faint etching. The name "Xavier" was scratched into the concrete, an uneven heart in the middle, followed by... "Fouzia"?

Now, that didn't line up.

Yeah. We were...friends. Fouzia's words echoed in my head.

Yeah. We were...friends. Again.

Friends. Again, again, and again. Her words kept swirling in my mind, every word, every pause she took to finish that sentence. It all clicked in an instant.

Friends, my ass.

CHAPTER THIRTEEN

Agnes and I had to wait two hours in the tiny roof access room, each of us taking turns banging on the door one after the other. One would think that such an experience would have trauma-bonded the two of us, but instead I was just left smelling like the girl's flowery perfume for the rest of the day.

"Jesus, you smell like a candle," I sneered while we made our way towards the principal's office, trailing behind Mrs. Quirk. She was the one who had finally noticed our incessant banging, and never had I ever wanted a photograph of something more than I wanted one of the look on her face when she had opened that door. *Priceless.*

Agnes looked appalled at my comment. "Do you even wear deodorant?"

"Nope."

She shuddered with disgust.

Mr. William's office was just as bland and dreary as I remembered it. Now that I was thinking about it, it reminded me vaguely of the hospital where Nan had done her surgery. There was the same lack of color, a soulless man in a position of power, and a whirring air conditioner above our heads.

When we took our seats across from the principal's desk, he did not say a word. Instead, he slid two identical pamphlets across the desk towards us. I leaned forward to read the front page.

Teen's guide to dealing with suicidal thoughts.

I looked at him, then back at the pamphlet, then back at him. "I'm not suicidal." I couldn't speak on Agnes' behalf so I left it at that.

"Then will you girls care to explain to me what you were doing trying to access the roof?" He tilted his chin downward, looking mildly bored. I doubted that this was the first time he'd dealt with such an issue.

"Sir, it's a complete misunderstanding," protested Agnes.

He glared down his nose at her. She seemed at a loss for words.

I sighed.

"We were making out."

Now this seemed to wake him up a bit, his eyes going comically wide. "Excuse me?"

"You heard me."

Though I wasn't looking at her, I imagined that Agnes was no less than shell-shocked. To my surprise, she remained absolutely silent.

Williams closed his eyes for a moment, his shoulders stiff. While he took a breather, I took a moment to notice a little picture frame on his desk of him and his blonde-haired wife.

He opened his eyes and stared each of us dead in the eyes. "Get out."

***

"Fouzia!" I zipped through the crowd of teens exiting the school, zigzagging on my bike. I had spotted the bright blue color of Fouzia's hijab and was following it like a beacon.

"Watch it!" hissed the boy whose foot I almost flattened with my tire. I didn't bother to apologize and continued pedaling forward until I skidded to a stop at Fouzia's side. I hopped off the bike and walked alongside it to match her pace.

"Hey," I said, waiting for her to acknowledge my presence.

She continued forward as if I were a ghost.

"Hey." I said it louder and stepped in her path.

She finally stopped and glared down at me. "Done ignoring me, then?"

I faltered for a moment. I had completely forgotten about how I had blown her off at lunch. It had never occurred to me that she would be so offended. "I got stuck in a closet."

Her expression didn't change. "Right."

A beat passed, and Fouzia began to continue towards her bus before I grabbed her arm and stopped her. "I'm sorry," I said. "Can we talk?"

She glanced from the yellow school bus to my pleading expression. "Sure," she agreed.

The two of us made our way farther from the school where Fouzia suggested we stop in the corner shop so that she could buy candy and a granola bar. She asked if there was anything I wanted and I told her no, but I didn't refuse the square of chocolate that she offered me once we left the store.

We took a seat beside each other on the curb, close enough to still see the school building from a distance. Fouzia made noises at every stray cat that passed by.

"Why didn't you tell me you dated him?" I asked.

Fouzia paused, letting the orange tabby finish the last of the granola bar in her hand before it darted away without a trace and she looked up at me. "How do you know that?"

"I asked you first."

She twisted her lips, looking conflicted. I saw the resignation in her eyes as she opened her mouth to speak. "You really think either of our families would have approved of each other?"

"What, 'cause he didn't wash his hair?" I scoffed, remembering the greasy-haired figure I'd seen wandering the halls.

Her gaze went cold again. "My family isn't exactly..." she paused. "We were from different backgrounds. My parents expected me to marry a certain way."

I could imagine. But if Fouzia thought that if she told me, I would somehow spread the news around school, she hadn't been paying attention. And anyway—the boy was *dead*. What did she have to worry about now?

"Wait," Fouzia stopped. "'He didn't wash his hair'? He transferred *after* you dropped out." She eyed me. "How do you know what he looked like?"

My first instinct was to lie and tell her that I'd seen his picture in the newspaper, but I had already scoured the newspaper and while there had been a section mentioning his name, there was never a photo. The only ones who knew what he had really looked like were those that had known him.

"I, um..." I hesitated, racking my brain for the best way I could explain it all. The most normal-sounding option there I could think of. "I know a lot of things."

She leaned in closer, taking another bite of chocolate. "Go on," she prompted in a mildly threatening way.

"You're going to think I'm crazy. Just want to preface with that."

"Don't pretend that you care what I think."

I nodded. "I'm a..."

"Yes?"

"A psychic."

She rolled her eyes, the disappointment clear. "Okay," she said, with a hint of *fuck you* in her tone.

"I'm not kidding."

"Okay," she repeated.

"Really, Fouzia."

"Are you on something?" she asked in all seriousness.

"Look," I said, trying to keep my voice steady, "I found something on the roof."

She raised an eyebrow.

"Yeah, the roof." I knew I was walking on unsteady ground here, and while Fouzia may have seemed like an unusually open person, I knew that she wasn't always what she seemed. "But seriously, I found something there that you may know about...."

"And what is that?"

"Xavier's name. And yours."

I could tell that she was getting more and more fed up with me. "So you saw that while you were screwing around doing god-knows-what on the roof. That doesn't make you psychic, Ophelia."

"But I was led there. I was trying to find something that would help me learn about Xavier since you've been less than helpful." She scoffed at that. "And I got a sense that I should go to the roof. So I did. And then I found your carving."

She still seemed skeptical, and I was bordering on desperation, so I leaned forward and mustered as much bullshit as I could. "Don't you get it? It's a sign. We're the ones that are meant to solve this."

She was silent for a moment, and then she shook her head. "You're a terrible liar, you know."

I considered the option of telling her the truth of what I saw. I could imagine how the conversation would commence as I began detailing the first time I'd seen my mother's ghost when I was seven. That way, I supposed she would be more inclined to believe that I was telling the truth. Or, more likely, that I *believed* I was telling the truth. Unfortunately, she'd probably be more inclined to report me to the counselor, as well. The word *psychic* had a more whimsical ring to it. And there were a number of self-proclaimed psychics in town already who made a considerable salary from bullshitting as I was doing now.

Honesty was supposed to be the best policy, wasn't it?

"But don't you want to believe me just a little bit?" I said.

She stared at me, her eyes searching for any hint of deception. Something told me that she'd already figured me out. It was scary to feel known.

"I need you to clear my name," I continued. "You need me to get justice."

She glanced at my bike, which had been lying on the ground for the past ten minutes. "You ride well?" she asked.

"I guess so?" I was confused.

"I missed the bus because of you," she pointed out. "If you give me a ride home, I will *consider it*."

It wasn't an answer, but it was plenty enough for me. I was filled with a sense of triumph. "You wanna ride on the handlebars?"

She nodded, "Just don't kill us. Otherwise I'm definitely not helping."

"Deal."

CHAPTER FOURTEEN

Connor visited the diner again on Saturday evening. The second I laid my eyes on him, my heart seemed to jump into my throat. I tapped Janie on the shoulder and offered to cover the table where he sat, the same one he'd taken last time. Had that been on purpose? *Maybe.* I ventured to hope that he'd sat at the same table because he thought it would be in my section again. After all, I'd never mentioned that I had covered another girl's section. Thankfully, Janie was too busy flirting with her own table to question my offer, and promptly waved me away.

I approached the table with my notepad in hand. "Funny seeing you here."

He looked up and smiled. *Ugh.* He had a wonderful smile, which seemed to transform and light his face so completely. "Hey."

"Hey." I gathered myself. "What can I get you?"

"Coffee," he said. "And a waffle."

"Anything on it?" I said as I scribbled it down.

"Ice cream. If you have it." He paused. "I like the apron, by the way."

I glanced down at myself, feeling mildly self conscious. "No, you don't. It's hideous and smells like hamburger grease."

"You're admitting to smelling like hamburger grease?"

"I said the apron smells like it. Not me."

"Sure, I believe you," he nodded with false sincerity.

"Asshole."

I looked up at him to find a pleased grin still lingering on his lips. God.

I put in his order and checked on the other four tables in my section. I snuck a look at him every time I passed, and half the time, he was already watching me. He pulled out a book eventually, and I began trying as discreetly as I could to discern which book it was.

"Watch it," one of the assistant cooks hissed at me as he passed, balancing hot plates on his arms. I heard him mutter something rude as he turned away from me. Surprisingly, I was in too good of a mood to care.

As I refilled the coffee at another table, I stole a glance at Connor. He was still engrossed in his book, his brow furrowed in concentration. Curiosity gnawed at me—what was he reading? Finally, I couldn't take it anymore. I approached his table with a fresh pot of coffee.

"Need a refill?" I asked, trying to take a peek at the cover.

He looked up, eyes twinkling. "Would be nice if you'd tell me why you're so interested in what I'm reading."

"Just trying to see if we have similar tastes."

He chuckled and closed the book, holding it up so I could see the cover. *Frankenstein*. A classic. *Not bad.*

"Good choice," I said, pouring his coffee. "A man with taste."

He took a sip, his eyes never leaving mine. "And what does a girl with taste do after her shift ends?"

"So, I say *man* and you say *girl?*"

"Sorry. Woman."

"Better." I put a hand on my hip, trying to fight a smile. My insides were bubbling with excitement, and I wasn't sure if I'd felt this many butterflies since I was thirteen. "So, you're asking me out?"

"There's that arcade around the block."

I hesitated for a moment, but the idea of spending more time with him was too tempting to resist. "You want to take me to the arcade."

He nodded, his expression earnest. "Yeah. We could...talk more."

The way he said it made my heart race. I couldn't fight the feeling that I was *winning.*

After finishing the last of my tables and cashing out, I grabbed my jacket from the back and found Connor waiting by the door. He looked relaxed, leaning against the frame, his hands in his pockets. He was wearing a blue denim jacket with matching stars embroidered on the shoulders. I wondered who had sewn them on for him—he didn't quite seem the type to embroider.

"Ready?" he asked, holding the door open for me.

"Ready," I replied, stepping out into the cool evening air.

We started walking side by side, the lights from the diner fading as we entered the park. The trees rustled softly in the breeze, and the path was lit by warm, dim lights. For a moment, as we neared the arcade, things were quiet and peaceful.

I was standing close enough to Connor to be able to smell him now. I took a deep breath, hoping he wouldn't think anything of it. He smelled like cinnamon.

"So," he began, breaking the silence, "how long have you been working at the diner?"

"About a year," I replied. "Do you work somewhere?"

"I did. I had a job at the second-hand store by the gas station. I was saving up for my car."

I raised an eyebrow, trying to hide that I was impressed. "You have a car?"

"Mhmm. Well, my uncle paid half of it. He's a nice guy."

The peace did not last, because soon, the erratic and overlapping game music filled my ears as the arcade came into view. He held the door open for me and we walked in.

The arcade was a riot of color and noise, a dimly lit cave of flashing screens and neon lights. Rows of game cabinets lined the walls, their marquees glowing like electric beacons in the dark. The air smelled like buttered popcorn, artificial cherry candy, and the faint metallic tang of quarters passing from hand to hand. The floor was sticky in places, worn thin in others, the patterned carpet absorbing years of restless footsteps.

A group of kids crowded around a Street Fighter II machine near the entrance, their voices rising in excitement as one of them landed a perfect combo. The screens flickered with pixelated action—spaceships soaring, characters leaping, cars speeding along endless highways. A few older teens leaned against a pinball machine, its silver ball ricocheting wildly under their distracted gazes. Somewhere in the back, the tinny, warbling voice of a synthesized announcer declared a *Game Over*.

Connor walked in like he belonged there, his head tilting slightly as he scanned the room. I followed, my eyes flitting from one machine to the next. It was overwhelming at first—the noise, the lights, the sheer energy of the place—but beneath it all, there was something thrilling about it. Like stepping into another world.

Connor leaned down slightly to speak to me. "Have you been here before?"

I exhaled, shaking my head slightly. "Never had anyone to go with."

His gaze flickered toward me, something unreadable in his expression. For a second, the noise of the arcade seemed to dim, the flashing lights casting shifting shadows across his face. Then, without hesitation, he reached into his pocket, pulled out a few quarters, and pressed them into my palm. His fingers were warm against my skin, brief but steady.

"Well," he said, his voice light but certain, "you do now."

I could see the challenge, the chaos, the unspoken competition humming beneath the surface of every game. And standing next to him, I felt it, too.

Tetris was open. When it caught my eye, I practically raced over, popping the quarter inside. "You haven't told me why you came back to the diner," I said as the game began, colorful geometric boxes filling my screen. "Especially after...."

"Getting the shit kicked out of me?" he said, using my own words. "Yeah."

"You know, I would have pegged you to have gone for one of the shooter games."

"I like the ones that make you think," I explained. "You avoiding my question?"

I saw him look at me in the reflection of the screen, a smile playing on his lips that told me he was indeed. "Maybe I was hoping to run into a certain waitress again."

Warmth tickled my neck. "You're so full of shit." I had to admit, my flirting skills did need work, but from the look on his face, he didn't seem to mind. "So, if you've got a car, how come you always walk to school?"

He shrugged. "It's close by. Why waste the gas?"

I paused and the yellow shape in front of me nearly fell into the wrong spot. "The west side isn't that close by."

"I don't live on the west side."

"I—" It took me a moment to realize what I had let slip. The countless days I had altered my course to cross with his in the mornings and afternoons. The course which led to the west side of town. I couldn't imagine what he'd think if he knew what I'd done just for the sake of seeing him.

My fingers faltered on the controls, and before I could recover, a long blue piece landed sideways, creating an awkward gap. I cursed under my breath, trying to fix it, but my movements were jerky, frantic. Another piece tumbled into the wrong spot, stacking the mess even higher. Connor chuckled nervously beside me, and I knew—knew—that he had caught on. My face burned as I fumbled with the joystick, desperately trying to clear the mistake, but it was too late. The screen flashed red. *Game Over.*

"I must have been thinking of someone else," I sighed, stepping away from the machine.

Once we left the arcade, having spent an unreasonable amount of Connor's money, we continued walking down the empty paths outside, everything eerily dark and quiet like any other night in Hinton. When we found ourselves back at the diner, the *closed* sign was already facing outwards. I internally thanked Janie with all my heart.

"I guess I'll see you at school," he said, turning to face me. The street lights lit up the top of his hair in a way that made him look angel-like. That same white light danced on the edge of his lips as he turned them into a warm smile.

I had only kissed a boy once before. It was so uneventful that I struggled to remember it now. I think I'd been eleven or twelve, right at that age before I began to hate everyone and everyone hated me. His name was Liam or Leo and we'd kissed on a dare. The experience had kind of put me off the whole thing, and I'd never had the urge to do something similar since. At this moment, however, I had a very strong and inexplicable urge to put my lips on his.

It had taken several years of self-reflection to realize that one of my main flaws was my lack of impulse control. I was aware of this. I rarely made any effort to fix it. Now, here, in this carpark, with a sickeningly beautiful person in front of me, I faced the inevitable consequences of such a flaw.

I leaned in, letting my eyes begin to lazily close.

"Oh." He took a half-step back. My breathing stopped.

I reeled back, blood rushing to my face at once. "Oh, my god." *Oh, my god.* "I'm so sorry." *Oh, my god. Oh, my god.* Never in my life had I felt such a sensation of complete and utter dread. The rush of fear and disgust I felt at that moment was worse than any dead spirit I'd ever laid eyes on. I had a very clear and distinct thought in that moment that I would do anything to be able to die right there and then.

"No, it's fine," he scrambled to say. "Don't worry about it."

I could not possibly express how little that statement meant. "I should go." I turned to leave, then paused one last time. "Sorry."

***

Me being who I was, shame was not a feeling I was particularly experienced with. The usual included rage, fear, disgust, and pride. I could handle those just fine. But shame? Shame was like a hole in my chest, like bugs crawling across my skin, like my blood boiling within with no relief and no way out. Shame was inescapable. Shame could be the death of me.

There I lay at three in the morning in my bed, eyes wide open, staring at the ceiling where I could see every inch of water damage above me. I'd been awake for twenty-four hours and yet sleep would just not come. I had been tossing and turning, my bones vibrating within my flesh. I had every urge to crawl out of my own body, to allow my spirit to separate itself and be free of its horrible prisons.

I could not return to that school, to that class. I would die before I did. Screw whatever my father said. Not even the money seemed worth my anguish.

When the clock struck five, I peeled myself from my bed. The pit in my stomach was too deep for me to have any sort of breakfast, so I buttered a single slice of bread and brought it to the room where Nan slept. I woke her and ignored her protests as I handed her her medicine, a glass of water, and the bread.

"Where on Earth are you going so early?" she grumbled as she swallowed the pills. Sometimes I could still see her as a teenager the way she easily got so moody. I wondered if she ever saw me as one anymore.

"To meet a friend," I told her. For once, it was the truth.

Standing in front of Fouzia's house, I couldn't help but feel a bit awkward. It was my first time at a friend's house in ages, and the unfamiliarity made my skin prickle. The front yard was small but well kept. I wondered if it was her or her parents who were in charge of the upkeep.

The garage was off to the side, its door partially open, casting a dim shadow over the driveway. The garage door was old and creaky, its paint peeling in places, but it still served its purpose. Following the instructions Fouzia had given me the day before, I made my way hesitantly inside.

I crouched slightly and slipped under the door, my heart pounding in my chest. Inside, the garage was a cluttered but oddly inviting space. There was a bright red couch against one wall and a mini blue fridge humming quietly in the corner. A workbench was strewn with various tools, and shelves were filled with boxes and random knick knacks. It was hard to imagine Fouzia fixing up cars or hammering wood, so I assumed the space wasn't hers.

Fouzia was already there, setting up a large map on the wall. She wore a pair of round purple glasses, balancing delicately on her nose. I'd never seen her with them before, and it had never struck me that she wore contacts. Her hijab was also nowhere to be found, long black curls falling loosely down her back like tar. She looked so different that I questioned for half a second if I had wandered into the right house.

She glanced up and smiled warmly as I entered. "Hey, you made it."

"Yeah," I said. "Nice setup you've got here."

She shrugged, a hint of pride in her expression. "It does the job. Ready to get started?"

I nodded, pushing away the embarrassment from yesterday from my mind. "Let's do this."

We began pinning down locations on the map, marking places and names. To the right, there was a black sheet of chalkboard where Fouzia wrote at the very top, *SUSPECTS*. She had a neat, bubbly type of handwriting, contrasting sorely with my scratchy, erratic script.

"Where do we start?" I asked, glancing at Fouzia.

"We start with him," she said. "Then draw the lines from there." Either oblivious or uncaring to the cliché, she retrieved a roll of bright red string and clear tape.

Full detective mode, I thought.

She picked up a small cutout photo of Xavier, his features blurred but distinctive. His hair was shorter than when I had seen him, but he still had the same slouched, unmotivated posture. She lingered on the photo, a wave of sadness passing over her expression before taping it up to the wall. "Here's his house. One thing you should know about X—his parents were horribly strict. They hardly let him out of the house over the weekend."

She reached over to the chalkboard and wrote beside the suspects column, *TIMELINE*.

"The police showed up to the school around 6:45 AM. Just early enough for them to have still been there when the buses arrived, but late enough that they were left with a hundred students that weren't allowed inside the building." She continued scribbling, adjusting her glasses on her nose. "That means that his parents must have called the police beforehand." She quieted suddenly. "I don't know *how much* beforehand, because they've refused to speak to me."

"You've tried to talk to them?" I asked incredulously.

"Twice." Her form seemed to deflate before she bristled and continued on. "We have to find out when they made the call, that way we can know if he came home that night or not."

"Why not go down to the station?"

"Have you seen the cops in this town?" she scoffed. "They're a bunch of incompetent nutbags and they're condescending as hell every time I pass them."

I couldn't argue with that. However...

"My dad is friends with the sheriff," I said. "Or *was.*"

Fouzia turned slowly towards me, her eyes lighting up. "Are you kidding? That's *perfect!*"

It was certainly perfect on the nights that I would find myself locked in a cell at the cold, damp police station at four in the morning with bruises on my fist, only to find my father shaking the sheriff's hand before driving me home. That was when he still lived in Hinton. These days, I would spend the whole night.

"You've gotta go down today and try to get those times," she implored. "Maybe if you go, we could get some *real* information."

"Well, time probably shouldn't be our top priority. What about—"

"No, the exact time is important. It will help us narrow things down."

"I really think—"

"Trust me," Fouzia interrupted again.

"What difference does it make if he went home or not? He died either way." I threw my hands in the air.

155

Fouzia quieted, and I realized instantly the mistake I'd made with my wording. She took a breath and spoke again. "I know you're very committed to this 'bitch who doesn't care what you think of me' act, but I'd really appreciate it if you could take it down a notch for a while." *Otherwise, I'm not helping you,* were the unspoken words there.

I shook my head. "I didn't mean to—"

"Just go to the police station. Today. The longer we wait, the less likely they'll be to want to pull it out of their records." She paused again, looking me up and down. Her eyes looked considerably bigger with the way her thick-lensed glasses warped them. "You know, I'm not trying to be mean, but maybe you really should work on the attitude."

"Yeah, I get your point," I huffed.

"No, I'm serious." She placed a hand on my arm. "If we're really going to do this, you need information, and the only way to get information is from *people*...which...are not your strong suit."

I tried as hard as I could not to be offended.

"How about Laura and Agnes?" she asked. "They're quite popular. What do you think are the chances you could fix things with them?"

I thought back to the chaos that had ensued the day Agnes *almost* apologized to me in the library. They were both undoubtedly insufferable, of course, and her apology hadn't been worth shit, but I couldn't deny the social leverage I could gain if I pretended that I no longer hated either of them again. The gossip might prove useful if I actually began to listen.

"I think I could," I said. *If I swallowed my pride.*

"Great," she said, running her fingers through her hair, "then you have homework, my friend."

CHAPTER FIFTEEN

My first task—as ordered by the very convincing Fouzia—took place at the police station, which just *had* to be on the complete opposite side of town. I was already sweating by the time I arrived, dismounting from my bike. The building itself was as unwelcoming as ever, a grim, gray structure that brought back unpleasant memories of my wrists in handcuffs and my father's angry voice on the phone. It had a dated sign out front that read *Hinton Police Department* in chipped gold letters.

Taking in the looming building, I realized this was the first time I was approaching it of my own accord and not in the back of a squad car, a firm hand around my bicep.

I steeled myself and walked in, the familiar scent of stale coffee and disinfectant hitting me almost immediately. The receptionist, a surly woman named Donna, looked up from her magazine and raised an eyebrow. "Can I help you?"

"I need to speak with the sheriff."

She looked me up and down, clearly unimpressed. "What's this about?"

"It's personal," I stated, trying to sound sure of myself. "You remember me. Michael's daughter?" I prayed that the name would only bring up friendly memories. I couldn't quite recall where he and the sheriff had last kept in touch, or on what note they left off.

Donna's skepticism was palpable, but she sighed and picked up the phone. "Sheriff, there's someone here to see you. Your old pal's little girl." After a brief pause, she continued. "That's the one."

Donna looked at me and nodded, pointing down the hall. "Last door on the right."

I walked down the narrow corridor, wrinkling my nose at the smell of cigarette smoke. I knocked gently on the door before hearing a gruff voice call out, "Come in." I turned the knob.

The county sheriff sat there, his ankle hooked on the edge of his desk, worn down by years of termites and an overzealous cleaning job. He looked older than the last I'd seen of him, his thick beard graying around his leather-skinned face. He put out his cigarette on the dirty ashtray in front of him.

"Michael's girl. Ophelia, right? Haven't seen your pop in a while. What brings you here?" he asked, motioning for me to take a seat. I breathed slowly, steading myself as I sat down in the worn out chair opposite the sheriff. His eyes, a sewage green, had a mix of curiosity and concern.

Sitting in front of him made me feel like a kid again. It wasn't that he had a particularly domineering presence or that he intimidated me. It was just that the sight of him brought back memories of when my father still pretended to care—when he lived in Hinton. I remembered the late night family dinners where the sheriff would sit across from me at the table, laughing and talking, looking at me just like he did now.

"I need your help." I was about to ask for a big favor, a really *big* favor. I recounted to him what had happened at school. The rumor that had spread to everyone, how I got entangled in the entire mess, and how deeply unfair the situation was. I had to resolve the issue on my own because the adults, instead of helping, were merely shifting blame onto others and refusing to take responsibility. All of it just led to me having to handle the whole thing all by myself.

His expression softened, probably out of pity. "Ophelia, I understand that all of this is just not a fair game for ya. But you're—what? Sixteen? This is a big case, bigger than any other, and it's best to stay away from it and not get any more involved. Ya understand? It's not safe. I can't do that to your father."

I clenched my fists, trying to keep the same expression I had the whole time.

Don't be bitchy about it. Fouzia's voice echoed in my mind.

"I understand, Sheriff. But I need to—"

He sighed. "I get you're concerned, but there are procedures and protocols we have to follow for situations just like this. I feel for ya, I really do, but think about it this way. Soon you'll be graduated and this'll all seem like a load of inconsequential crap." He looked me in the eyes, driving his point home. "Let the police take care of this."

I forced a smile, swallowing my disappointment. "Thank you for your time, Sheriff. I appreciate it."

He nodded. "Stay safe, kid. At least for the sake of your sick nan waiting for ya at home."

I stood up and made my way to the door, my mind racing with frustration. What was I supposed to tell Fouzia? I had one job, and yet my utter lack of charm seemed to stand in my way. If only I could—

My thoughts were interrupted as I stepped into the corridor. A couple feet to my left sat Patrick, the insufferable boy from my class, the one who had jumped Connor with his friends that day at the diner. He was slouched in his chair against the wall, fiddling with his watch. When he noticed me, he looked up and grinned, running a hand across the back of his neck where his pale skin contrasted his dark brown hair.

"Hey." He rose to his feet. Now that I was up close, I could see that he was several inches taller than me, and considerably wider too.

Why are you smiling at me, dumbass? I almost shot you. Those were the words I wanted to say to him, but I had to remind myself that I *was* capable of learning. I would not start a fight that wouldn't do me any good, especially not in a place of law and order with the sheriff right on the other side of the wall.

And so instead of replying, I looked him up and down, and walked right past him.

***

The next day of school was no less painful than the last. I had been met with another night of tossing and turning, and when I looked in the mirror to brush my teeth, I found that the dark purple circles beneath my eyes had only deepened. When I really took a moment to think about it, I wasn't exactly model material. My hair was greasy and

162

my teeth were crooked. When I leaned in even closer to the mirror, I realized that I had what one might call a unibrow.

Frowning at my reflection, I thought back to Fouzia's commentary on my current social life.

I caught a glimpse of my mother's figure behind me, her watchful eyes meeting mine. Here, in the house where she had raised me, her image was so much clearer. I could see every detail of her face, every rise and fall of her chest as if she were really breathing. As if she were really alive. When I was younger, people raved about how similar the two of us looked. I could hardly see the similarities now. She was tall and slender, her sleek hair so dark it almost looked blue in the light. She had a strong nose with a little bump in the middle, just like mine, but her nose made her look graceful and almost divine. Mine had no semblance of beauty when set on my face. It was the deadly beak of a bird of prey.

I looked down at the clock on the edge of the table. I had an hour and a half before my first class.

"Fuck," I whispered before grabbing a pair of tweezers from the medicine cabinet.

I spent half an hour in the shower beneath the searing hot water. I shaved my legs and underarms with an old, dull razor. I found a bottle of half-empty hair conditioner under the sink and spread it through my hair until my fingers slid easily through the strands. I scrubbed my entire body clean until my skin was red and angry. When I finally turned the water off, I ventured into the living room, only a towel across my body, and retrieved a small bottle of vanilla extract from the cabinet to dot on my neck and cover whatever was left of my body odor. It was a trick I'd seen my mother do when she ran out of perfume. While my hair was still wet, I combed it gently just like I'd seen her do so that it would dry sleek and straight. I used coconut oil on the places where I'd shaved, and then, leaning over the sink to get my face as close to the mirror as I could, carefully plucked the scraggly hairs around my brows until they formed dark, delicate lines arching above my blueish eyes.

When I finally finished, I felt as if I'd peeled back an old layer of skin and here was the new and fresh version of me, like a snake.

When I looked in the mirror, I nearly mistook myself for the ghost standing beside me. It was a feeling I could get used to.

I set out Nan's medicine and hopped onto my bike before zooming to class.

When I arrived, I walked away from my bike feeling a bit lighter, my hair felt softer, and my skin—though a bit raw from the scrubbing—was smooth and supple, breathing in the sunlight. I had on a shirt Nan got me for last christmas that was never worn. It was red and hugged my curves in a way I wasn't used to, and so I had been letting it rot in my closet for the past three months. As I strutted through the hall, feeling virtually naked for the first time in years, I did nothing but pray that this would be worth it. I caught glances in the hallway, open jaws and raised eyebrows followed by murmurs to a nearby friend.

I stopped at my locker, spinning the lock and opening the door. As I grabbed my books and shoved them into my bag, I was suddenly knocked off balance, my bag slipping from my grasp and spilling most of its contents onto the floor.

"Whoa, my bad," came a voice above me. I looked up to see Patrick with his dark brown hair sticking every which way. He crouched down and began helping me gather my things. His eyes flicked up to mine and he gave me a crooked grin. He had nice teeth. "You look different."

I eyed him. I didn't choose to stay silent just because I knew it would give me a sort of edgy-girl mystique, but rather because I worried about the poison that would leave my mouth if I chose to speak. There were several insulting things I could say to this boy if I wanted to.

"In a good way," he clarified. "A *really* good way."

With that, he handed me my things and disappeared off to his class. I turned to watch him go, only to see that he looked back, too.

I was still feeling unnerved by the time I walked into my first period, a minute or two later than usual. By the time I opened the door, all the other students were already at their seats, and the history teacher, Mr. Roberts, was organizing notes at his desk.

The class quieted when I walked in.

It was a different kind of quiet. They weren't watching me to make sure I wouldn't steal their things, or so that they could snicker to the friend next to them. The eyes on me at this moment didn't even seem intentional. It was as if they couldn't help themselves but look. I hated it.

I sat in my seat as quickly as I could, shooing away the tendrils of Xavier's spirit with a waving hand. Fouzia, sitting at my side, slowly leaned sideways to whisper in my ear.

"You look hot."

I rolled my eyes.

"I'm serious," she insisted. "I mean, you were hot before, but now it's just a lot more obvious."

"Thanks," I said. Since Mr. Roberts still seemed occupied, I spun around in my chair to face her. "I went to the police station yesterday but the sheriff wouldn't give me anything. We're going to have to try something else."

Just as I began plotting internally my new heist plan to break into the station, Fouzia waved a dismissive hand in my direction. "I've got that worked out already."

I frowned. "How?"

"After you left, I was eating lunch, right? And all the sudden my dad comes barging in with these papers in his hand and he starts complaining about the phone bill being high this month." She sat there waiting, looking expectant.

I shrugged. "So?"

"The *phone bill*," she repeated, but when she realized I didn't have a clue what she was going on about, she went on. "If you've ever looked closely at your phone bill, it will have every call you made over the course of a month. Date, time, and everything."

"Oh. *Oh.*" It was something I never would have thought of on my own. My house phone had been out for months, and when it came to the monthly bills, I usually forwarded them to my father so he would know how much he'd owe us. And so he wouldn't forget about Nan and my existence.

"So," she continued, "I realized the mailman must have delivered them at the same time. I bolted out of the house and ran to X's house. It was a slice of cake, I just reached into the mailbox and there it was!"

I blinked at her. "You do know that's a crime?"

"Yeah."

"Okay. Just checking."

Fouzia pulled out a sticky note and stuck it on my desk before writing out the numbers. "Six sixteen AM. That's when they called the police, meaning that he came home that night, and they found him missing from his bed in the morning. They couldn't have found him any earlier, or else they would have called earlier. They're insanely over-protective."

Beaming, I picked up the sticky note with the number. "Our first clue."

"Our first clue," echoed Fouzia.

Chapter Sixteen

My next mission began when the lunch bell rang. I rose from my seat and shared a knowing look with Fouzia. As we filed into the cafeteria, I didn't make my way to my usual seat at Fouzia's table with her and her friends. Instead, I crept towards where Laura and Agnes sat, both of them chatting away with their own friend group, noses in the air. Patrick sat with them, surrounded by his usual protective circle of jocks—the guys who had attacked Connor at the diner. Even Connor sat at the opposite end of the table, looking very focused on his low-quality, school-provided meal. I tried my best to tear my eyes away from him.

"Hey." I stood before them, my lunch tray in hand. Their conversation quieted and their eyes fell on me. I tried to focus on Agnes, hoping that she was the weak link I was looking for. "Can I sit?" There was an empty seat before me. All I needed was to sit my ass in it and then I'd win.

Agnes and Laura glanced between each other. The boys didn't look away from me. I stole a glance at Connor, who remained transfixed with his food. I imagined myself tackling him in the middle of the cafeteria, ripping his hair from his scalp and bashing his head against the tile. Shame was a strange, ugly thing.

"Sure, why not?" chirped Agnes, and all the tension left me at once.

Laura watched me carefully as I lowered myself into the chair. They all did. I wondered if she would say something, but she seemed intent on keeping up the silent treatment for as long as possible. In the month or so that I'd known her, I'd learned that this was not as easy of a task as she tried to make it seem.

I had a deep-seated hatred for Laura and the way she acted. The longer I knew her, the stronger it grew. Beneath the surface, she was hardly the meek, gentle, feminine beauty she presented to the world. Next to her sister, she may have seemed mild, with her natural blonde hair and her "refusal" to wear makeup—though I still often spotted flakes of mascara beneath her blueish eyes. I noticed the way she deliberately slouched her shoulders, how she'd make a conscious effort to soften herself, skipping meals at lunch, as she was doing now, until her arms were as thin as twigs. If I had to guess, I doubted that she kept down the majority of the food she did eat. I imagined her hunched over the toilet, reveling in the guilty pleasure of reducing her size, or diminishing herself to sickness. I imagined her finding a romantic aspect to it, and showing up to school and seeing girls like me—all rough edges, taking up so much space—and then feeling overwhelmingly validated. Maybe that was why she sought me out in the first place. I wondered if she liked me less now that I looked the part of a girl.

The days continued in suit. Rather than plot with Fouzia during class, I would pretend to be fascinated with whatever new gossip the twins had in store, and save the plotting for after school in Fouzia's garage. Our map grew, detailing our timeline and filling the board with sticky notes. Fouzia began to talk about Xavier more, and I got the impression that talking about him comforted her in an unexpected way. It seemed like she enjoyed reliving the good memories with him. Her stories, along with the glimpses I saw of the boy in the halls, made me begin to feel like I really knew him. It was strange to know a person so deeply that you'd never met.

I worried more about Nan and her health. Every evening when I'd return home after a day of productive sleuthing, I would have a paranoid image of her frail figure dead on the floor when I walked in. My imagination would haunt me until the moment I'd see her, the same as every day, seated in her chair, knitting or watching television with a smile on her face—a smile that often felt taunting, as if she knew what I'd been thinking. With each day that passed, I was taking care of her less and less. I hoped that with the surgery and the new medicine that she might be improving and not need my care anyways, but I hardly spent enough time at home to monitor her and know for sure. Of course, every time I asked, her response was always the same.

"Oh, I feel fresh as a daisy," she'd chuckle. "Don't worry about me, dearie. So, tell me. How are your friends? Any boys?" She gave me a suggestive wink. Clueless, I thought.

I turned away and rolled my eyes. "No, Nan. No boys," I'd reply flatly. So far, it had been the truth. Connor hadn't shown up at the diner in days, and I had only seen him in passing at school, and he never seemed to notice me then. Part of me believed that it was for the best, for if he never wanted to speak to me again, I could let go of the shame and anguish, but the other part of me knew this was only worse. If I could have made him speak to me, if I could have brought him down on his knees and forced him to explain himself, I would have. *Why say the things you did if you didn't like me? Why make me believe that you did?*

The moment repeated itself over and over again in my head while I sat in Fouzia's garage, watching her pin different names up to the board. "How about Connor?" I asked her.

"I don't think I ever even saw them speak to each other," Fouzia replied. "But he's in our class, after all. I'll add him to the list."

Seeing *CONNOR SMITH* scribbled in big letters on the suspect list eased my anguish a bit. The idea that he might be a raging homicidal psycho certainly made me feel better about my own actions.

I picked at my nails, which Fouzia had recently helped me file properly. I thought hard, racking all the information stored in my brain, examining the map before me. "What do you know about that guy Patrick?"

"Patrick McCarthy?" asked Fouzia. I shrugged, for I never paid much attention to last names. "He's not exactly a rocket scientist. I've heard he's a bit of a jerk, so I try not to mess with him personally, but if you're asking if I think he'd kill, I don't."

"Why's that?" I thought back to the night at the diner.

"He's all bark. No bite."

"He seemed to have plenty of bite to me."

"Did he?" Fouzia frowned. I explained to her what I'd seen that night, leaving out the part where I'd come at them all with a shotgun. "Maybe I underestimated him. I don't know. He and his friends are a tricky group. Xavier would never tell me straight out, but I knew they bullied him. It was mostly words, but I guess sometimes things escalate." She paused and then wrote below Connor's name. *PATRICK McCARTHY.*

"The thing that throws me off," I began, leaning forward in my seat, "is that this was a cold-blooded murder, and it was obviously calculated, or else the killer would have been caught by now. Look at what we've got here. The author says that he was stabbed with a knife that still hasn't been found. You don't stab someone *accidentally* in a fit of rage—or at least, you don't show up in the middle of the night with a knife without a plan to do something with it. With that in mind, take a minute and picture our class, the oldest kids in the school, supposedly the smartest public school kids in Hinton."

Fouzia nodded. "I see your point."

"They're a bunch of hard-headed idiots. I'm finding it hard to believe that one of the students could have done this."

"You think one of the teachers?" she asked.

"Well, Mrs. Quirk doesn't exactly seem like serial killer material, either, but I definitely think we should be looking into the staff. From the administrators to the custodians."

"Good thinking." She then disappeared for a few minutes before presenting the school directory, filled with the names and number of every student and staff. I may have had the same book laying around somewhere in my house, but I didn't have a clue where. "So, what classes have you got tomorrow?"

I listed off to her the ones I remembered. When I'd first come to the school, I had memorized my timetable only so I didn't look like a bumping idiot every hour trying to figure out where to go.

"I don't know which teachers Xavier had. I can't think of any possible motive for any one of them, either, but if he really did have a problem with someone, I would look into Mrs. Whitlock first. She's trouble."

"So I've heard." I'd certainly seen a few students shudder in her presence in passing.

I thought back to the endless math classes I'd had with her. I didn't pay attention to any of her lessons if I could help it, and neither, it seemed, did the rest of the student body. I remembered one day that she'd caught a boy sleeping during her lessons and poured a pitcher of ice cold water over his head.

"I think I have an exam with her tomorrow," I said.

Fouzia glanced sideways at me. "You *think*."

I shrugged.

She sighed. "Don't you know how well you could do if you put in more effort? I mean, you washed your hair and you're practically on your way to being prom queen. It took you one exam to get yourself bumped up into your year. Imagine the grades you could get if you just *tried*."

I tried to take her seriously, I really did, but an amused smirk was already pulling up at the corners of my lips. "Sure. I'll try."

***

I finished my exam early, and so I waited by Whitlock's desk as she graded the twenty questions. It was only a minute or two before she slid the paper back over to me, a big letter A drawn in red pen across the front.

Only one mistake. I'd forgotten to add a negative dash on one part of the eighteenth equation, which had screwed me over halfway through. It was the consequence of trying to finish too quickly. Still, I knew if Fouzia saw it she'd eat her words.

"You're dismissed," Whitlock chirped.

"Actually, I was wondering if I could speak with you." I locked my hands behind my back, trying to look as sweet as possible.

She glanced up at me from her papers. "My office hours are during fifth period."

I smiled. "Great. I'll be there." I was sure that my English teacher wouldn't miss me.

When fifth period arrived with the ring of the bell, I waltzed into Whitlock's classroom, book bag hanging over my shoulder. I dropped it on one of the empty desks and dragged a chair over to her. She watched me carefully as I did so, raising a lethal brow. I could see why the other students described her the way they did. She certainly had an intimidating aura to her.

"Make it quick," the teacher snapped. "I have two other meetings after this and then it's my lunch time. My *personal* time."

Mrs. Whitlock, though she was a physically small woman, had not been described as such by anyone who had ever truly met her. She had shoulder-length bleached hair and bangs that swooped across her forehead. It wasn't bleached in the California bombshell way, but in a cool, silver tone. She wasn't trying to pretend that it was her natural color. I respected that—the authenticity of it. Her outfits had the same slight edge to them. She wore something different each day. Sometimes it was a skirt, sometimes striped pants, usually paired with loose-fitting blouses or V-necks that went just deep enough that administration probably did a double take. However, she was well into her forties and I doubted she cared.

"Understood," I said. "I wanted to ask you about Xavier. The boy who—"

"I'm well aware of last month's incident. Thank you," she cut me off quickly.

I pursed my lips. "I was going to say, the boy who was in this class before me."

Her icy eyes were digging daggers into me. I thought that maybe that look she was giving me now, the one that sent a chill down my spine, was the one that Mr. Williams had been trying to imitate those times he had called me into his office. Only sitting here now and seeing the real thing did I realize how poor of a job he'd done. It was almost laughable.

After a moment, the woman relaxed. "Ophelia, I know what you're going to say."

That was a possibility. But she didn't know what I *wanted* to say. "You do?"

"I've heard that someone is spreading a nasty rumor around," she said, "and I understand that you might be upset, but there's nothing I can do for you. I teach math, not social navigation."

I blinked at her. For some reason, it hadn't crossed my mind that a teacher could be so up-to-date on the recent social drama. Perhaps, if she was the killer, she really *did* have a motive.

"It's not really about that, either," I said. "I guess...I heard about what happened to him when I first came, and someone told me that he really respected you as a teacher. I know it's silly, but it's just so *sad* that this happened. Was the school always like this, or did it change when he died?"

Fouzia had reminded me that when I spoke to a suspect, my main job was to observe their body language as carefully as I could. I watched her closely as she crossed her legs and narrowed her eyes at me. She dropped her pen for the first time since I'd come in, finally putting her full attention towards me. I wasn't sure if that was a good thing or a bad thing.

"I will admit, there's been a certain change to the atmosphere." She pursed her dark red lips together. "Did you happen to have any *math* related questions for me?"

I had already planned out the questions I was going to ask before I had arrived in this classroom, but at that moment my brain lagged behind in a strange way. Instead of processing her question, my mouth spoke before my brain.

"It must be tough for everyone. Have there been any recent changes in the dynamics between students and staff? Anything unusual?" I leaned back in my seat, attempting to seem as casual as possible. Fouzia had mentioned before that the more relaxed I seemed, the more relaxed it would make the other person. She had also reminded me not to seem too robotic when I recited the questions that we'd prepared.

Whitlock narrowed her eyes again and it suddenly seemed much less like she was the suspect here and more like *I* was. *What did I do wrong?* I wondered, trying to mask my rising panic.

"Ophelia," the teacher began. Suddenly, the sound of my name was not comforting. "I'll give you the benefit of the doubt, because the other teachers have told me about your history, but if you're looking for advice, this is what I'll say. Don't get involved. Just ride out the year, lay low, keep your grades up, and start thinking about your future. You could go to a good college if you wanted to, but playing detective and getting involved with a tragic incident that had nothing to do with you is not doing you any favors."

I didn't reply. As much as I didn't want them to, her words were hitting me hard.

"You're smart, Peterson," she told me. "Start acting like it." She picked up her pen once more and tapped out her stack of exams to make them flat. "Dismissed."

I had to bite on the inside of my cheek to keep from blurting something out. Having a filter was not something I was used to, but I slowly rose from my chair and began to turn away. But just as I grabbed the door handle to leave, I stopped and spoke again. "I know you've got other meetings today, but can you tell me what your schedule is tomorrow so I can stop by?"

She raised an eyebrow at me from where she sat.

"To talk about math," I clarified.

"My office hours tomorrow are first period."

"So you'll be in early?"

"Six forty-five, yes."

"Great." I smiled. "Thanks.

Xavier had been murdered on February third, which was a Tuesday—and tomorrow was also a Tuesday. If Whitlock came in early every Tuesday for her office hours, she had to have done the same the morning of Xavier's murder.

Another clue.

CHAPTER SEVENTEEN

I t might not have been the most discreet location for Fouzia and I to do our scheming, what with the crowds of gossiping teenagers passing us by, but we met by my locker to reconvene.

"She didn't tell me much," I admitted, "but I found out that she would have arrived at the school by six forty-five on the day of the murder."

"What does that tell us?" asked Fouzia, leaning against the locker beside me with her books hugged against her chest. After seeing her with her big purple glasses at home, it had become strange to see her without them. It also made her look considerably less detective-like with her face naked.

"A lot of things," I said, biting my lip to think. "It means that if she arrived like normal that day, then she would have arrived at the same time as the police, and if she was already there when they arrived, no one would have questioned her."

"Good thinking," she praised.

A smile pulled at my lips as I swung my locker open. "Who needs—" I stopped.

"What's wrong?"

I didn't answer. There was a little folded piece of paper sitting inside my locker that must have been passed through the vent. I reached inside, my mind already flooding with possibilities. The threats and notes left in my locker had subsided as of late, especially now that I'd healed my relationship with the twins and the rest of their crowd, but perhaps they were more persistent than I'd hoped.

The note read:

> I'm sorry. Meet me after school?
> –C

"'C'," said Fouzia. "Who's C?"

I folded the note back up, my heart racing. "It's nothing."

When I looked back at her, her eyes were widening. "Well, if it's someone from our class, it's either Connor or Chloe." She tapped her chin, looking me up and down. "Judging by your style, I wouldn't be surprised if it were Chloe, but I'm already, like, ninety-five percent sure she's hooking up with Daniel, so Connor it is."

I quickly hid my hands in my pockets. "It's *nothing*."

She grabbed my shoulder, her gaze sparkling. "Are you going out with Connor?"

I yanked away from her, curling my lip in fake disgust. "*No.*"

Her smile widened so big that her mouth nearly touched her ears. "You're blushing."

"Fuck you."

She squealed with delight. "Oh, I don't even know the context but I am *begging* you to go see him. Ugh, I am *elated*." She paused. "Wait. Unless he actually did something inappropriate. If he hurt you, don't give him a minute of your t—"

"I tried to kiss him," I hissed. I glanced around to make sure that no one was listening. I could already feel the shame creeping back up my neck. "I tried to kiss him and he pulled away."

"Ophelia, that's even better," she laughed. "He's apologizing for not kissing you. You know what that means? You make him *nervous*."

I frowned. Could that be true? He hadn't seemed nervous when we had walked together in the park. In fact, the only time I'd seen him even remotely nervous was when I'd had a gun pointed at his head.

"I don't think so," I told her.

"Well, he is on the suspect list," Fouzia reminded me, "so you might as well talk to him and rule him out while you can."

"Sure," I replied, if only to humor her.

***

Three hours later, I found myself waiting by my bike, leaning up against the lock rail. Students were filtering out of the school around me, and I could see Fouzia in the distance stepping onto her bus. The twins were across the sidewalk, starting their car which they'd parked next to Patrick's pick-up. Patrick waved me goodbye as he pulled away, the sound of his engine practically shaking the ground beneath me.

Connor was nowhere to be found.

As the crowds got thinner and thinner, it crossed my mind that someone could have sent me the note to mess with me, or perhaps he had sent it himself just to spite me one last time. *Figures,* I thought. *Everyone always wants the last laugh.* I took the note out of my pocket and read over it again. The handwriting was impeccably neat, written in generic blue pen. Now that I thought about it, I had never seen a boy with handwriting that nice. It could have been Laura, but she hadn't seemed particularly smug when she passed by me before. Maybe it *had* been Connor, and he was, in fact, g—

My thoughts were interrupted by his soft, articulate voice. "Sorry I'm late."

I spun around. There he stood, the sun falling over his golden hair perfectly. He wore the same denim jacket as the day I'd tried to kiss him. I wasn't sure why that surprised me, since I'd already seen him today in the halls. I guess it just seemed more relevant now that he was, once again, one step within kissing distance.

I meant for something romantic or flirtatious to be the next thing to leave my mouth, but instead I said this:

"What do you want?"

"I wanted to apologize," he said. "I didn't mean to make you feel bad the other day, it just caught me off guard. That's all. I guess I felt really embarrassed, and I know I should have told you that before." He paused, perhaps waiting for me to say something and fill in the gap, but when I didn't, he went on. "I was wondering if you maybe...wanted to go on another walk?"

"A walk," I repeated carefully.

"Yeah."

I stepped forward. "Tell me, Connor." I looked up at him. Now that I was closer, I could see the ever-so-slight five o'clock shadow across his face. His eyes had flecks of green in them. "Are you doing this

182

because you think it's funny, or because you're only interested now that I look different?"

His mouth fell agape and he furrowed his brow. "I—Neither." He seemed to be thinking of what to say. "You do, um. You do look nice, though."

I was trying so hard to read him, to figure out what he could possibly be thinking.

"But maybe just start as friends and...go from there." His Adam's apple bobbed, and for the first time I realized that Fouzia had been right. He *was* nervous. I wasn't sure why it had never occurred to me that he acted the way he did out of intimidation. For some reason, the thought made me like him more.

"So...friends," I said.

He nodded, glancing nervously to the side.

We were absolutely, without a doubt, *not* going to be friends.

"Let's go then," I said, and we began to walk.

First, we walked by a dingy café closest to the school where he could buy himself a coffee to-go. I was beginning to catch onto the fact that he may have a mild addiction to caffeine, but he bought me a cookie without asking, so I couldn't find it in me to care.

"No allergies, right?" he asked as he handed it to me.

"No." I took it from him. "Thank you." I normally made a point of not allowing anyone to buy me things, (not that many offered) but since he had caused me a considerable amount of strife, I made an exception.

"Anytime," he said, sipping on his rich-smelling coffee, radiating warmth just like the rest of him. He leaned in close to say, "Don't ever, under any circumstance, buy coffee from here." When I looked at him, I could see he was trying to conceal his grimace of disgust.

"Noted," I said.

He took a pause, straightening. "You smell like vanilla."

"Do you like vanilla?"

"Love it."

"Convenient."

There was a second-hand shop next door, so we stopped by there next. We strode in silence, bending down at each shelf to inspect the individual trinkets. I was content with the silence—it made me feel comfortable. I could recall the couple of days that I'd gone out around town with the twins and how they had constantly criticized my silence, perhaps under the impression that I was shy. It was as if some people simply could not comprehend the notion of finding fulfillment while your mouth was closed. Not Connor, though. We seemed to understand each other perfectly.

In the early Spring, the days were always short, but it wasn't until the sun began to set that I realized how long I'd been with him.

"I have to go home soon," I warned him. "My Nan's supposed to get her meds at seven."

"I won't keep you if you want to go," he assured me.

I bit my lip, looking out at the burnt sienna sunset. I hadn't seen something so beautiful in a while. "Why don't we wait a little longer?"

When I looked back at him, he was smiling into his cup.

He and I sat together on the curb behind the singular run-down gas station at the edge of town. We sat close enough for our knees to touch, looking over the grassy drop in front of us, every blade illuminated by the sunset's golden hue. If I could have stayed in that spot forever, I would have.

I glanced over at him. He wore a slight grimace.

"You okay?" I asked hesitantly.

It seemed like he was trying to disguise the discomfort with a smile. "I'm fine." For a moment, it seemed he was going to leave it at that, and an ache clawed at my chest at not knowing, but then he spoke again. "I've got a bad leg. Ever since I was twelve. It just acts up sometimes, but it's no big deal."

I glanced down at his leg, and then at the spot where the denim of our jeans rubbed against each other. "What happened when you were twelve?"

He paused for a long time. When I followed his line of sight, he seemed to be looking at our knees as well, but I couldn't discern if it was because of me or whatever memories were bubbling up to the surface for him now. Selfishly, I hoped it was because of me.

"My parents took me and my little brother up into the mountains one Summer. It was just supposed to be a couple days, and my dad was teaching us how to hunt." His gaze remained pointed downwards as he spoke, and his voice had gone down an octave, a quiet and low tone I could have fallen asleep to.

He went on, a rueful smile playing on his lips. "It was a nice trip at first. We would sit out there for hours while Dad was gone, hoping to have something to present when he got back. I hadn't caught jack shit, but Dylan—that's my brother—he shot this huge deer in about twenty minutes.

"He was always really good at everything he did. It didn't matter what it was, you'd think he was an expert on his first try. He did badminton, chess, swimming, piano... Whatever nerdy gifted kid crap you can think of. He was...He was great. I guess I kind of envied him, but I also did a lot of taking care of him, and you can't really envy the person you take care of. Hell, I fed him more than our mother did.

"But we were out in the woods that day when my dad left us alone to grab something from the cabin. And we were really close to this, um, cliff. But neither of us fully realized just *how* close. That's when Dylan...he was trying to be funny, pushing me around and all." He glanced over at me, his eyes glossy. "Y'know, he was a smart kid, but he was still an eleven-year-old."

I chuckled lightly. I wasn't sure if I was supposed to.

"Anyway," he went on, "he ended up falling. And he might not have if he'd had his boots on, but he was wearing some flimsy sandals because he'd gotten hot, and I hadn't said anything to him about it because he was right. It was hot. And I was an idiot. But yeah, he fell, and like I said, I was an idiot, so I tried to grab him as he went." He stopped himself, sucking in a breath. "Then somehow I fell over the edge with him."

I wanted to tell him to stop. It was the kind of story that he shouldn't trust with me, but I just watched him, mesmerized. There was something beautiful and charming in the way he blinked tears away, how he avoided my gaze, but kept speaking, as if now that he'd started he couldn't stop. Instinctually, I began to raise my arm to stroke his cheek, but stopped myself half way.

"How did you survive?" I asked.

"My leg caught on the edge of this stone and kept me from going all the way over. It hurt like hell, but it saved my life. Found out after that I'd gotten a dozen fractures and a messy break, so it never healed right. But I can't complain. Dylan wasn't so lucky."

He tilted his head to the side in a sort of self-deprecating way, like he wanted it to seem like it was no big deal. But it was. Anyone could see that it was. "He would have been seventeen this year. Our birthdays were 364 days apart, so there was one day that we were the same age."

"I'm sorry," I said.

He just shook his head. Another long silence passed between us. The sun continued moving down, turning bluer by the second. After another minute, he turned his head to look at me. He stared for a while before speaking. "What are you thinking?"

I nudged his knee gently with mine. "That I just realized I'm older than you."

He laughed. The sound was sharp and thick, like it had been pulled out of him by surprise. I liked it. "Didn't realize I was consorting with a cougar."

"Yeah, I'll rip your throat out like one, too." I shoved him to the side playfully and he pushed me back. His skin was warmer than I'd expected, and I wanted very badly to be sitting closer to him.

"So, now that I have successfully made things awkward by talking about *my* personal life," Connor began, "may I ask you an equally personal question?"

I narrowed my eyes at him, weighing my options. "Go on."

He slowly reached over and the tips of his fingers met the skin on my upper arm, just below the sleeve of my T-shirt. He looked down inquisitively. I was so absorbed in the feeling of his warm skin on mine that I didn't realize he was pointing to my scars. "What are these from?" he asked.

I did not dare move. My heart began to beat faster.

"You don't really want to know," I said. It was more likely than not that the truth would only scare him away, but I didn't want to lie either. I worried that if I lied, he would know, and if I told the truth, he would think I was lying.

He met my eyes. "I want to know you."

Shit.

There was a heavy rock of dread sitting in my stomach. Connor was not aware that he had just voiced the most terrifying thing he could have said at that moment. He wanted to *know* me? To be known was to be seen and to be seen was to be vulnerable. I wasn't sure that I could afford vulnerability at that moment.

But then I looked into his eyes, his searching, warm eyes like two blue beacons lighting the way. This was the moment where I decided if I was going to leave him hanging in the nothingness, or answer his call.

"Ever since I was little, I've been able to see ghosts." I said it so quickly, so quietly, that I wasn't sure he would have even been able to hear me. His expression didn't change. "And when I summon them...it leaves scars." It was the truth. Part of it, at least. He didn't need to know the rest.

He stared at me still, as if waiting for me to say more. Maybe it was the punchline he was waiting for, the sudden *gotcha!* before I admitted that I'd been messing with him. But it didn't come, and slowly, he looked away.

"Wow." That was all he said at first, one breathy word as he furrowed his brow. Was he thinking of the fastest way he could escape this situation, or the easiest way to tell me he never wanted to see me again without offending me? I waited for the blow. "I remember the first day you came in, you thought there was someone sitting in your chair."

I thought back to that day. It wasn't really my first, but it was the day they'd put me in his class. I remembered how triumphant I had felt right until I realized that what I was seeing in the chair was a ghost. It surprised me that he had remembered that moment.

"A ghost," I confirmed. I left out exactly *who* the ghost had been. He didn't need to know about how involved with Xavier I was getting.

"Right. A ghost."

"It's fine if you don't believe me." I looked away, no longer able to bear seeing his face as he came to terms with my apparent psychosis. "I should probably get home."

I began to stand, but he stopped me. "No." He took my hand. "Ophelia, wait."

I looked down at him.

He stood to be at level with me. "I believe you."

I read his face closely, then shook my head. "No, you don't." I stepped back and he came closer again.

He sighed then, holding his hands out as if he were giving up. "Maybe I don't. I mean, it is hard to believe. But I don't think you're lying. I don't think badly of you."

I shook my head again. What he was saying just didn't make sense. "Why not?"

"Because I—" he seemed at a loss for words, looking around him as if some external force could possibly help him in this difficult situation. "Because I like you. Because I don't think I've ever met someone that I can just *talk* to. Like a person. Like, without all the performance and bullshit. Ghosts or not, that doesn't change that."

The two of us standing there, helpless beneath the purple sky, I supposed we must have seemed absolutely ridiculous. But at that moment, I found that I didn't care. I didn't care at all.

I had the very startling and unnerving realization just then that I *really* liked this boy. Much more than I should have. Much more than I wanted to. And it seemed that he had a very similar epiphany, because just then, without warning, he took a step towards me.

And then I was being kissed.

I was being kissed.

He was *kissing* me.

My hands wrapped around the side of his neck like it was the most natural thing in the world, snaking around to lock my fingers in his hair. Everywhere he touched me came alive, sparking like lightning. With his lips pressed against mine, he pulled me closer by my waist. I wanted to melt into him, to forget everything else, to stay just as we were for the rest of time.

I was being kissed.

And then I wasn't.

Before I truly understood what I was doing, I pushed him away. My skin was on fire, my heart pounding like a drum against my ribcage. *I can't, I can't, I can't.*

There were ghosts all around me, glowing, spectral figures circling around me as if trying to swallow me whole. I was in the eye of the tornado, dozens of faces clouding my vision all around. I could no longer see Connor, though I knew he was close by. *I can't, I can't, I can't.* The words continued chanting in my mind, drowned out by the screams of the spirits encircling me.

I tried to form the words *I'm sorry,* but I wasn't sure if they ever left my lips. I could not stay to find out. I was already running away.

CHAPTER EIGHTEEN

I made the decision that I was not going to speak to Connor ever again. The facts were simple—he was wonderful and bright and selfless, and I was a psycho bitch. The fact that he could not see these facts, or maybe *did* see them and simply didn't care, was highly unsettling.

The ghost thing had been the last straw. Where anyone else would have called me out on my bullshit and run the opposite way, he had chosen to stay. He had put prejudices aside and had gone for the kiss anyway. (God, the *kiss.*)

One thing was unequivocally true: If I ever came close to that boy, I would most certainly break him.

And so I ran. I ran as far as I could, back to the school, my calves screaming in protest, until I mounted my bike and rode away before I could make any more terrible decisions. Like the kiss. (God, the *kiss.* I hadn't known *that* was how it was meant to feel.)

I was having a very difficult time silencing my thoughts. They lasted for the next couple days, overwhelming me to the point where I couldn't think of anything else. The dark circles beneath my eyes which I had finally gotten to disappear were beginning to rematerialize. I wasn't getting enough sleep, and I had blown off the following days of school. Exam week was over and I was burnt out, so I felt justified in doing so.

It wasn't long before Nan noticed the change. She gazed up at me from across the dinner table one evening, her wrinkled face twisting into a frown. "I heard you tossing and turning all night last night, honey. Are you sure you're doin' well?"

"I'm fine." I stabbed my fork into a fresh piece of rabbit and shoved it into my mouth. I wanted to curse at her and tell her to leave me in peace, but the new Ophelia would never do such a thing. The new Ophelia, the one that was popular and perfectly able to solve the murder of Hinton High would never scream at her own grandmother. *Fake it 'til you make it.*

But then she pressed further. "You don't seem f—"

I slammed my hands on the table and stood, scooping my plate and fork up before storming out of the room. So much for that.

Ever since the kiss, I'd been seeing more ghosts. My mother was practically glued to my side, always watching, observing my every mood. I would have screamed at her, too, if I didn't already know that it wouldn't do any good.

Things did not change until one day, when I was walking down to the store, a girl walking down the sidewalk caught my eye.

She saw me before I could dash out of sight. "Hey!"

"Hey, Fouzia." I stuck my hands in my pockets.

"Where in the world have you been?" She seemed concerned, and perhaps just as tired as I was. I figured that exam week had been hard on her. Maybe she would think I was on the same boat.

"Home," I said.

"We're supposed to be in this together," she reminded me. "We haven't done any work in days."

"I'm sorry. I've been busy. With my Nan and all."

Fouzia sighed. "Right. I forgot about your Nan. How is she?"

"Fine."

Silence hung in the air for a couple more seconds. It wasn't the type of silence I had rested in with Connor, but the uncomfortable, suspenseful kind. I could already tell Fouzia was weighing her options, perhaps deciding if I was worth it, if she had made the right decision in the first place by becoming my friend. My guess was that the answer would be "no."

Finally, she jutted her chin to the side. "Let's go, then."

"What?"

"I don't have all day. Come with me."

"Where, though?" I asked, utterly baffled. But strangely enough, I found that my feet were already moving.

"My house."

And sure enough, I was soon standing in Fouzia's garage. The map and chalkboard on the wall was now filled practically to the brim. There were dozens of photos tacked up on the wall, some of faces that I recognized, and others seemed to be old newspaper cutouts. There was red pen scribbled all around the map of the school, indecipherable X's and circles across the whole board. Even the suspect's list, which had only held six names the last I checked, now reached the bottom of the board. Half of the names she'd added were crossed out or blurred out, but the work she'd done was absolutely mind-boggling.

"It's barely been a week," I marveled.

"While you've been sitting on your ass at home," she looked back at me over her shoulder, sliding her glasses on her face, "I've been busy."

There was very little that could surprise me anymore, but I was coming to terms with the fact that that would change if I were to continue hanging around this girl.

Fouzia whipped out her notebook and began scribbling on the board within one of the last blank spaces. "For one thing, I've gotten a mostly accurate list of every relevant person who was and wasn't at the school the morning Xavier was found. Some of this is off of my own memory, and some is just by asking around. Human memory is fickle, but this is the best I could do. Now, comparing *this* list," she tapped on the list she had just written out containing every person who had not shown up that morning, "to *this* one," she tapped on the suspects list, "there is only one name in common. That we know of, at least."

I gazed up at her handiwork. "Patrick."

"Patrick," Fouzia echoed, crossing her arms with a proud smirk.

"It's circumstantial."

"Maybe. Maybe not." She looked back up at her board. "By the way, I'm going to break into Xavier's house tomorrow and see if I can find anything that might help us."

I gawked at her. "His parents won't even speak to you, and you're going to break into their home?" My tone held disbelief, but in reality I was becoming more and more impressed with the girl. I was quite certain that I had chosen the right person to do this job with.

"Hence why I have to take matters into my own hands," she said.

"Right. Keep up, Ophelia," I said in a sing-songy imitation of her voice. It earned me a sour look from the girl, in response to which I held my hands up in surrender.

"So," she regarded my worn-out figure, "you in?"

I had to take a moment then and reflect on the slew of odd situations I had been able to get myself into in the past couple of months. It was a talent, really.

"I'll free up my schedule."

***

Xavier's house stood like a shadow in the night, towering over us with an almost malevolent presence. Every instinct in me screamed to turn back, to run, to just stay away from all of this, but I forced myself to stay rooted to the spot. This was our only chance—to sneak in and get answers. Beside me, I could feel Fouzia's determination radiating off her, but I knew she was just as nervous as I was. If we got caught tonight, I would be fine. It wouldn't be my first night spent in a jail cell. But Fouzia? Her and her big round eyes had probably only spoken to the police to offer them girl scout cookies.

I took a steadying breath and glanced over at her. She seemed to be biting her cheek, a nasty habit that I myself had had to get over a while ago.

"We don't have to do this," I whispered, the words barely making it past my lips. But even as I said it, I knew it was a lie. We had no choice. I had already decided that if she backed out, I would go in alone. No hesitation.

"Yes, we do," Fouzia replied. "We need answers. This is the only way."

I nodded. All things considered, if we got caught, it wasn't a scolding or a slap on the wrist. The police would be called. Worst case scenario, I'd be hauled off to jail, leaving Nan alone to fend for herself. And Fouzia? Her parents would kill her if they found out. I had gotten a hint of how strict they were, and her sneaking into her dead boyfriend's house—one she wasn't even supposed to have in the first place—wasn't something they'd go easy on.

We moved closer to the house, crouching low as we approached the side where the ivy clung thickly to the walls. Fouzia kept glancing over her shoulder as if she were convinced that the sheriff was right around the corner, waiting to jump out of the shadows. I could practically hear her heart pounding from three feet away. I considered passing her some words of encouragement, then decided against it. With my social ineptitude, whatever I said was bound to only heighten her nerves.

Fouzia reached for the back door, her fingers hovering over the handle for a moment before she took a deep breath and tried it. Locked, naturally. I sucked my teeth in frustration, but she pulled out a small set of lockpicks. Watching her work, I could see her hands were shaking. *Pull it together,* I thought.

The lock clicked open, a sound which seemed infinitely louder within the tension. We both froze in fear, listening to any sign that we'd been heard. Nothing. Fouzia pushed the door open, just a crack, and a rush of stale, cold air greeted us. I followed her in.

The house was nearly pitch black aside from the moonlight seeping in through the windows. It was eerily silent as well, but I thought I could hear the dull sounds of someone snoring upstairs.

Fouzia glanced back at me, as if to say, *Are we really doing this?*

I nodded back to her. *You've made it this far, now hurry the hell up.*

While I wasn't sure if my message translated, she seemed to understand well enough and carried on through the foyer. Interestingly, I hadn't realized how well off Xavier's family was until just then. Judging by the quality of the furniture and the endless marble kitchen counters, you would have thought the boy would have gained a few popularity points among his peers. I wondered—not for the first time—what it was that Fouzia had liked so much about him.

I motioned questioningly towards the stairs before us. *His room?*

Fouzia gestured in the affirmative, though her face was much paler than normal. We moved as silently as possible, every step feeling like a thunderclap in the quiet night.

Fouzia paused before the second door in the upstairs hall. Now that we were this close, I could hear the snoring more clearly. It came from the room at the end of the hall, a low and rhythmic tone.

We stopped and I gave Fouzia a questioning look. She pointed at me, and then down to the ground, then up to her eyes. *You stay here. Keep watch.*

I grimaced. *Why me?*

She gave me a firm glare. *Just do it.*

I rolled my eyes. *Fine.*

With that, she slowly opened the door to Xavier's bedroom. There was a small *KEEP OUT* sign across the front, which I assumed he'd taped there himself when he was alive. Sadness threatened to rush in, but I quickly shook it away. I wasn't doing this for him.

With Fouzia gone, and me left out in the open, I rolled my shoulders uncomfortably. Sneaking around I was fine with, but standing here in the dark with his parents a breath away, just waiting? It was making my skin crawl. While Fouzia rustled gently through Xavier's things, I distracted myself by focusing on the picture frames in front of me, barely visible even with my eyes adjusted to the dark.

There was the usual there; family photos, a beach pic, a print from last year's yearbook. I was shocked at how different the pictures of Xavier looked here. He looked so much more...well, alive. Even in the pictures they had used of the boy in the newspaper, he had looked gloomy and depressed. So, he hadn't always been that way.

I leaned in closer to one particular photo, taken in front of some sort of cabin. It could have been a summer home or a kind of camp, about a dozen of Xavier's family members standing there, smiling for the photo. When I squinted my eyes I could make out a young Xavier towards the left. The principal stood above him, a hand on his shoulder. So, he could be affectionate. Who knew?

My gaze caught on one particular face towards the middle. I knew that face.

What?

Was that—?

A finger tapped on my shoulder and I nearly leapt out of my skin. My whole body went numb as I spun around to see Fouzia behind me, her eyes wide and nervous. She had something in her hand, a small piece of half-crumpled paper. I frowned as I took it from her and brought it close to my face to read

Meet me at school.
Fouzia ♡

I looked back up at her. She pointed to herself, and then wagged her finger. *I didn't write this.*

I furrowed my brow. *Then who the hell did?*

She pressed her lips together tightly. *You know who.*

So that was how the killer had gotten Xavier out of the house. As we already knew, he had gone home that night, retired to his room, and then he must have found this very note. Believing that it was truly written by the girl he loved, he could have valiantly climbed out the window or snuck out through the house and driven to the school in his father's car. And that's where the killer got him. Stabbed him to death.

But the most unsettling part was when I looked back down at the letter, it was so familiar to me. The handwriting, it wasn't some random scrawl or typed-out message. It was Fouzia's writing. I was sure of it. I'd seen her letters written up on the wall enough times that I could see it was an exact match. I could practically envision her small hands writing it out right then.

Who in the world had the capacity of a killer, a reason to want Xavier dead, and the ability to copy anyone's precise handwriting?

Fouzia pulled at my arm. *We need to go.*

Finally, we agreed on something.

CHAPTER NINETEEN

I wouldn't have gone to school the next day if not for Fouzia's insistence. It seemed that she was still convinced I was failing half my classes like the rest of the student body, when in reality my grades were so high that I was pretty sure most of my teachers thought I was cheating. Tried as they did, they had never caught me doing any such thing, and so I hadn't been called to the principal's office for weeks. Nevertheless, the day was bound to be filled with misery and anguish.

I had yet to tell Fouzia about what had happened that day with Connor, nor had I mentioned what I had seen in the hallway the night before. I had already decided on things, and while normally I would have taken some time for myself to think everything over, that was no longer the case. I had done enough thinking, enough wallowing in my house with Nan and my ghosts. The decision was made, and now was my time to get up off my ass and act.

I was going to put an end to this case if it was the last thing I did.

And as for our latest clue? Neither of us had any idea who in the school could have mimicked Fouzia's handwriting so perfectly. We finally had a physical, concrete piece of evidence to who had murdered Xavier, and practically no hope of finding out who had actually written it.

As I strolled through the main doors of the school, I felt like I was walking through a dream. Half of the people around me were dead, half of them were alive. Half were real and half weren't. The less sleep I was getting, the more difficult it was becoming to differentiate between the two.

But when a shrill voice greeted me from behind as I turned a corner, I was fairly certain it came from someone living.

Agnes was there, joined in arms with her twin, wearing a bright smile. "Good morning!" she beamed.

"Morning." I tried to match her smile, watching her body language to find things to mimic. It was one of the pieces of advice Fouzia had given me. *Speaking of, where is Fouzia?* I hadn't seen her since I'd gotten to school.

"We've got something to tell you," said Agnes, wiggling her eyebrows with anticipation.

I leaned against the lockers, hoping it would be worth my time. Perhaps a sliver of gossip containing another clue? "Shoot."

"There's a party tonight," she informed me. "Out in the woods by the skating rink. A bunch of us are going to hang out. I mean, it's just what we do every Friday, but—"

Laura nudged her twin in the ribs, painfully lacking subtlety. I didn't know what made her think I would care that they'd been hanging out without me. I had assumed that they did, anyway, and it hadn't bothered me—until I realized the advantage to my mission that came with it.

"Anyway," Agnes went on, "we thought you might want to come."

"It could be fun," piped up Laura.

Agnes then leaned in close, her voice lowering as if she were telling me an exceptionally interesting secret. "Actually, *Patrick* was the one who suggested it."

A spark of excitement shot up my spine. "Did he, really?"

Agnes nodded, her lips pressed together as if trying to repress her smile. I thought she must have been almost as excited as I was, but for a very different reason. "We'll pick you up at eight," she said with a wink, and then they were off.

***

It had been a while since I'd ridden in the twins' car, and I was relieved to not have to work my calves to get somewhere for once. It was a tiny, silver cabriolet that made me feel like I was being chauffeured despite the effort it took for me to squeeze into the back seat. As I sat there, my hair flowing behind me in the wind, music blasting as we drove through the dark, I thought that perhaps I could get used to this.

"Hey, change the song," insisted Agnes, raising her voice above the sound of the rushing wind.

"I like this one," argued Laura as she drove.

Agnes reached forward and the tune halted to a stop before resuming with another pop beat. "Ophelia, what do you think?"

"I love it." I didn't. But I was enjoying myself regardless.

It wasn't long before Agnes was taking a flask out of the pocket of her leather jacket. She took a swig, and upon Laura's protest, handed it over so she could do the same. "Take some," she told me as she passed it into my hands.

I took a moment to pause, looking down at the flask. I'd never drunk before. But they didn't need to know that, did they?

I took a sip. It burned all the way down but I didn't make a face. Agnes was grinning when I handed the flask back to her.

Miraculously, we arrived at the edge of the woods alive. Laura parked the car on the gravel beside Patrick's black pick-up truck. Now that we were away from the town lights, and all the wind and music had quieted, it was eerie. The twins, however, didn't seem to notice.

"There they are," Laura pointed out as she stepped out of the car. I followed suit to see that there were dim flames peeking out between the trees, dancing idly against the moonlight. I spotted people's silhouettes crowding around the bonfire.

"How many people did you say there'd be?" I asked as Agnes came to my side.

Either she didn't hear me, didn't care, or didn't know, because she strolled right past me, locking arms once again with her twin. I followed behind them silently, taking in my dark surroundings. Normally, a place like this was where I'd feel the most at home. Warm darkness, the smell of dew and smoke, and a certain sense of impending doom were all the perfect recipe to make me feel like I was in my element, but tonight it was just unnerving.

We zigzagged through the trees towards the fire to find ourselves face to face with the so-called party. There were about twelve or fifteen washed-up teenagers dancing around the flames of the bonfire, empty bottles of various alcoholic beverages discarded at their feet. One girl, a redhead that I recognized from my biology class, tripped over one of the broken bottles, and she cried out before another boy helped her to her feet. The boy was Patrick, wearing that same idiotic grin as always, fluttering his lashes like a common whore at the redhead. But then he looked up and spotted me.

He let go of the other girl, and while she stood left behind and confused, he sauntered over to me and the twins. "Glad you could make it, ladies."

God, he was a dick.

"So are we," chimed Agnes.

He gave her a sideways glance and I got the distinct impression that he wasn't really talking to her. His eyes rolled back to me. "You excited to party?"

Agnes chuckled. "Definitely."

"Come on, then," he urged. And then his arm was wrapped around me, holding me as we made our way to the bonfire. His skin was warm against mine, but not in the way Connor's had been. I suspected the heat permeating from his body had more to do with intoxication. Being this close to him, it was now difficult to ignore how much bigger than me he was, with rounded biceps peaking from his shirtsleeve, fabric tightly hugging his pectoral muscles which probably required a bra size larger than my own. All things considered, he wasn't *un*attractive, but he wasn't Connor, and I didn't need him holding onto me.

He leaned in close. "You don't do the party scene very often, do you?"

"How did you know?" I joked.

"Lucky guess." He took a plastic cup from a spot on a log where I assumed he'd been sitting and handed it to me. "Try it."

I brought the cup to my nose and sniffed it. It was definitely alcoholic. "You don't have an unopened bottle?"

He raised an eyebrow.

"That's fine, then." I handed it back to him. "I had some in the car, anyway." And it was true. I'd taken only a sip, however the tips of my fingers were tingling, and whenever I moved my head too quickly, my vision blurred slightly. Still, I wasn't drunk enough to drink from any random cup someone handed to me.

Patrick looked at me, and then back to the cup. Without breaking eye contact, he lifted it to his lips and drank. I saw the liquid flow into his mouth before his Adam's apple bobbed with a swallow. He then took my hand and placed the cup back against my palm. A challenge.

I lifted the cup and drank. He smiled.

"That was disgusting," I said, licking my lips.

"Never taken a shot before, princess?"

"I have," I lied. "Just none that terrible." It wasn't until I finished speaking that I realized he'd actually called me *princess*. It gave me almost as much urge to gag as the alcohol had.

He laughed, but I got the impression that he didn't really think I was all that funny. He held out a hand to me. His hand was calloused and scratched-up, so it felt like sandpaper when I took it. "Dance with me?"

It wasn't a question I could say no to. I nodded.

And then I was being pulled away. He lifted me off of my feet with ease and a surprised cry escaped from my throat. Before I knew it, I was standing among the others, Patrick dancing along to the music in front of me. He took my hand and spun me around. I was laughing then, more out of surprise than amusement. But when I really thought about it, it was all sort of amusing, wasn't it? The music, the dancing, the buzz flowing through my veins. I couldn't remember the last time I had danced. Why didn't I do it more often?

As I swayed my body to the beat, my back against Patrick's chest, he was whispering compliments in my ear. I didn't really process exactly what they were, but I couldn't deny that they made me feel a bit warmer inside.

The longer the alcohol flowed through my bloodstream, the less I began to care about if I smelled, or if he smelled, if I was acting weird or stupid. I thought less about my mission and more about the music, my hips, and my hair. Why hadn't I noticed how soft my hair was?

"You smell like vanilla," murmured Patrick.

"You said that already."

He frowned, spinning me around again as an overwhelmed giggle escaped me. "Did I?"

No, I remembered. It was Connor that had said that to me. *Don't think about Connor,* I reminded myself. "Yeah," I said. "You did."

He shrugged and continued to dance. I was fairly sure that I'd stepped on his toes at least three times, but he didn't seem to notice or care. And neither did I.

"Ophelia, dance with me!" squealed a voice from behind me, and then Agnes had taken my hands and we were swinging each other around in the air. The pink of her hair was blending so beautifully with the fire light. It reminded me of cotton candy, which made me suddenly very hungry.

"I wanted to tell you," began Agnes, grabbing me by the shoulders. She was very drunk. "Ever since that day up on the roof, I have been so...*inconsolable.*"

I frowned. "I shouldn't have dragged you into it."

"No!" she cried. "You don't get it. I've been searching for something to give me that feeling again. The *rush.* Doing something that I'm not supposed to, being a million feet in the air, I've never felt like that before. It's the...whatsit called..."

"Adrenaline," I offered.

"Yeah! Adrenaline."

My head fell into my hands. I had stopped dancing. "Jesus, you're turning into an adrenaline junkie." I didn't realize I had said it out loud until the words left my lips. I didn't feel like the sort of stupid-drunk I saw in movies, but I was beginning to notice that my inner monologue had suddenly turned into my outer monologue.

"Your mono-what?" asked Agnes.

I shook my head. "Nothing." I suddenly thought of Laura. If Agnes had gotten this drunk, where was our designated driver? I looked around and then spotted her at the edge of the woods, bent over and grimacing. "I thought she wasn't going to get drunk."

Agnes glanced over at her. "Oh, she's not. It's from the food." She nudged her chin at the plate of chips and other assorted junk food sitting by the fire. "She can't keep anything down."

"Oh." So I'd pegged her right. I tore my eyes away from the girl and back to Agnes. "I'll be right back."

I had completely forgotten about the food until she'd mentioned it, and the look of her hair really *had* made me hungry, so I bustled over to the chip bags laying on the ground and popped one open for myself. As I stood there, basking in the heat of the fire and munching on the flavorless corn chips, I began to think that this party wasn't really as bad as I had feared. As long as I could stay right there in that spot forever in my own silence.

The mission. I had forgotten about the mission. While attending the party was all well and good for my reputation and getting closer to these people, I was currently wasting the gigantic opportunity in front of me right now to get more information about Patrick and the rest of his idiotic friends.

I looked around to make sure that nobody was watching me. Patrick was now lighting a cigarette (at least, I thought it was a cigarette) to pass between his friends.

Without another word, I crumpled up my bag of chips and slipped away from the party, back into the darkness of the woods. I reappeared out on the gravel where our cars waited. I neared a red Jeep, which I thought belonged to a kid named Aiden or Alvin. I crept around the side and cupped my hands around my eyes to look in the windows. The interior, though poorly cleaned, held no murder weapon or any other incriminating evidence. I tried to pop the trunk but it wouldn't give, so I removed a bobby pin from my hair and jammed it into the lock until it released. I examined the contents within, but found nothing of interest.

Strands of my loose hair licking my face, I slammed the trunk closed and continued down the line of cars. I approached Patrick's pick-up next. It was a nice car, large and robust, teetering on the edge of obnoxiousness. It was the kind of car I would have gotten myself if I had the money. I could load all my furniture up in the back and leave

Hinton for good. It was a nice fantasy. Impossible for the time being, but nice.

I had to stand on my toes to see inside the truck. The front seats seemed empty at first, with no sign of any murderous intent behind Patrick's travels, but then I got a closer look. There was something reflecting the moonlight down in the footwell, but from where I stood, I couldn't tell what it was.

I started to retrieve my bobby pin again to work at the lock, but the snapping of a branch behind me made me pause.

I turned to see Patrick there, keys in his hand.

"Wanna see inside?"

CHAPTER TWENTY

It wasn't long before I was sitting in Patrick's passenger seat, trying to get a look down the footwell as he stepped into the car from the other side. Whatever I had seen seemed to be half-wedged beneath my seat , but I could barely make it out in the dark.

"What are you looking for?" asked Patrick.

"Nothing," I lied. "I like the car."

I nudged it with my foot and I saw another flash.

"Ah, sorry about that." He leaned across me, his chest pressing against my legs so he could stick a hand down in the footwell. He retrieved a metal crowbar and quickly threw it behind his seat.

"What do you need that for?" I asked.

He shrugged. "Never know what situation you might find yourself in on the road, you get me?"

"Sure," I agreed halfheartedly. "Hey, do you remember that kid that died a while ago?" Normally, I might have been more subtle with my interrogation tactics, or at least made an effort, but tonight I was nothing but blunt. The alcohol wasn't helping.

He picked at his teeth. "That nerdy kid? Yeah, why?" His words were slurring, and he may have been more drunk than I was. I could use that to my advantage.

"I never knew him. What did you think of him?"

"I thought he was a nerd," he said with a chuckle. "I don't really give a shit, to be honest. Why are we talking about this, again?"

"I just felt bad for him."

He placed his hand over mine. "You can't spend your whole life worrying about other people. Enjoy the time you have, ya know? Live...freely."

"Are you always this philosophical when you're drunk?"

"No." He furrowed his brow as if he had come to a great epiphany. He didn't seem to have noticed that I was mocking him.

"Patrick." I took his hand between two of my own, looking meaningfully into his eyes. At least, I hoped it looked meaningful. If I scared him away tonight, I was sure I would never hear the end of it from both Fouzia and the twins—each for different reasons. "Do you know who killed him? I just...I can't wrap my head around it."

He stared at me for another moment, his lips slightly parted.

And then he leaned forward and kissed me.

Warm lips pressing against mine, I broke away from him and dropped his hand, groaning disappointedly. "That is *so* not what's happening here, bud."

He frowned. "What?"

"Did you even hear my question?"

"You were asking about the nerd."

"Yes..." I urged.

"If I talk to you about the dead kid will you let me kiss you?" he asked in all seriousness.

I paused, weighing my options. I knew, factually, that people had a great tendency to make stupid decisions when they were drunk, and yet in the grand scheme of things, it didn't actually seem like the end of the world. After all, if Patrick had any valuable information, I could be done with the wretched murder hanging over my head soon. The principal as well as those bothersome detectives would *finally* leave me in peace. It was also worth noting that there were much worse things in the world than kissing a boy who looked like Patrick.

"Sure," I said.

He grinned. "It was his sweet old uncle. Obviously."

I raised an eyebrow at him. "What?"

"The whole school knows it," he insisted. "Didn't you hear that Willaims' car was outside the school when they found him? I mean, the cops and all said that the nerd must've stolen it, but there's no way he had the balls."

"So, what? You think they drove there together?"

He shrugged again. "What do I know? I didn't kill him." He rolled his eyes lazily. "Anyway, for a while we all thought it was you, which was why we left those funny notes by your locker, but you turned out to be cool, so I figure we were right the first time and it was uncie."

I racked my brain for a moment, trying to connect it all together through the drunken fog. Fouzia and I had already suspected that Xavier had gotten to school with a family car, since it would have been too far to walk in the middle of the night, but Patrick did make a good point about the boy's lack of testicles. Thinking back to the smiling pictures of Xavier that I'd seen in the hall before, I simply couldn't imagine that same boy doing something so rebellious as to steal his uncle's car in the dead of night to go see the girlfriend that he wasn't supposed to have. But his own nephew? What possible motive could he have had?

My thoughts were interrupted when Patrick's hand came around to cup my cheek. My heart stuttered in my chest.

I looked up at him and envisioned his face as Connor's.

Our lips made contact again. At first, it wasn't so bad. He did a lot more movement than Connor had done, but it was still an upgrade from the boy I'd kissed on a dare when I was eleven. Still, as I brought my hand to his hair, I found myself wishing that it was blonde, that the nose touching my cheek had that little hook that Connor's did. As I parted his lips with my thumb I thought of golden light hitting Connor's skin. As his tongue melted into my mouth I pretended that I was tasting coffee and cinnamon.

While we kissed, I was not thinking of Patrick at all, which was why I began to pull him closer.

But Patrick, unfortunately, was not Connor, and took it very much the wrong way. First, his hand made its way to my thigh, and then his lips met my neck, and everything was all of the sudden very *wrong*.

"Patrick," I said. He didn't seem to hear me. "Patrick, I'm done." Once again, no acknowledgement.

Rage and fear flaring up in my chest, I grabbed him by both shoulders and shoved him away from me. Under any normal circumstances, I doubted that the push would have done anything, but with the condition he was in, he practically went flying away from me. He looked baffled, his hair now an unruly mess and his lips pinker than before. "What?"

"That was more than enough," I said, catching my breath.

"Come on." He leaned towards me again, his hand returning to my thigh, moving higher and higher—

I smacked his hand with my palm, but this time I didn't catch him off guard. He clasped my wrist and in a moment, the world seemed to flip underneath me, fear crackling up my skin like electricity.

I was not going to test my chances. I twisted my wrist from his grip, then swung the door open, thankful that I hadn't locked it, and stumbled out of the car. My knee hit the gravel, but I was too dizzy to acknowledge the pain.

"Ophelia, wait! Come on!" he called back to me from inside the car, but I was already running back into the woods.

When I glanced back, I saw his figure, a black silhouette, racing behind me through the trees. He was running fast, his movements suddenly sharp and determined. Had he somehow sobered up?

I quickened my pace, my mind racing. The woods were getting darker and Patrick was getting closer. If I was correct about which part of the woods we were in, my house would be eastward from here. I *thought* I knew which way was east, but I could hardly think now. Everything around me looked the same except for the bonfire still burning in the distance. *East, east, east. Where is east?*

Suddenly, I crashed into something. The breath was knocked out of me and I came tumbling to the ground. Choking and coughing where I lay, I looked up to see Laura standing above me. She must have been puking again.

"Are you okay?" she asked softly, offering me a hand.

Someone else stood beside her, a boy with black hair and tired eyes. She didn't seem to notice him, his form fading in and out of my view as he gazed down on me.

"Run," he whispered, and then vanished back into the shadows.

Xavier.

A jolt of clarity hit me. I took Laura's hand and rose back to my feet, whipping my head around to try and get a glimpse of Patrick. Could he still be chasing me? I looked back to Laura. "Go back to the group. *Now.* What are you waiting for? I said go!"

While I may have warned her to spare my own conscience, I wasn't going to wait around and see if she had decided to take me seriously. I was off in a second, and this time I did not look back. I raced through the unruly, dark forest, moving as quickly as I could while only being able to see about six feet in front of me. My heart was still pounding against my ribcage, my throat burning itself raw.

I just have to get home, I just have to get home, I just have to—

My thoughts were interrupted by the sound of movement.

I froze in place.

"Patrick?" A sober me may have been smart enough to keep my mouth shut, but I was at least smart enough to not move for a moment, waiting, trying to focus on anything other than the blood rushing in my ears.

Another *crunch* of a leaf came from my right, and without thinking, I darted left.

I ran as fast as I could, my legs swinging like wings below me. Every muscle in my body burned, powered by fear. I could hear whoever it was behind me—I was sure of it. It wasn't a deer or a rabbit. It was a person. I was being chased. I was being hunted.

I made the mistake of looking over my shoulder and I *saw* them. Not Patrick—it couldn't be. Sprinting like a shadow, too fast and too dark for me to see. But the shock slowed me, and the figure bent down when the opportunity presented itself.

Pain shot up my leg as something cut across my calf. Hot liquid poured over my skin, but I continued running. I could not stop running.

Something caught on my hair. Whether it was my pursuer or simply a hanging branch from a tree, I didn't know, but it sent me reeling. I internally cursed myself for not having pinned my hair back up. But it didn't matter now. Now, I was crawling around on the forest floor, desperately trying to find my grounding, trying to tell up from down.

In my blindness, I clawed desperately and my nails met skin. I heard a gasp from the person above me, a sharp, voiceless inhale from my faceless attacker. I'd done damage.

I rolled onto my back, and when I looked up, I saw the glisten of metal. A knife, held within a gloved hand.

The knife began to come down on me, and in one swift, desperate movement, I rolled out of the way.

I was on my feet again, and I was running. There was blood flowing over my forehead and into my eyes, but I did not let it stop me. I ran for my life, I ran for my soul, I ran until I could not run anymore.

PART 3

April, 1989

Pepperback Press, Inc.

Chapter Twenty-One

I was shaking when I walked through the front door. The house was dark, but I didn't turn the lights on. I couldn't risk drawing attention from outside. The first thing I did was shut the blinds, taking one nervous glance out the window. The coast was clear, but anything and anyone could have been hiding at the treeline. I wasn't sure how far I'd been followed.

Next, I checked on Nan to make sure she was still asleep in her bed. I closed her window, too. I passed by my own room and retrieved my baseball bat. I waited in the kitchen with it, crouched beside the sink, watching through the window. There was no movement outside, no sense of disturbance. The world was asleep. The forest seemed to be, as well.

I released a trembling breath. I did not realize that I was crying until the tears hit the backs of my hands. Fear was a funny thing—it didn't quite hit you completely until you had no need for it.

I waited there in the kitchen for another twenty minutes before my wounds throbbed too much to bear. I limped my way to the bathroom and flicked on the light, a tiny bulb that buzzed idly above me.

I was a mess. My black hair was tangled into a nest above my head, mixed in with dirt and blood that had dripped from my scalp over my forehead. I wasn't sure when I had gotten the head wound, but it would explain why the room swam around me.

I leaned over the sink, both arms braced against its edge, and spit blood onto the white ceramic. I might have bitten my tongue at some point during the fight, because I could taste nothing but that warm, metallic liquid. I glanced down at my hands gripping the sink. There was blood beneath my fingernails. This blood, however, was not mine. I raised my hand to see it better.

This blood represented everything I meant to destroy, everything in my way. The skin and cells of my attacker rested on my nails.

I turned on the faucet and washed it away, down the drain.

There were cuts across my arms and legs, as well, the worst one being along my calf, a long gash split through my jeans. I pushed the bathroom door slightly ajar to see that I had left a trail of blood behind me, and more was still pooling on the bathroom floor.

I swore under my breath as I dug through the medicine cabinet, searching desperately for bandages and alcohol. I took off all my clothes and sat in the bathtub where I began to work on the wound.

I considered calling an ambulance, but too much time had passed already, and the phone wasn't even working. I could have tried to make my way into town, but I couldn't ride my bike in my condition, and I was too terrified to go outside anyway. I was all alone here. My life was my own responsibility.

By the time I had finally stopped the bleeding, the tub was stained red and my head was pounding like a drum.

I took a steadying breath as I hung my head between my knees, chills running up my spine every couple of seconds despite the warm air permeating through the bathroom. I turned on the faucet and let lukewarm water hit my back, washing away the blood and grime from my body.

I looked down at my hands again. There remained blood beneath my fingernails, red and crusted to my skin. I held my fingers under the water, scratching away at my hands in an attempt to remove it. And yet the red would still not go. No matter how I scrubbed, how desperately I picked it out from my nails, it stuck to me like glue. Tears were streaming down my face, my vision blurred with red as I watched the blood droplets fall to the tub, until I finally realized that the only blood on my fingers now was my own.

I wrapped my bleeding, agonized hands around my middle and stifled my sobs.

What have I gotten myself into?

***

I jolted awake, the baseball bat falling from my grasp. I had fallen asleep standing, leaning on the bat with my back to the door. Every muscle ached, as if the act of pushing the blood through my veins and the air into my lungs was using up all of my strength. My head still throbbed within my skull, the dull pain of a hangover creeping through me as the night went on. I knew that I could not afford sleep, not with the risk of my attacker still roaming the woods and my grandmother in the room next door.

The night went on in stops and starts of consciousness. I paced around the living room and hummed to myself to keep myself from falling into a desperate sleep. Eventually, when a couple more hours had passed, I worked up the courage to turn on the noisy coffee machine and downed a cup of dark brown energy.

When the sun rose, I tucked my baseball bat away behind the couch so that Nan wouldn't see it when I roused her out of bed. I did my best not to make her worry, but she did anyway, of course.

"Sweetheart, are you sure you're all right? You look so pale," she remarked as I forced her medicine into her hands.

"I'm always pale. Just sit tight here for a minute, okay?" I flashed a tight smile which I was sure she saw right through. At least she hadn't yet noticed I was limping. I then left the house, checking my surroundings constantly. When I was sure that there was nothing around me but woods and morning dew, I hopped onto my bike and drove into town where I could pick up the first payphone I saw. I called a cab, and then returned to her.

When our ride arrived, I had the driver take us down to the hospital, where I claimed she had had a seizure in the night and forced the doctors to admit her.

"But dear, I feel fine," Nan insisted with her voice lowered as a nurse pulled over a wheelchair for her.

If I cared less, I might have told her the truth, but instead I shook my head and dropped her hand. I told her that she had to stay in the hospital until she had improved, and then promised that I would come back for her.

And then I left. I had the cab take me straight to Fouzia's house. I knew I'd made the right decision as soon as she opened the door.

"Ophelia?" She looked me up and down. "What happened to you?"

"Someone tried to kill me last night."

She opened the door wider. "Come in. Lower your voice."

We soon found ourselves back in her garage, standing face to face with the nearly illegible map on the wall. The more clues we collected, the less clear the answer became. The truth no longer felt just within our grasp.

"Explain yourself," Fouzia demanded.

I turned to see her. "I told you."

"No, tell me *everything*."

I did as she ordered, recounting everything that I could remember from the night before despite my intoxicated haze.

She listened to me with an incredulous look on her face, every word seeming to hit her like a punch. She stopped to ask, "You didn't see the killer's face?"

"No, I couldn't see anything. Just a knife." I racked my fingers through my hair, trying to self-soothe. It wasn't the first time I'd been attacked. Why had it shaken me so much? I looked up. "Wait, you said *killer*."

"Who else could it be if not the person that murdered Xavier?" she ran her hands across her map and list of suspects. "It's clear that they found out what we're trying to do. Maybe your sudden rise to popularity gave it away."

"Maybe someone saw us that night at his house."

"Maybe. Who was at the party?"

"A lot of people."

She shoved a pen and paper into my hands. "A list. Now."

I wrote out every name I could remember, and if I couldn't place their face, I put *scrawny brunette kid with the eyebrow piercing,* which Fouzia later matched with their actual name.

"So whoever did it...has to be one of these people," she said softly, staring down at the list I'd written out. "What did you find out about Patrick?"

I nibbled at my fingernails. "That he needs to brush his teeth more often."

She snapped her gaze back to me.

I took a breath. "He had a crowbar in his pick-up. And he thinks the principal is the one that killed him."

"He thinks Xavier's uncle murdered him?"

I nodded.

"Does he have a reason to think so?"

I shrugged. "Not really. I didn't buy it. Although, I was mildly drunk, so you probably shouldn't trust my judgment."

"Don't worry, I wasn't going to."

I flipped her the bird.

With that kind exchange between friends, the two of us began to form a plan, both of us well aware of the stakes. The plan was that Fouzia would go to the principal's office while he was away and look for anything incriminating. I could tell that the idea made her uneasy, but she had a certain resolve that I couldn't argue with. My job was the students. She gave me the role of searching through the things of every student whose name was on the list I'd written out. Everyone who had been at the party.

I spent the night in a sleeping bag beside Fouzia's bed, since I was fairly certain my nerves would not allow me to sleep in my own house, and she didn't mind the company anyway. The next morning, we both woke up to her alarm and brushed our teeth side by side. We did everything in a comfortable silence as if we had been this way for years. It was a strange experience to share my morning routine with someone, and yet I found that I didn't hate it. I didn't hate it at all. The idea of marriage had always unnerved me, though I couldn't say exactly why, but that morning that I spent with Fouzia made me begin to think that perhaps I wouldn't mind spending my life with another person.

When we arrived at the school, however, the two of us parted ways. While Fouzia headed for Williams' office, I went looking for a fire alarm I could pull.

School had not been in for ten minutes, and chaos was already erupting when the alarm began to blare throughout the halls.

As students we had all been taught the proper way to exit the school building in the case of an emergency, however the majority of students hadn't yet entered their class, and so what was meant to be a series of straight and uniform lines calmly making their way towards the doors, had become a frenzy of panicked and half-asleep teenagers desperately rushing to escape. I grinned as I watched them flood towards the exits, tripping over each other in a prepubescent stampede. If it weren't for the alarm blaring overhead, a noise that pierced through my skull like a nail and hammer, I might have actually been able to enjoy the chaos.

I pulled my hood over my head and began to work my way through the crowd toward my first period classroom. I slipped into the empty classroom and looked around, scanning for familiar backpacks left at desks.

It was pink that caught my eye first. A small backpack the exact same shade as Agnes' hair, not-so-coincidentally. I unhooked it from the back of the chair and began rifling through it in search of anything suspicious. When I was left empty-handed, I moved on to the bag beside it. I didn't have to guess who had been sitting beside her with the plain gray bag, decorated with only one small kitten pin on the front. I searched through Laura's bag just as I had done with Agnes'.

My eyes caught on one paper sticking out from the rest. I pulled it out and set it on the desk to get a better look. It was a report card marked with her name, but strangely, only half of the teachers' notes were filled in.

I thought back to the last few days of school. I couldn't recall our class receiving our report cards yet. I frowned down at the paper. There were only three boxes of teachers' notes already filled in, and each of them seemed to have been written by different people.

> Amber Whitlock:
> Extraordinary student, meets all standards, very knowledgeable in advanced mathematics.

That certainly didn't sound like Laura. My suspicion was growing by the minute. I looked over to the other side of the classroom. Whitlock was the teacher we were meant to have class with *now.* Those were her notes sitting on top of the desk. I rushed over to the teachers desk and set the report card beside Whitlock's handwritten notes, my mind racing.

The handwriting was an exact match. Down to every stroke and unique dot. The imitation was seamless. Scanning the text for flaws, I nearly began to doubt myself, wondering if I had assumed wrong, and the report card was indeed real. But it wasn't possible. Whitlock never would have written these words about Laura. Hell, she wouldn't have written it about *me*, and I was acing her class.

I searched further through Laura's bag, moving quickly now that I was becoming more aware of my limited time. I shook out every paper and sleeve, looking for inconsistencies, handwritten notes that didn't match her own delicate scrawl.

I found a doctor's note detailing her need to be absent from gym, a field trip form supposedly signed by her father, and even a love letter addressed to one notoriously unpopular girl that seemed to be written by Patrick. I gawked at the evidence before me. *Not her. Could it really be...?*

Suddenly, the alarm blaring above switched off, and I was left in utter silence. I swore under my breath and returned the papers to the girl's binder.

I flew out of the classroom as quickly as I'd come into it, out of sight before anyone could catch me here.

CHAPTER TWENTY-TWO

If there was one thing I hated more than anything else in the world, it was pretenders. I loathed the idea of people who pretended to be something they weren't, who would go through the world with a crude mask. In short, I hated liars. It was the one thing that had made me suspicious of Fouzia in the beginning—her innate ability to put on a show and present the personality that best suited the occasion—but I guess I had kind of gotten used to it. For her, it was more of a survival skill than anything. Fouzia wasn't necessarily a liar, but a chameleon. That was something I could bring myself to respect.

Laura, on the other hand.... Somehow, finding the forged report cards in her bag made sense. The fake delicacy of her every action, the rare slip-ups that showed the true rage she harbored within. I recalled the day she'd made a scene in the halls, the day she had begun the rumor that I was Xavier's killer. It was very clear when someone had shown their true colors, when their true self was slipping out of them, and that was what I had seen that day with Laura. If only I had been able to recognize it sooner.

I had taken only one of the forged documents from Laura's bag, an old doctor's note dated from a week ago that I was sure she'd already used, and so was unlikely to notice was missing anytime soon. At lunchtime in a dark corner of the library I presented the note to Fouzia.

"Do you know what this is?" I said after slapping it down on the carpet between our bean bag chairs.

Fouzia frowned down at the doctor's note. "I didn't know you had asthma."

"It's not mine," I said, pointing down at Laura's name at the top of the text.

She shook her head, furrowing her brow. "Since when does *she* have asthma?"

"Fouzia," I said, "it's fake. The signature is forged. I found a million other faked documents inside Laura's bag, including a note from Whitlock referring to her as a golden student that matched the woman's handwriting *perfectly*. Don't you get it? Who else could have written a note that looked exactly like your writing except for her?"

"You think Laura—that she—?" Fouzia still seemed in disbelief.

"Who else if not her? I..." I had begun to say something, but stopped short as my mind reeled. "The night someone tried to kill me. I almost forgot. She was there, in the woods."

"There were a million other people there," argued Fouzia. "We can't jump to conclusions."

"No, you're not listening," I insisted. "She was standing in the woods throwing up, and as I ran past her I told her to get back with the others because I didn't want her to run into Patrick, but what if *she's* the one that followed me, not him?"

"She's built like a twig. If you fought in the woods, how could she have gotten the best of you?"

"She was the only one sober that night. Come to think of it, I never actually saw any vomit. I never even saw her eat anything at the party. Don't you get it? She's a poser, she shows everything but her real personality so that people will like her, but she's always been a psycho deep down."

"Then why Xavier?" Fouzia asked. "Why would she..." I could tell she was hurting now, painful memories being brought back up to the surface. In all the time we had been trying to track down this murderer, she'd been as emotional as a cast iron pan about it all, but now that we were close, now that I may have found *the answer,* she seemed to be falling apart. Was it denial?

"You want justice, don't you?" I asked her. I reached forward and took her hand in mine, the same way she had done for me that first time we'd really spoken. "It has to be her. We have to confront her. Or get more evidence to prove it to the police."

"Ophelia," she began, "you don't know the people at this school like I do. I'm telling you, I've got a gut feeling. Laura, she might be crazy, and everyone knows it, but she's never been the type to get her hands dirty."

"Then maybe she had an accomplice."

"Or maybe it's a coincidence."

I let go of her hand, frowning over at her. "Why are you defending her all of the sudden?"

"It's not about defending her," said Fouzia. "I just think you're wrong."

Anger sparked in me. I breathed the poisonous feeling away. *How fucking dare—*

"I'll prove it, then," I stated. "*We'll* prove it. We can find evidence, and if we come up empty-handed, I'll let it go, but if I was right, then we'll have gotten justice for Xavier."

She looked up at me through her lashes, looking more tired than before. It seemed that this job was finally getting to her, that the girl was reaching her limit, but I was determined to get her to keep powering through. I needed her.

"And what happened to your so-called 'psychic abilities'?" she asked with air quotes. "Why don't you conjure him up and we can ask him now?"

I glanced nervously to the side. "It doesn't work like that."

Fouzia sighed, but I couldn't tell if it was out of disappointment in me or disappointment in the mission. In the back of my mind, I hoped it wasn't the former. "Right. Of course it doesn't." There was a new venom in her tone that she's never had before, like there was something else she wanted to say, but had decided against it. "Let's find your evidence then, *madame.*"

Oh, how I loved when things went my way.

But before we could continue our detective activities, I had to check on Nan. I went down to the hospital the same way I'd come, in a tiny yellow cab with a driver that gave me funny looks in the rear view mirror every now and then. I braved the miserable journey to the hospital and paid my fee, using up the last of my father's check. His next one was due soon, and I was already anxious. My salary at the diner could only go so far despite the torture of working there.

The atmosphere of the hospital never brought back good memories. I had been getting better at disguising my limp so that when I approached the front desk, which was decorated with cat stickers and framed family pictures, nobody felt tempted to admit me or ask questions. I stuck my injured hands in my pockets.

"Agatha Peterson," I said to the receptionist, who led me down the long, empty hall. White lights buzzed above our heads, casting a ghostly hue across the beige wallpaper and bland tile. It was strange how this was meant to be a place for restoring life, and yet it seemed more lifeless than the ghosts pacing at the edge of my vision.

In fact, I always saw the most ghosts at the hospital. Their figures were always clearer. Sometimes they even muttered words.

A pang of guilt hit me for having put Nan in this place, but I knew it was only temporary. I knew she'd be safer away from that house, away from Laura—or whoever had killed Xavier.

"Just the girl I wanted to see!" exclaimed my grandmother in her soft, scratchy voice. As I approached and the receptionist whose name I'd forgotten left us in peace, she flashed me a toothy smile. I bent down to embrace her, but kept it brief. I didn't want the smell of her medicine-like perfume clinging to my clothes and skin.

"How are you?" she asked, but something about her overly-gentle tone made me think that she already had a suspicion. How could she not, with the state I was in? My hair was knotted and greasy from sweat, my face colorless and shiny, and I was wearing long sleeves despite the Spring heat to hide the cuts and scrapes around my arms and hands. Not to mention, just standing upright was making me feel light-headed at that moment. I took a seat beside her, concealing my pained grimace as my calf made contact with the side of the bed.

"I'm great," I reassured her. My answer didn't seem to satisfy her, but I went on anyway. "I should be asking you."

"Oh, I feel normal as ever," she told me. "No worse than usual. I really do think I'd be better back at home. More bills aren't doing us much good, are they?"

"No, they're not," I sighed. "But it's for the best. You should stay in for a couple more days until you're discharged. There's just something I have to do before we can both go back home."

She frowned at me. "You're not living at home?"

I pursed my lips. "Not at the moment, no." I raised a hand before she could question me more. I didn't need a lecture, nor could I afford to recount everything that had led us here. "I promise I'll explain all of it when it's over."

Her chest rose and fell with an anxious breath. Her eyes filled with a dull disappointment, a rising fear. "Ophelia," she said, reaching over to place her bony hand on my knee. "Ophelia, my strong-headed girl, are you in trouble?"

I opened my mouth to speak, but she continued. "Your mother and I have done nothing but try to make a good life for you. That's all we want. Not just for you to survive, but to *live*. If there's something endangering you now..."

"Come on, Nan..." I tried to stop her.

"It's not an accusation, sweetheart. But I know you wouldn't tell me if you were." She gave a knowing smile, and then hardened again. "You need to know when to leave. When to *stop*. You're a smart girl. You know many things. That's never been one of them."

I looked up at her. It hadn't slipped my noticed that she still spoke of my mother in the present sometimes. I wonder if it was a coping mechanism she employed for her own well-being, or something she did completely thoughtlessly. "You shouldn't worry about it," I told her. "I'll fix things."

Nan shook her head, like she was beginning to get frustrated with me. "I would be betraying Georgia to let you live like this. This isn't who you're supposed to be."

It had been so long since I'd heard my mother's name spoken aloud.

"Maybe I'm tired of doing the things I'm supposed to."

At that, she laughed. A full, genuine laugh. "How can you be tired of something you've never done?" She said it almost as if she were speaking to herself, as if it were a private joke.

"Well, I'm not gonna start now."

Nan went quiet for a moment, staring down at the beige covers draped across her and the IV attached to her arm. "When I say you can leave, I mean it." I listened to her closely, not understanding, so she went on. "We have savings. Under the floorboards in the attic. They're not meant for me, they're meant for you. It's enough for you to be able to leave Hinton."

My mouth had fallen slightly open. How had such a thing escaped my notice in all the years I'd lived in that house? Her words did not process immediately, but when she looked up at me, her eyes stony, I knew that what she was saying was true. I felt myself pale.

All these years. And freedom was waiting right above my head.

My chin fell. Would it really be so bad to do what she was suggesting? I could envision the scenario in my head where I packed up the old suitcase sitting in the back of my closet with my few possessions. It would be so easy, to then take that suitcase and leave the house behind, to drive down to the train station and move into the city. Get a real job. Maybe even go to college. Find a real passion that didn't just involve giving people dirty looks on the street and starting stupid fights with people that probably knew my father. If I left, there was a chance that... A chance at what? Oh, I didn't know.

"I can't," I told her.

"Why not?" she demanded, ready to scold me again.

"Because I can't leave you." If I left her behind, if I left behind that house, I would no longer be the same person that my mother had had those dreams for. Without her, without this town, without that house, without the abandoned shell I returned to every week, without the ghosts I saw, I would be unrecognizable. It would be a betrayal to myself.

"Oh, Ophelia," she sighed. "Since when have you cared so much?"

I curled my lip at that. What did she know?

In any case, my feelings did not stem from compassion nor self-lessness. My need for my grandmother had nothing to do with my grandmother herself. But what choice did I have when it had been my entire life's purpose to keep the woman in front of me alive? I thought of all the things I'd given up in her name, all the opportunities I had missed. If I left now, would it mean that I'd done it all for nothing? That I'd obeyed my father's orders no matter how ridiculous, that I'd dropped out of school the moment I could, that I'd taken that wretched job, that I'd allowed myself to turn into the dark, twisted girl I was.

I stood from my seat. "I'm going to fix this," I swore again. Then I left the room without another word.

CHAPTER TWENTY-THREE

Fouzia and I decided that before committing any more crimes, we try another route. I got the impression that she'd been a bit shaken up since the day we broke into Xavier's house and found the forged note.

"They invited me to go shopping on Friday," I told her one night as we sat in her garage, staring aimlessly at her map as always. It had become a jumbled mess at this point, filled with seemingly random names, pictures, and newspaper clippings. I would bet that Fouzia herself was now the only one that could actually understand it anymore.

"Shopping?" she echoed, tapping her chin. Her hair was down again in those flowing waves.

"For prom dresses." An amused smile pulled at my lips. Priorities differed, I supposed. While the two of us sat here, working our brains tirelessly to achieve justice, I was sure that Xavier's name would not pass either of the twins' minds even once.

"Well, obviously you should go," Fouzia told me. "In fact..." she took a long pause, "I could go with you. Maybe to monitor things. Help you out if things get ugly."

"*Ugly?*" I asked. "I thought you wouldn't want anything to do with the ugly. And besides, we'll be in public. Unless she has a weapon, I can take her." Thinking about it now, I was almost embarrassed about how afraid I'd been the day she'd been outside my house—if it had been her at all.

A flash of doubt shot through me as I remembered how I'd been pinned to the ground for that one, fleeting moment in the woods. The near certainty that had passed through me that I was about to die as the knife had come down.

I shook the thought away. "Anyway, I think I'll be fine on my own. They're not the nicest people in the world, so I'm sure you won't be missing out on anything besides a few snide comments from each of them throughout the night."

"I think I can handle it," she said with a scoff.

"Really, it's fine." I began to stand, but suddenly she jumped out of her seat and faced me.

"You know..."

"What?" What had gotten into her?

"I'm only asking because I'm trying to get you to help me find my own dress," she admitted.

"Oh." I balked. "I didn't even realize you were going."

Fouzia bit her lip and sighed, falling back into her chair. It seemed there was something she hadn't been telling me, and I could sense a confession coming. "Actually...I have a show that night."

"A *show?*"

"I'll be singing at prom. You know, right after the king and queen are announced."

I searched her face, trying my absolute best to tell whether or not she was kidding. When her expression didn't change, and no punchline arrived, I straightened. "That's great."

She rolled her eyes. "You know you don't have to hide what you're thinking around me, right? You're not very good at it, anyway."

I dropped the guise. "Why the hell didn't I know that you sing?"

"Well, you never asked."

I huffed. "When would I have asked if you sing?"

"You never ask me anything about my personal life." She stopped me before I could protest. "It's fine. I don't care. I know we're not best friends and I never expected you to pay attention to my stuff. I'm just...I was wondering if you might want to come see me. And maybe help me pick out a dress."

"I—" I had to stop myself and reflect for a moment, taking in everything she'd said. Perhaps I really had been overlooking what was actually important. "No, yeah. I'd love to."

And that time, she didn't have to call me out for insincerity.

***

Friday rolled around quickly. While the twins had, in fact, invited me to ride to the little boutique down the street from the diner where I worked, in the end I opted to walk with Fouzia—that way saving the four of us from a rather awkward car ride. And the walk was actually nice. We strode side by side wordlessly, and Fouzia didn't seem at all offended that I slipped my headphones over my ears so I could listen to music instead of making an attempt at small talk with her. Both of us remained utterly content until the moment we approached the boutique.

The storefront fit in with the other run-down shops around town, all of which were either on the edge of bankruptcy or were run by a family-owned business and were most likely to stay up until the day the world ended. This building seemed more of the former, judging by the lack of movement I saw within. There were mannequins lined up in the windows dressed in ridiculous frilly outfits, each one more vibrant and over-the-top than the last. It was almost fascinating, but in a way that settled just between a work of art and a car wreck on the side of the highway.

"This is where you want to get your dress?" I asked her as I slipped my headphones off. I tried to disguise any judgment from my tone, but as always, I wasn't quite sure if my attempt had done any good.

"Just turn off your overly critical tomboy brain for one moment and go along with me, alright?" She looked over at me. "You can focus on Laura and try to get as much information out of her as you can, and I'll supervise while I find my dress."

"Fine," I said. "Let's go in, then."

Agnes and Laura were already waiting inside when a happy little bell rang above our heads at the pull of the front door. They stood over in the corner, chatting with a woman there. The woman caught sight of us and bustled over in her obnoxiously high heels. She beamed with her row of pearly white teeth. She had a little mole next to her mouth and her hair was perfectly styled into a French twist. She also wore a white dress with a pencil skirt bottom, black trim along the edges. Thinking back, I was fairly sure that I'd had a doll that looked exactly like her growing up.

"How may I help you two beautiful ladies today?" She gave us a wink. "Shopping for prom? We just got a new shipment of dresses I'm sure you'd like to see!" She gave a bittersweet sigh. "I remember when *I* went to prom. The dancing, the decorations, the lights. It's lovely!"

Listening to this woman speak, I was almost beginning to understand why someone like Laura might feel inclined to end another human being's life.

"I'm good, thanks," I said, then motioned to Fouzia, who was promptly whisked away over to a rack full of outrageous dresses. I might have been worried for her, but by the way she was beaming with delight as she fingered through the rack, I knew I'd left her exactly where she wanted to be. Why had it never crossed my mind that she might like these things? Looking at her now, she seemed exactly in her element—not to say that was uncommon.

"Ophelia, over here!" called Agnes.

I strolled over to where they stood. Each of the girls held at least three dresses in their arms. I sat there with them as they waited for the dressing rooms to open up, revealing more teenage girls spilling out. I retrieved a book out of my bag to read as Laura went in first, and Agnes sat by my side.

"So, you're not going to try anything on?" she asked me.

"Maybe another time." I knew that telling her I didn't plan on going at all would only spark protest and then I would have to explain how agonizing the thought of actually attending a highschool dance seemed to me, murderer on the loose or not.

"You know the dance is only a couple weeks away, right?" Agnes glanced at me as if she were questioning my decision making skills. In the months we'd known each other, it seemed she was still convinced that I was an idiot.

"I know," I assured her. "I'm super excited."

"Me too," she agreed. "And if I were you, I really wouldn't worry about not having a date. I know it can be hard, but just remember that you're still *worthy*, okay?"

"Thanks. Super inspiring."

She didn't seem to catch my sarcasm. At least I could pull off a convincing lie when Fouzia wasn't around. Not that she would have been very proud of my comment.

Laura emerged from the dressing room after several minutes of what I assumed was dislocating her joints to fit into the impossibly tight dress she now sported proudly. It was a floor length dress with a slit down the leg and crooked ruffles along the collar line that seemed to be poking her in the chin. The dress was bright blue that clashed with her skin in a way that made her look sallow and pale beneath the white store lights. Or maybe that was just the dress cutting off blood flow.

"What do you think?" she asked us, turning around in the mirror so she could get a better look at the curve of her behind. "Should I get a smaller size?"

"It looks great," marveled Agnes, though her amazement might have simply been her own projection of excitement to try on her dresses. Unless she really did have such awful taste. Judging by the color of her hair, it really could have gone either way.

"Aren't you worried the ruffles will poke your eye out?" I asked her.

"I think they're kind of cute," Laura replied.

To each their own, I thought.

At that very moment, Fouzia came walking out of her own dressing room. She wore a sort of floor length ball gown that swayed below her as she stepped forward. It was a mulberry color that contrasted darkly against the white hijab she wore. She ran her fingers delicately across the silky material on her long sleeves. I had never in my life seen a girl look so classically, simply, unequivocally *pretty*. I thought to myself that all she was missing was a tiara and a royal title.

I stood from my seat and walked over to her. She glanced up at me.

"Is it too much?"

I looked her dead in the eyes and was suddenly very thankful that she would know every word I said was the truth. "If you don't buy that dress I will kill you and then me."

She blinked confusedly at me. I, too, was not quite sure what had compelled me to say it.

The store clerk cleared her throat, looking rather more nervous than before. "Why don't you come over here to the mirror, dear?"

I was then left to go back to Agnes and Laura, who were gushing over the ruffled dress as if they'd never seen anything more beautiful in their lives.

"You should definitely buy it," Agnes insisted. "How much is it?" She began digging at Laura's back in search of the tag.

"Doesn't matter," said Laura with a shrug. "I'm not paying for it, am I?"

Agnes frowned and then went red in the face. "Dad's paying for yours?"

"No! No," Laura denied, chuckling lightly. "Connor is."

I stopped. *What?* I knew she was more or less deluded, but I couldn't figure out for the life of me what could have possibly compelled her. "What in the name of hell are you talking about?"

Slowly, Laura turned to face me. Her face had taken on a new twisted smugness and the air in the room seemed to have shifted. "That's right," she said, pulling at the straps of her dress. "Oh, don't get all worked up. We're not dating or anything. We agreed we're both better off as friends." She sniffed. "Not that you have any right to be jealous."

"Then why the fuck is he paying for your dress?"

Laura glanced off to the side, a smirk playing at her lips. "Jeez, Ophelia."

Before I really knew what I was doing, I stepped forward and grabbed her shoulders, clasping her so firmly that she jolted back, knocking over a glass decoration from the table behind her. It tumbled to the floor and shattered, amplifying Laura's sharp squeak of fear.

"Tell me." I could see my reflection in her light blue eyes, beginning to warp into something strange and ugly.

She bristled at my action, pursing her lips with offense. "Let me go."

I did, and something flashed in her eyes, a realization that she had some sort of power here. I could tell that she liked to see me squirm.

"It's really funny, actually." She turned to the mirror once more and smoothed out her hair. "You know how I'm really good at copying handwriting? Actually, I guess you wouldn't know since Agnes always thought you'd snitch or try to get me to do something for you or whatever."

"Oh, don't tell me you wouldn't," teased Agnes, adjusting her bra behind Laura. I ignored her.

"Anyway." Laura's gaze returned to me. "As for the dress thing, he was having me write out a bunch of stuff for him, and in return..." she gestured to the clown's outfit draped over her, her mouth contorting into a smug grin.

My heart was beating so hard in my chest I was sure it would crack my ribs. I was sure they could hear it. I could feel the blood being sucked from my face, every inch of my skin going cold.

It couldn't be. It just couldn't.

Not him.

"What...What stuff?" I managed to say.

Laura waved her hand dismissively. "I don't know. I didn't really pay much attention. I think it was just, like, letters and stuff. A dress is a dress, right? And who could say no to that *face?* Seriously, what a dreamboat."

No.

Fuck.

"Laura." I was struggling to even stand, but I had to speak. I had to know. "What *letters?*"

She looked at me funny through the reflection in the mirror, still faced away from me. "Gosh, what do you care?" She sighed, looking like she'd finally had enough. "You know what? I feel like you'll never be happy until you've successfully made everyone around you miserable. Ever notice that? I mean, first you *have* to take Connor from me, and for what? To boost your ego? You didn't even keep him!"

249

How much had he told her? *How fucking dare...*

"You don't know shit," I growled, stepping towards her.

"No, he told me all about your little episode," she said, rolling her eyes. "And then there was Patrick. Everyone knows you led him on and then blew him off. After the party, he was practically in tears when you ran away, poor thing. He wanted to go after you but I stopped him because I *know* what you *do.*" She turned, jutting a finger at me. "And then we *kindly* invite you here just for you to pollute the air with your judgy attitude as if you know better than the rest of us! Well, guess what? You don't. You stand there in your ugly clothes and stupid look on your face and you just *judge.*"

"Laura, maybe—" Agnes began, taking her arm.

"No! I'm done pretending like we're actually friends when every-one knows you just started out as a *freak* before we took you in! Just 'cause you picked up a hairbrush doesn't mean you get to treat other people like shit, okay?" She cocked her head to the side, pursing her lips as she looked me up and down. "And besides, none of that hair or makeup or less-shitty clothes can cover up the fact that you're still the weird girl you were on that first day of school."

I reeled back my fist and punched her square in the nose.

Gasps flooded the store. My hand burned with the impact, but I didn't care at all. Nothing could overpower the pure satisfaction I got from that one, solid hit. She fell to the ground as if I had body-slammed her, and there was the sudden and distinct sound of fabric ripping.

Looking down at her, I took a moment to imagine what it would be like to pounce on her, to straddle her with my legs as I bore my fists into her jaw over and over again until I was sure that she wouldn't run

250

her mouth off again. I imagined how satisfying it would be, how *right* it would feel.

But I released my fists. I stepped back. I walked out of the store.

The happy little bell jingled above me before the door fell shut.

CHAPTER TWENTY-FOUR

I t was safe to say I wouldn't be spending my lunches with Laura and Agnes anymore. And this time, I meant it. I was done with the attempts at talking to them, at trying to stay close with the popular crowd, dotting my neck with vanilla and shaving my legs. I had absolutely nothing left to prove.

I now had a new mission, one possibly more difficult than the last. I had to prove Connor's guilt. It was the only way to clear my name once and for all and for Fouzia to get the justice she deserved. I wanted justice, too—now more than ever. Not just for the notes in my locker, the spray paint, the endless snickers and sneers, or the accusations and threats from the principal, but for that night after the party, for my grandmother, and for him to have dared make me feel the way I did. Never had I felt fear like on that night in the woods. Never had I felt hope like on the day he kissed me. He would pay for both.

The first order of business involved finding out where Connor lived.

One thing I had failed to mention to Fouzia, yet only later realized how relevant it may have been, was the picture I had seen the day we had broken into Xavier's house. The family picture taken out in front of some sort of cabin. When I had looked closer that day, squinting my eyes in the darkness of the hall, I had spotted the unmistakable image of Connor's face among the family. With his golden hair standing out among the rest, and the sharp line of his jaw, it couldn't have been anyone else.

So, somehow they'd had a connection. Maybe they were related, maybe they'd simply been family friends. Either way, it was the clue we'd been missing. It was my ticket out of this nightmare.

Before that first day walking with Connor, I had assumed that Connor lived on the west side of town. After all, it was the direction I'd seen him walking in every afternoon and morning I took my bike to school. It was the entire reason I'd started taking that complicated, hilly route. To see him. But the day that we'd walked together he had corrected me that this was not the case. What this meant, I wasn't sure yet.

That afternoon, after the last bell had rung, I took my normal route home on my bike. But I did not at all intend to go home.

I took the usual hills and turns, leaning and braking against my rusty bike. My backpack—although I wore it today for the sake of appearances—was completely empty. I'd skipped all my lessons that day, unable to sit through a class with *him*.

I stopped suddenly at the corner where I always intersected with him. I placed one foot on the ground and looked left, then right. There was no one there, no one down the road, and no one coming.

I frowned down confusedly at the ground. It had been every day without fail that I'd seen him walking along this road. Fouzia had already confirmed to me that he'd been in class today, so why wasn't he here now? I worked the question through my mind for a moment as rain began sprinkling down.

I took a turn towards Xavier's house, biking as fast as my legs would take me. A couple minutes later, I arrived onto the road where he lived. The last time I'd been on this road was in the middle of the night, weeks ago, and it looked different now.

That's when I saw him, the blonde head of hair trailing down towards the house at the end of the road, only a block down from Xavier's.

I moved to begin biking down towards him, and then I stopped again. If he lived here, *how* had his path ever intersected with mine all those days? This spot was nowhere near the west side.

My heart dropped as things clicked into place.

All this time, I had thought that I was the strange one, that I had been stalking him for months on end, constantly worried that he would realize what I was doing. And in reality...

He had been doing the exact same to me. Going out of his way every afternoon and every morning, just to come up on that one path.

A crazed, exhaustion-powered laugh ripped itself from my throat and I had to slap a hand to my mouth. The irony of it all was too perfect. Here I was, thinking myself a psycho, when meanwhile the two of us had actually complemented each other better than I could have ever imagined. I wondered if he genuinely believed that that was the route I was meant to take on my way home just as I had thought the same of him.

Oh, I really was going to kill him.

***

"Okay," I said, spreading out the notes and every piece of information we had on the workbench. We had taken down everything that may have led back to Connor, abandoning the miscellaneous information tying to Patrick, Whitlock, and Principal Williams back up on the wall. Now was the time to look at the simple facts.

Connor had killed Xavier, and he'd used Laura to do it.

Fouzia leaned in, her eyes scanning the chaotic spread of information. "We have all these detailed accounts of the events surrounding the incident, but Connor's name only pops up once or twice, and it's always incidental. There's no evidence linking him to anything directly."

"There has to be," I argued, shuffling through the papers and cut-outs. "Do we know if he has an alibi?"

Fouzia shook her head. "We'd have to ask him ourselves."

"But then he'd know what we're doing."

"If he was really the one that attacked you in the woods, I'm sure he already knows we're close," she pointed out. "Maybe he's even scared because he knows how close we are. Why else would he have attacked you?"

"It's been going on longer than that," I told her. I thought back to every afternoon that I'd obliviously passed by him on my bike. "I think he's been stalking me since before any of this started. Back in February."

Fouzia frowned. "Why didn't you tell me?"

"I wasn't exactly aware of it," I said. "I don't know how much of this all was him. I mean, we know that he didn't even write the letters himself."

"How about Laura?" asked Fouzia. "Maybe we could get her to tell us something."

"You heard that airhead before. She doesn't know shit. She doesn't even remember most of what she wrote, and I doubt she would confess to the police to get him caught. She's obsessed with him."

"There has to be some way that we can prove it."

"This is ridiculous," I muttered. So far, we had found absolutely nothing to prove his guilt, even though *we* already know the truth. We searched for hours through all the evidence we had and yet still could not find any detail where he had failed to cover his tracks. Yet—whether it was his brain or his luck—no matter how smart he thought he was, he must have left behind something—a clue, a misstep, anything.

"How about the note that we found in Xavier's room?" I asked her. "That's gotta be something."

Fouzia shook her head as if my statement was utterly ridiculous. "Then we would have to explain why we were in his house at all, and we both know that wouldn't go well. Anyways, even if we could show it to them, who's to say they'd believe me that I didn't actually write it? It *is* an exact match, after all." She set down a piece of paper beside the handwritten note and scribbled out the exact same words written there. When she finished, and both texts turned out nearly identical, she dropped the pen, her point proven. "Without Laura's testimony, most of the evidence we have is worthless."

"So we search for more," I stated, because I knew it was true that we had very little chance of being able to get through to Laura. "We know where he lives now. I'm sure he's left some loose ends if we can only track them down."

She paused. "You mean break into his house?"

"We've done it before."

"I'm not doing that again."

"Oh, come on," I urged. "It's the only way. We weren't caught last time."

"I said I am *not* doing that again." Fouzia stood.

"Then I will."

She turned to look at me, eyes wide. "Oh, no you're not."

"You can't tell me what to do," I reminded her.

"It's too dangerous. It's...it's *insane.*" She looked down at all the papers on the bench in front of us, scattered into absolute chaos. I could see the severity of the situation processing in her eyes. "Ophelia, this has gone too far."

I stood to face her. "What do you mean *it's gone too far?* He's a *murderer,* for Christ's sake!"

"No, no," Fouzia smoothed her sleeves nervously. "You don't understand. Look at all this. I've looked over it a million times. Every night, I'm awake, trying to solve this case to find whoever it was that hurt him. Everything that's here, everything you see, I've memorized it ten times over. I'm—" She took a breath, holding her fist to her mouth. It seemed that I was finally beginning to break her, that her composure was teetering on the edge. "If there was something here that could prove his guilt, I would have found it by now. There's nothing."

She threw her hands up in the air and repeated, "There's nothing."

I pressed my lips together. "There has to be something."

"I've gone over it *hundreds* of times in my head. You don't understand. I'm dreaming in sticky notes and red string." She laughed dryly, a sound devoid of humor. "He didn't leave any loose ends."

"Then we talk to him."

"He tried to kill you, Ophelia!" She stepped forward and grasped my arms, her eyes glistening with tears. "You can't just talk to him."

"Why not?" I cried.

"Because then I'll have lost you, too." A sob escaped her throat and she slapped a hand over her mouth as if the sound had shocked her just as much as it had me. A moment of silence passed over us, her hand still clasped onto my arm.

I guess the thought had never really crossed my mind. I'd never really tried to accept that Fouzia might truly care for me. Maybe it was a foreign concept to me, or maybe I really was just as dumb as everyone else seemed to think. In all the days that she and I had spent in this very garage, why had I never noticed that we'd grown close? Why had it never occurred to me that the girl might truly care if I died? I thought for a long, hard moment. Would *I* care this much if I were in her position?

"I'm not going to stop," I told her.

Her mouth slowly fell open. "You can't break into his house. I won't support you."

I had spent eighteen years of my life without support from anyone else. If I had to bet, I thought I would do just fine.

259

"I don't care."

But that was a lie.

Chapter Twenty-Five

D ays passed, and Fouzia had still not spoken to me. I'd moved back into my own house. Nan had, too. If it were up to me, I would have kept her in the hospital where I knew she was safe, but she'd been there long enough for the doctors and nurses to have realized that there was nothing wrong with her aside from her arthritis and generally poor health tied to her age, which they could do nothing about. They had sent me home with a refill of her pills and a "good luck".

I'd been mostly solitary for the greater part of my life, and yet there was something about this that felt different. I sat in my living room beside Nan and her knitting needles at work, staring off into the distance, wondering where I had gone wrong. When I looked around the room, I found that every spot on the two couches were filled with unfamiliar faces, a new group of ghosts now following me wherever I went. They had never lingered for this long, and I was beginning to worry.

As I rode down to the diner for the afternoon shift, I passed people that I knew for certain were not there. I wanted to scream at them, spit at them, beg them to tell me what it was they were waiting for, but I kept my composure until I arrived and hung up my sweater to replace it with an apron.

I got to work, blurting out my bland, monotone speech to every customer that walked through the door, and the horrible feeling that I'd made a terrible mistake continued to eat at me. Every time the bell at the door rang, I expected Connor to be standing there, a knife in hand, his eyes wide and crazed, ready to try and take my life again. I kept thinking back to the moment he'd come so close in the woods, his face now plastered onto my memory of the event—even though I knew for a fact that I'd never seen those crazed, blue eyes that night. My mind was beginning to convince me that I had.

Even Janie noticed that something was off, even through the clouds of poofy blonde hair. When she came around the corner and asked me, I brushed her off dismissively.

"I had a late night," I told her. It wasn't a lie. I'd been sleeping between three and five in the morning for the last couple nights.

"Oooh," she crooned, leaning over to set her elbows on the counter. "A late night, huh?"

"Get your mind out of the gutter," I snapped, setting a plate of fries onto my tray.

She batted her long eyelashes at me. "Does it have anything to do with that good-lookin' guy that was at table five?"

"No." I picked up my tray and turned away. Now *that* was untrue, but after all, she wasn't Fouzia. No one was.

I finished the rest of my shift as normal, and wasn't surprised when Janie clocked out early. I watched her as she fluttered her fingers at me in a wave and walked out the door with her bag over her shoulder. I wanted to be angry at her, but I couldn't summon the feeling. The sun was lowering into the horizon and the light that always pooled into the diner was dimming. I had never noticed how creepy this place looked at night, but I was sure as hell noticing now. It put me on edge more than usual.

When the night finally ended with no other strange visitors to the diner and I spotted no lingering figures outside waiting to pounce, I closed out the building faster than I ever had.

As I biked back home in the dark, I was beginning to come to the strange revelation that I was no longer okay on my own. And it was a terrifying thought—that I might have allowed myself to become dependent over the past couple of months.

On Monday, I knew there wouldn't be many lessons actually given, since the majority of the Juniors and Seniors were too preoccupied with organizing prom. I wondered if Fouzia had ever ended up buying that purple dress.

My questions were left unanswered because I chose not to go into school that day. I stayed home the next, too. At what would have been lunchtime, when I would have been sitting in the library scheming with Fouzia, I instead was stalking around Connor's house, studying every door and window, every possible opening. It was the second day I had loitered here, imagining all the ways I could break into the place and what I might find within. A creepy basement with murder weapons on the wall and bloodstains on the carpet, a bag of chains hidden beneath his bed, a shrine of my face with the eyes burnt out. The possibilities went on.

But though I was here, though I was thinking about it, the past two days I had not been able to bring myself to do the actual thing. I had yet to break in and see for myself. Be it a mental block or a deep-seated fear, I could not bring myself to do it. On the second night, I watched the sun go down and soon saw the light from his bedroom window flick off. I imagined him lying down in bed, closing his eyes, so vulnerable.

Maybe it was the fact that Fouzia's words were still echoing in my head, maybe it was the spirit of Xavier holding me back, maybe I was afraid to admit how wrong I'd been about Connor, how stupid I'd been in deciding to trust him.

I approached the front door. I stood there with the cheap lock pick sitting in my pocket, feeling significantly heavier than before. I stared at my reflection in the frosted glass of the door, my own blurred face gazing back at me. I looked so much like my mother's ghost then—it was uncanny.

I turned away from the door, stuffing my hands in my pockets.

I began my walk towards the graveyard.

***

The graveyard wasn't what I expected. It wasn't creepy or eerie, like something out of a horror movie. Instead, it was quiet, peaceful. Standing there, I realized how long I had avoided this place. I'd always had my excuses. Too busy, too tired, too overwhelmed, but deep down, I knew the truth. I was scared. I'd been terrified of facing this part of my life, of confronting the reality that my mother was truly gone. And all I could have was her ghost roaming around me. It was easier to see her ghost, a blurry figure, rather than accepting the fact that her body was lying here, in this silent, lonely place.

I knew my grades were slipping. I knew I was making internal excuses to skip school—all because I was afraid of reality. All the progress I thought I'd made, all the change, felt meaningless now.

My feet crunched on the gravel path as I made my way through the rows of headstones. After a couple of wrong turns, I finally found her, and I froze. The stone was smaller than I'd imagined, its edges creeping in on themselves with moss. The name carved into the flat stone sent a shiver down my spine. Georgia Peterson.

"Hey, Mom," I whispered, my voice sounding strange to my own ears, like a song you were sure you'd heard before, but could have sworn had a different tune the first time you listened.

I was almost surprised that she didn't reply. The thought sent a dry laugh through me. Too much time spent around ghosts.

I supposed this was a classic moment, the part where I would finally reach out to my parent for help and support. It had felt right to come here for help, but now, I wasn't sure what I was supposed to do or say. Standing here at her grave, I was only reminded more of how alone I was. The silence hung too heavily in the air.

"I don't know what to do."

It had been a while since I'd been completely honest. Not just with those around me, but with myself, and so I'd said the truest thing that came to mind. The thing that I felt in my soul.

"You know, I should probably be asking Dad, not you. You're dead, after all. But I guess there's a joke somewhere in there about how you still manage to be more present." Still, no response.

What did I feel? I felt angry, but that anger was always there, resting right at the front of my mind, waiting to escape in whatever form seemed fitting. I was angry at my father for his role in bringing all of this on, in forcing me to go to this horrible school that offered me nothing but strife. I was angry at Fouzia for leaving, no matter if she had the right to do so. I was angry at the twins for their blindness, for their inability to see anything that wasn't right in front of them. I was angry at Connor. I was fucking furious with him. I'd spent too many nights lying awake imagining what it would be like to kill him—almost as many as I had imagining kissing him.

But aside from the anger, there was something dull there, waiting idly in the back of my heart. Some sort of emptiness. Desire for something more.

I used to envy other kids growing up. Those who played with their dads at the park, those with warm homemade lunches at school while my stomach rumbled for hours. The anger stemmed from the constant waves of jealously that smacked me in the face every time I stepped outside. The anger stemmed from desire.

What if—just *what if*—my life had been different? If both of my parents had been alive and present, my grandmother healthy and dependable. And what if the boy I liked wasn't a cold-blooded killer?

When I looked back down at the rotting gravestone, my vision was already blurring with tears.

"If I do nothing, I'm going to die," I said.

A long pause. No response, again.

"I don't want to die."

I was crying now. Low, gentle sobs pulled me down towards the mossy hill where my mother's body lay. My knees hit the ground and

I placed my hand over my chest to steady myself, worried I would fall. My bones were aching as they had the night in the woods, as if the wounds across my body were fresh all over again.

"What are you waiting for, then?"

I looked up. *Mom.* Hope rose within me and then—

"It's you," I breathed.

Xavier stood there beside my mother's grave, his arms crossed over his chest, dark, greasy hair covering half of his face.

He brought his chin forward slightly in a slow and controlled nod. I imagined the action alone cost him some effort.

"How come you can speak?" I asked.

He stretched out an arm and pointed over to the side, where another grave lay. "My grave. Makes it easier...I guess."

"All this time," I said. "I could have just come here and spoken to you." I inwardly cursed myself. How could I have been so stupid? How much time would it have saved me if I would have had the courage to walk down here?

"I've...been trying to tell you." The words came out stilted. "His face. Your book."

"His face?" I frowned, and then it dawned on me. I thought back to the sketches I had found in my textbook months ago filled with senseless scribbles, Connor's distinct features within them. It was the thing that had led to my obsession with him, making me think it was some sort of sign that there was something more to him. It sparked my curiosity. But not in the way it should have. Shame creeped up my neck.

Xavier's figure rippled in the air a bit. His ghost was fading.

"Can you tell me what happened?" I begged, standing up off the ground and leaving my flowers behind. "Anything that could help me? Was it Connor?"

A whisper of a smile pulled at the corners of his mouth. "I'm already dead." He paused, formulating the words. "Just tell her...you know."

I shook my head. Did he mean Fouzia? "I don't."

"Just that...I'm sorry." His voice was quieter, as if it were coming from a distance, as if it pained him to vocalize it. The individual features on his face were blurring into each other, the edges of his figure blowing away into the wind.

"That I can do," I told him, just before he disappeared.

CHAPTER TWENTY-SIX

I arrived on Connor's street that night in all-black clothing, a new resolve swelling inside me. Things had changed. I had nothing to lose.

I stalked along the edge of the house, dragging my fingertips along the brick wall's surface. The sound of the night's crickets filled the air, wind rustling the leaves on the trees in the family's backyard. After jumping over the short fence, my feet landed gently on the grass of the backyard. I crept forward towards the sliding glass doors, maneuvering around the sunflowers in the garden. I was careful not to make a sound. Although it was well past midnight, you never knew who could have been awake.

The door slid open easily and breathed a sigh of relief. I imagined Fouzia at my side with her neverending vocalizations of doubt. I could practically hear her whispering in my ear, wondering if we should maybe turn back. I waved the thought away and continued onward.

Every step seemed like the click of a gun in a game of Russian roulette. *Click, step, click, step.* The wooden floorboard creaked lightly beneath me, threatening to expose my presence.

I found myself in the living room, circling around the small coffee table. Curious, I crouched down beside it and began rifling through the various papers scattered on top of the table. What I found were invoices, checks, and scribbled notes, all quite useless to me, especially since I could barely read them in the darkness of the room. My eyes were adjusted enough to be able to see where I was going, but not so much that I could read text so small. I discarded a sheet of stamps back on the table and made my way towards the door.

At the front door, there hung various jackets that I'd seen Connor wear. There was the denim one with the stars that I'd wondered about the first day he'd asked me to the arcade. I ran my fingers along the material, a dull pain running through me once more.

Beside the jacket, there was a hat. Just a simple, navy blue cap hanging off of a hook on the wall, the postal service logo printed across it. I let my vision wander further down the line and spotted a brown bag hanging beside it. I reached forward and peaked inside the bag. There were envelopes inside. Nothing but plain, white envelopes.

Mr. Smith. The same man who brought me my mail every month, wearing that same blue postal cap and brown bag full of mail. Connor Smith. Connor *Smith*.

Standing there in the dark, I wondered how I had never worked out the fact that Connor's father was the very same mailman who would go raving on about how his stepson would have made a good husband for me. The thought almost made me laugh now, thinking back to all those years when I had imagined what the man's poor stepson must have looked like, a small, worse-looking version of the already unpleasant man who delivered my letters. *If I had known....*

I continued down the hall towards the stairs and regarded them with a determined look. I imagined the house around me as the forest that led to the abandoned house I so adored. I imagined what was waiting for me upstairs as my rabbit, oblivious and unsuspecting.

And so the hunt begins, I thought, moving upwards.

If there was one thing I had learned over the years, it was how to mask my footsteps, how to hunt quietly. I could disappear when I wanted to. I felt like a shadow drifting down the hall.

I approached the bathroom door, left slightly ajar, revealing a glow from the nightlight that seeped into the hall. I carefully closed the door, turning the handle before I did so that it would not make a noise. I did not want that dim light peeking into any other doors I opened, for in darkness this deep, even the slightest hint of brightness could draw attention. I had to be smart.

I looked around, thinking hard. I had already gone around the whole of the downstairs, and there had been no basement that I'd seen. Above me was the door up to the attic, but I doubted anyone would be in there at this hour. The bathroom was empty as well. All of this meant that everyone in the family was most certainly lying in their respective rooms. Asleep, hopefully.

Based on the layout of the house, I could guess that the room at the end of the hall was the largest of the two bedrooms. I doubted that Connor's room was the largest, and so I turned towards the one adjacent to it. There was no sign or poster on the front of the door that might have indicated my guess was correct, but I was confident as I moved. I took the round door handle in my fist and turned it inch by inch, lifting up slightly in case the door were to creak on its hinges. When it stopped turning, I pushed the door open.

I did not hear breathing.

I took a step forward ever so carefully. There was no sound at all besides the blood pumping in my ears. I took another step, and the shape of a bed came into view.

It was empty.

Shit.

I moved further into the room and shut the door behind me. I glanced out the window to make sure he hadn't somehow heard me and snuck out. Though I doubted he would have run from me if he knew I was here.

There was no way he was in the house. It wasn't possible. I had scanned every nook and cranny already, so unless he was sleeping in his parents' bed, he was—for some odd reason—not home. Was he sleeping at someone else's house? I would have thought sleepovers would be a bit too juvenile for him—unless, of course, he was out for another reason. He could have been with Laura, paying off the rest of her favors. He could have been at school, in the process of murdering his next victim. He could have been waiting outside the door for me to come out, ready to finish the job he'd started.

I dismissed the thought. I'd covered all my bases. I'd been smart.

And so I began searching through the killer's things. I looked over his desk, in his drawers, under his pillow, and beneath his bed. I looked for anything incriminating, anything relating even remotely to Xavier or me. Maybe one of the letters Laura wrote would be laying around, forgotten somewhere, or yet to be used.

I could have been more careful about not leaving any tracks, about keeping everything in place so that the next morning when he went through his things, there wasn't the slightest possibility that he would notice anything was off. But today was different. I didn't care if he knew. In fact, I was almost amused at the idea of him realizing it, of him finally coming to terms with the fact that *I was dangerous, too.*

As I searched, I found no weapon and no bag of bloody clothes stuffed in a corner. No matter how he may have stabbed Xavier to death that night, it seemed he'd disposed of everything correctly.

I paused when I opened one of his desk drawers. *Odd*, I thought. Following my gut, I reached in and pulled out the plain white envelope sitting inside, already marked with a stamp. It was not yet sealed and so I opened it and shook the contents out onto the desk.

I struggled to read in the dark, but I saw that the letter was dated back to early February. It began with my name.

Dear Ophelia,

I trust this letter finds you well. Your grandmother, too. I am currently in DC on business and may not be back for the next few months. Your February payment attached.

I double-checked the inside of the envelope but there was no check inside.

I thought back to February. The letter I received had demanded that I return to school. He had been so adamant, going as far as to withhold his financial support, and I'd had no idea why. After his letter, he hadn't sent the February check until after I'd enrolled.

My knees were beginning to feel weak.

There was no check inside because it had been removed before I could receive it. And I did get it eventually, but not attached to this letter.

The letter. The piece of paper that had started this whole mess.

Had been *fake*.

The real one was before me, staring me down with that taunting black ink.

I looked back towards the door, thinking of Mr. Smith and the bag full of envelopes hanging at the door. How easy would it have been for Connor to sneak down in the night and snag an envelope with my address, and then ask Laura to write out a copy with his own version? A version where my "father" would demand that I enroll? How *easy*?

And Laura. Oh, I doubted she even cared. She was dumb, sure, but not that dumb. She had to have known this whole time why I had really returned, how Connor had been pulling the strings. But after all, she got what she wanted, didn't she?

The letter ripped in my hands, shreds falling down onto the desk. I didn't even realize I was doing it until it was too late. The sound of the paper ripping rang out like a bell in the utterly silent house and I had to freeze for a moment to make sure that I hadn't alerted his parents sleeping next door.

I had been so stupid. So *dumb*. Too absorbed with my own hatred towards my father to realize it, to see past the absurdity of it all. In what *world* would he have worried about my education? In what fucking universe would he have preferred that I further myself and my person goals rather than be making money? How stupid could I have been to think that he *cared?*

The truth was laid out in front of me.

I had been played.

I looked back down at the open drawer, and leaned down to get a closer look. There was a notebook, not like one of the large notebooks you might use for school notes, but rather it was small, used, the cover not too worn so it didn't look as if he'd taken it anywhere, but the pages within were crumpled and tattered with signs of constant use. I picked it up out of the drawer and opened it.

My eyes struggled to make it out in the dark—not to mention I hardly believed what I was seeing—so I retrieved a tiny pen light from my pocket and pointed it at the scribbled text across the pages.

Holy shit.

***

I arrived home as quick as I could, my legs burning with effort. I was fairly sure I was on the verge of ripping my leg wound open again by the time I jumped off my bike and walked in the door.

I stopped in my tracks, my breath catching. The door had been left unlocked. When did I ever leave the door unlocked? For a moment, I stopped there, standing right at the threshold, looking into the eerie darkness of my living room. Everything was silent within.

I closed the door behind me.

Something was wrong.

There was light peeking out beneath my bedroom door to my left. Thankfully, my baseball bat was sitting right by the front door, so I swept it into my hands within the span of a breath, letting it rest above my shoulder.

I crept toward my bedroom. I was absolutely positive I had turned off that goddamn light before I'd left.

I reached my free hand towards the knob, took one steadying breath, and then swung it open with all my might, so hard that it slammed against the wall opposite.

There was no one inside. However, my window was hanging open, a cool breeze passing through. Otherwise, everything seemed untouched.

I stepped further into the room and checked behind the door, in the closet, beneath the bed. Anywhere that a person—Connor—could have been hiding, waiting for me to slip up. I looked out the window, scanning around the treeline, but I could not see anything from where I stood.

When I was finally sure that the room was empty, a sharp, crazed laugh escaped from me.

He'd been here. He'd come in—probably to kill me—and I had been at *his house,* hoping to do the same.

If I hadn't been so terrified, I might have thought it was almost romantic. Poetic, even.

But then my heart stopped, struck with a horrifying realization.

I flew out the door and sprinted across the house towards Nan's room, all without taking a single breath. It was stuck in my chest, and I could not inhale until the moment I opened her bedroom door.

I found her lying there peacefully, her chest rising and falling with breath just as I had left her. She hadn't even been woken by the noise I'd made in my room. I took a shaky sigh of relief.

But he could have, I thought. *He knew she was in here. He could have hurt her if he wanted to.*

And yet he hadn't.

CHAPTER TWENTY-SEVEN

I stepped through the front doors of Hinton High the next day to find a mountain of change before me. The last time I'd been here—before things had gotten too serious for me to continue my educational career, and before I'd found out that the entire plot requiring me to enroll in this godforsaken school had been fabricated—the atmosphere had been very different. Last month, students had roamed the halls as if it pained them to do so, bags beneath every eye, and the only chatter heard throughout the building revolved around some stupid piece of gossip to get people through the day. I had imagined that things hadn't been so on edge before the incident with Xavier, but I had never imagined such a drastic change until I walked in on that last day. *My* last day, at least.

The walls were covered in posters and decorations, the halls filled with so much color that it hurt my eyes. There were banners and streamers hanging down from the ceiling and confetti strewn across the floors. It must have been the custodial staff's nightmare, but there were nothing but smiling faces everywhere I looked. Students practically skipped through the halls as bouncy music blasted through the intercom.

The banner in front of me read, *PROM NIGHT TONIGHT.*

I had been well aware that today was the day, but I hadn't expected it to be taken quite so seriously as this. Even in my past years here, I didn't remember the day of prom being such a fiasco.

"Oh, hey," a brunette girl with freckles paused at my side, yellow streamers falling over her shoulders. I recognized her from my class. "We don't have class today. It's just the prom committee and celebrations."

"I know," I told her. "That's what I'm here for."

She looked me up and down, then shrugged. "Alright." She then made a beeline around me and disappeared into the crowd.

I supposed they were moving on. This celebration was meant to be the turning point for everyone where they hoped to stop dwelling on the past, and move forward with the future. It was what they needed.

Not that anyone but Fouzia had ever talked about Xavier as an actual person. But whatever.

With a new sense of determination, I made my way through the crowd towards my locker, my toes nearly stepped on twice. I then took in the metal door in front of me, wondering what new notes I would find inside today.

I put in the combination and opened the locker. There was only one folded-up piece of paper sitting on top of my history book. I hesitantly took it and read the single word written inside.

Prom?

I frowned.

"What do you think?" He had appeared at my shoulder, leaning against the row of lockers beside me.

My expression must have given away my shock, because he laughed when I looked up at him. "Jesus, don't look so horrified."

"Connor." I said his name aloud, as if trying to convince myself that he was really standing in front of me, really asking me to *prom*. I shook my head, trying to read his expression, trying to comprehend what the hell he was thinking. I slammed my locker shut. "Don't fuck with me."

He held his hands up in a mock surrender. "Was I?"

I crumpled his note in my hands. "Do you think this is some sort of game?"

He shrugged, grinning. "Kinda fun, no?" He then bent down to my level and leaned in close. "I've gotta say, I had such a good laugh when I got home last night." He looked up, tilting his head. "This morning. Technically."

Out of all the situations in which I thought I would have seen him next, this was low on my list of guesses. It became clear to me then that I had truly never known him at all.

I studied him closely. "Are you not worried that you've been found out?" I asked him, almost exhilarated by the fact that his eyes did not leave me once. "It doesn't scare you that I could have told the police already? That I've been in your room?"

He pressed his back against the doors, hands in his pocket. "Why would it? You've got nothing on me."

"Are you sure?" I said the words smoothly and carefully, pronouncing each syllable like parts of a song. I wanted them to hit in just the right places.

And it worked. I saw his eye twitch slightly, his posture shifting with a sudden discomfort, but he brushed it away so quickly I almost wondered if I'd imagined it. If there was one thing he was good at, it was pretending. "Absolutely nothing," he repeated. "Otherwise you wouldn't be here."

"I'm not here for you."

If my attention was what he wanted after all these months of stalking me and trying to control my every move, I would not give it. I let my vision wander away as if he was of such little importance to me that I was so easily distracted. I then turned away and let myself disappear back into the crowds.

A hand clamped on my arm and I spun around, fear spiking through me.

"You didn't answer my question," said Connor, his teeth pressed together tightly.

"Get your hand off me before I chew it the fuck off," I spat.

He hesitated, his grip loosening. A flash of excitement passed over his expression, like a wolf realizing this would be no easy prey. He looked me up and down, and I wasn't sure if the action was out of lust or bloodthirst.

"I doubt you want us to be seen fighting," I challenged quietly. Whether he'd realized how much I knew now, I wasn't sure, but it seemed to strike a chord within him.

He then let go and I stopped myself from rubbing the spot where he had been grasping me, wondering if it would leave a bruise.

"You didn't answer me," he repeated.

"What do you want?"

"Prom." He smiled. I used to think there was something pure about that smile, something beautiful. Now, though nothing had changed in his face—even his mannerisms were identical to before despite the facades—the sight of that grin was so different. It sent a chill down my spine. This was not the same boy.

I had to take a moment to weigh my options. Which answer was least likely to get me killed tonight?

He waited.

"Sure," I told him.

And there was that grin, wide and victorious. I wanted to rip his teeth out of his skull and watch him bleed on the ground. But I didn't. I walked away, and this time, he did not stop me.

***

I knocked gently on the door with the handwritten sign reading *PROM COMMITTEE* taped across the front. I swung the door open and looked around. A dozen students were kneeled around a half-painted banner laying on the floor. When I asked about Fouzia, they directed me to the bathrooms where she'd disappeared to only minutes before. I thanked them and left. I then waited outside the closest girls' bathroom until I heard the sound of a toilet flushing within.

Fouzia stepped out from around the corner, shaking her hands dry. She stopped short when she caught sight of me.

I had expected her to say something. A *hi,* maybe. Even a respectful nod or *some* kind of acknowledgement. Instead, she took one look at me, and then turned away, walking back down the hall.

"Your group is the other way," I reminded her.

"I know, but you were standing in that direction," she muttered, continuing on.

"What are you going to do?" I shouted down at her, throwing my hands in the air.

"*Make a circle!*" she hissed over her shoulder, and then disappeared around the corner.

So, I was alone.

I'd always been good at pushing people away, at building walls so high that no soul could surpass. But Fouzia had been different. She had seen those walls, and she had tried to tear them down. And she had failed. I understood why she was walking away. It was fair, really. I had taken this whole thing too far, dragged it out longer than anyone should have to endure. And now, she was setting boundaries, choosing herself over me, and I couldn't blame her for that—I'd have done the same. I had thought of her as selfish when I'd left her house. Now, I saw her actions for what they were. Walls. Walls like mine.

But the truth was, *I* didn't have a choice. I couldn't just step out like she did. I had gone too far, and the only way out was through. Whether I succeeded tonight or not, this game would end. Him or me. And I'd already accepted what losing may entail.

I stopped by a couple more of my classes and finished the last of my business before leaving, then left school early, quickly enough that no one would notice my absence. Lastly, I rode down to the diner.

Janie was too busy to notice the oddness of my arrival at first. "Hey, O," she said without looking up from the counter. "Nick wanted me to ask you if you saw what happened to the shotgun." She nodded over to a space on the wall.

"Not a clue," I said.

She finally looked up, and then cocked her head in confusion. "Wait, it's not your shift.".

"I know. Have you seen John?"

"He just left for lunch. He'll be back in an hour. Probably."

I could not wait that long. In an hour, I would already need to be getting ready. "Alright." I made my way around the counter and plucked the ring of keys from Janie's pocket.

"Hey!" she cried, but rather than try to take them back, she just watched me open up the register.

"I'm taking the last of what he owes me," I told her, shuffling the bills in my hands before closing the drawer and tossing the keys back to her. "Just tell him I quit, will you?"

Her eyes widened. "You can't do that."

"I can and I am." I stepped towards her and placed my hands on both her shoulders. "If you knew what was good for you, you would, too. I know you don't want to be working in this diner for the rest of your life."

She frowned. "How do you know what *I* want, kid?" She'd loved calling me *kid* ever since I'd started working here, as if the five or so years between us really made any difference.

"I know you don't want to turn out like Pam. I mean, Jesus, you might not have many big hopes or dreams but I know you aren't hoping for *that*. And if you don't make the decision, things won't change themselves for you, you know?"

She took one good look at me, a hint of understanding passing across her eyes, and then she lost it as soon as it had come, shaking my hands off. "Don't go telling other people how to live their lives."

I had realized a long time ago that some people simply enjoyed being miserable, and I'd had a feeling about Janie, that inexplicable gut feeling that she could be something else if she really wanted to. But I also knew that she was right. It wasn't my place. So I let it be, and only hoped that my words had struck a chord.

"I'll see you around," I told her, but I knew it wasn't true. When she didn't respond, I left through the front door, the money in my pocket.

A couple months ago, I might have been more than pleased at the idea of never having to see any of these people again. I could have envisioned myself then, grinning as I walked out the door towards my new sense of freedom. Now, while I certainly felt free, I felt no triumph.

When I arrived home, my first stop was to the attic. I got on my step stool and pulled down the door above my head, revealing the stairs on the other side before climbing through the dark gap. When I had made my way inside, I searched blindly for the pull cord dangling from the ceiling until the room around me burst into color.

I followed the instructions Nan had given me, digging deep into the boxes stored in the corner, rifling past my mother's books. After another painful minute of searching, my hand caught on the edge of one of the floorboards, and I pulled.

Nan had been telling the truth. All this time, this had been waiting here.

I began packing my bags. I tore photos down off the wall and loaded half my things into garbage bags, and the other half into the old suitcase I'd kept under my bed.

I then made my way into Nan's room and turned on the light to find her still sleeping. I called to her as I searched in her closet for her own suitcase. "Come on, Nan. I need you to pack."

I found the old suitcase behind her row of dresses hung up in the closet and used my bodyweight to lean back and yank it out of its spot. It had been sitting there for so long, it had practically been wedged into the floor.

"Nan, I said you've gotta get up." I turned around, the case in my hand.

I paused.

With care, I slowly set the suitcase back down on the ground. I turned towards the bed and found it empty. Making my way back to the living room, I instead found her there, sitting idly on the sofa, knitting needles in hand.

"Nan." I neared her.

She made no response, continuing to knit. The yarn in her lap had partially unwound, a long strand snaking down the length of her dress and onto the floor. I kneeled down and grazed the yarn gingerly with my fingers, but it seemed to disintegrate in my grasp.

"Nan," I said again, looking up at her from where I kneeled.

Looking at her then, seeing the blurred edges around her wrinkled skin, the way her gray hair seemed to float in the hair even though there was no wind in the house, the dots began to connect in my mind.

And suddenly it made sense. Why I hadn't felt the need to administer her shot in the last couple of days, why Connor hadn't touched her when he'd broken in the night before, why I couldn't seem to remember when exactly she had returned from the hospital.

I stood back up and returned her suitcase to its place in the closet.

CHAPTER TWENTY-EIGHT

I could not bear to stay in that house. My things were already packed, and every inch of my skin was numb. I had a knife strapped to my thigh beneath my periwinkle dress that I'd taken from Nan's things. It went a couple inches past my knees, unfurling gently at the bottom. I had unbuttoned the first two buttons at my neck so that I would both be able to breathe and also not look like I was going to be selling bibles.

The dress still smelled like her. I remembered how I used to be disgusted by her sickly medicine smell that she left behind wherever she went. But now, in the back of the taxi I sat in, I found myself pressing my nose to the fabric.

I had not cried when I realized she was gone. I had not cried when I changed into her dress. I had not cried when I left her ghost alone in the dark, empty house. But now, as the town lights came into view,

I felt the threat of tears in my eyes. Horrible, humiliating, wretched tears.

Nothing was ever supposed to happen like this. This was not what freedom was meant to feel like.

Not that I was free yet.

Two more tasks, and then I was done with this town. I mouthed the words under my breath.

I could see the lights emitting from the school gymnasium the second the car turned the corner and I had to take a breath to steady myself. I paid and stepped out, looking out at the building sitting idly in the dark. A dull beat of music sounded through the air. The cab drove away and I was left standing there in the darkness, my heart heavy. I took a step forward, and then another, and then another.

This ends tonight, I thought to myself for the hundredth time as I approached the doors and swung them open. The music swelled and purple lights fell over me, spinning and flickering off of the disco ball hanging from the ceiling. The scene inside was such a stark contrast to that of the outside night view, with crazed teenagers jumping up and down in the middle of the floor, tables with colored punch bowls decorating the edges of the gym, and streamers hanging down from every inch of the ceiling. I began to think of how fun this might have looked from an outside perspective, how excited I might have been at seeing the celebration if my heart wasn't already palpitating with fear.

I quieted my incessant anxieties and stepped forward with an artificial smile. Even if I couldn't actually enjoy myself, I could pretend for the time being.

The girls all around the room wore dresses of every color of the rainbow, and I guessed that most of the cliques must have coordinated their colors so that no one was matching too closely, and yet they all looked more or less the same with their fresh tans, teased hair, and polished nails. The boys were even worse. To me, they were practically identical in their black and white suits, none of which really fit any of them quite right. Taking in the scene before me, it dawned on me that it was going to be very difficult to locate Connor if he was truly among them tonight.

"I must admit, I didn't expect to see you here tonight, Peterson."

I turned my attention toward Mrs. Whitlock who stood at the snack table, plucking a potato chip from a large plastic bowl and popping it into her mouth. She wore a black dress that fell just past her knees like mine, paired with a bright red scarf draped over her shoulders. Wearing that, paired with her dangerously high heels, she actually looked quite nice. While she usually had her hair twisted into an updo so tight that her skin seemed to be yanking her cheekbones into her ears, tonight it was left down, falling over her scarf in gentle waves.

I made my way over to her and took my own handful from the row of snacks, hoping I wouldn't regret it later. "Neither did I."

She looked at me oddly. "Any special boy you're waiting for?"

I opened my mouth to speak but she stopped me.

"Nevermind. Don't answer that. I just realized I don't care."

And just when I was beginning to wonder why she was being so nice to me. I looked down and grinned. "I'm not coming back after this, just so you know."

"I figured," she said. "I noticed the rest of your classwork was left on my desk this morning."

"All of it," I nodded. "Everything I need to graduate."

She eyed me for a moment, almost suspiciously. I always felt sort of naked under her gaze, but I didn't let it bother me now. Why should it? I would never see her again after tonight, one way or another. She looked back down at the paper plate in her hands. "If you find yourself having any difficulty while trying to do so, don't hesitate to give me a call. I'll facilitate it to the best of my abilities. I can also send you any letters of recommendation you might need—if it's college you're interested in."

"Thank you," I told her. I was quite glad that it hadn't ended up being her who had murdered Xavier. It would have been unfortunate to lose such an ally.

After that, she left to go patrol the rest of the gym with her newly-stocked plate of snacks, heels clacking loudly against the beat of the music. I stayed behind at the snack table, looking over it with interest. I eyed the punch bowl to the side and scooped up a plastic cup before pouring myself a small serving. I took a sip and then ventured deeper into the gym.

As I neared, I spotted mulberry fabric within the crowd and my heart skipped a beat. Fouzia was there in the middle of the dance floor, her face lit up in a smile, swaying to the music as her purple skirt danced beneath her like a complement to her rhythm. Everything about her looked utterly *right,* like she was just meant to be there, at the center of attention, enjoying every fleeting moment.

Stepping off to the side, I kept my distance and took another sip from my cup, the motion becoming an anxious tic.

"You know, when I didn't see you at first I thought you might have been screwing with me." The voice came from over my shoulder, a few inches higher than my head.

I was right, he wore a suit with the exact same cut and style as every other boy in the room. Except there was one difference. He wasn't wearing any white. His outfit was all black, through and through. I thought it must have looked quite edgy compared with my grandmother's dress beside him. But that wasn't the point. The point was that red didn't show on black.

"You would have deserved it," I said flatly, but it wasn't true. He deserved worse than getting stood up at prom. He deserved what I had planned for him.

"You're probably right," Connor said, leaning against one of the tables. He looked off to the side, a kind of amazed yet baffled grin on his face. "So, why *did* you agree?"

"Why do you think I did?" I asked.

"Well, you're not *that* stupid, so I'm guessing you've planned something," he said lazily, as if the topic almost bored him with its simplicity. "You've probably got a wire recording everything I say in the hopes that you'll be able to frame me for murder. Oh, or maybe the police are already waiting outside. Actual police. Not dead ghost police, I'm sure."

So, he was full of shit when he said he believed me. Now, it was almost comforting to hear. "None of the above." I stepped closer to him, holding my cup to my chest as I leaned in to whisper in his ear. "I'm going to kill you." I said it plainly and simply, as if it were the most natural fact in the world. It wasn't even really meant to be a threat, I just said it because it was true.

When I pulled away, he was smiling still. "Now, *that's* good. Really, I got chills."

I didn't let his words provoke me. Frankly, I didn't really care if he thought I was kidding. If anything, it was an advantage. My gaze wandered back out to the dance floor.

He watched me carefully as I raised the cup to my lips again.

"So, what's *your* plan?" I asked him.

He didn't answer right away, which was the first sign that whatever he wanted to say must have been at least half true. "Do you want to dance?"

I looked at him.

"If it's all going to come crashing down anyway," he pushed. "Why not enjoy ourselves?"

Slowly, I set my cup down on the table, and when he offered out his hand, I took it. Disgust crawled over my skin where he touched me, but I followed him towards the middle of the room anyway. Distantly, I wondered if Fouzia was watching, or if she had even noticed that I had shown up, but my eyes were locked with Connor's.

"You know," he began, his voice smooth, "if things were different, we could have been good together."

I stared at him. There was a time when the thought might have appealed to me. But it had long passed. "Maybe. Except I'm not like you," I replied. "I'm not a murderer."

He chuckled. "Not yet, anyway."

"No, not yet."

The song shifted. Slowing to something more somber, and Connor pulled me closer, his hands pressing into the small of my back. I sucked in a breath.

"Do you *really* think you can do it?" he whispered, his breath warm against my ear. "Do you think *you* can take *me* down?"

My mind went back to the night before, the darkness that had surrounded me as I had crept into his room. That same sense of determination was still within me, waiting for the perfect opportunity to jump out, to reveal itself. I thought of the night in the woods and the rage that had consumed me when I had realized just who had attacked me.

I pulled back slightly, just enough to look him in the eyes. "Yes."

Connor's grip tightened, and he spun me around, pulling me away from the dance floor to the side door of the gym.

"Let's go talk."

I did not try to pull my hand from his grip, following him languidly through the door. It was dark outside. Too dark.

While I registered this fact, and I understood logically that I should maybe be afraid or on edge, my body was not quite responding. My heart did not continue its incessant pounding in my chest, instead beating smoothly as it had. I had no goosebumps, and even my breath remained rhythmic.

"I have one thing I wanted to ask you," Connor began.

I began to blink my eyes repeatedly at him, as if trying to correct my vision. I couldn't see very well despite the street light beside us.

"What is it?" I asked, but the words came out much more slurred than before.

A knowing look passed over his face, and all hints of that smugness from before dropped away. "That worked faster than I thought."

I had to force the next words out, frowning with confusion. "What...did?"

"The punch."

And with that, my knees gave out from under me and my world went black.

CHAPTER TWENTY-NINE

C onnor Smith was perhaps the second smartest person in this awful town. In all the time I'd known him, I had been constantly amazed by his every step. Even in the way he had ended Xavier's life, there was something artful about it that I could admire. He was a mindless killer, but I supposed there was a reason I had fallen for him in the first place.

Still, he had a certain arrogance when it came to his own privacy. While he had a history of stalking, lying, and invading others' business, I was beginning to think that it had never once crossed his mind that the same could be done to him. It was clear that while he had been skillful in covering up his role in Xavier's murder, the entire process had given him the notion that he was invincible.

I was prepared to prove that this was not the case.

On the night that I broke into Connor's house, I made more than one revelation. Not only had I discovered the truth of my father's letters that night, but I had also found a very interesting notebook in his desk drawer. A book that I read as carefully as I could, memorized every inch of it, and then put it back just as I had found it, replacing every item within exactly as he had left them. Because the notebook had contained the extent of Connor's plan to end my life. *Plan B*, as he had labeled it.

While I didn't yet know what Plan A was meant to be, it *had* to have been better than that.

What I did know was that Connor planned to drug me the night of prom. And if I didn't have any drink, or if I refused one that he offered, he was going to take me to the back of the gym and knock me out with chloroform. If all of that hadn't worked, he was going to take me out to the woods behind the school and simply stab me to death. These were plans B, C, and D, because he had a taste for dramatics, and he would have much rather taken me to a more significant location before carrying out the act. Just like he had done with Xavier—luring him out into the school hall where he would undoubtedly be found. Like I said, dramatics.

Conveniently, I had taken my own drink by the time he arrived, and even luckier for him, I had turned my head away from it twice in the time he was standing beside me, giving him two clear opportunities to throw his little white pill into my cup. I hadn't made them too obvious though, waiting until I heard a noise on the other side of the gym, or turning so that I could hear whatever he was whispering better. Getting my drink spiked was not the difficult part. The difficult part was ensuring that he still thought me oblivious. Alert and aware, but ignorant to his true intentions. However cliché they were.

Then, once I was fairly sure he'd done his job, I had raised the cup to my lips, facing towards him so that he could not actually see the liquid enter my mouth, and then sealed my lips around the edge and swallowed my own saliva. Based on the ever-so-subtle flicker in his eye when I did so, I was pretty sure he'd bought it.

And then there was my fainting act. This was the risky part, since I didn't know what drug he planned to use on me or how long it would take to kick in. It was a gamble, but I assumed once he took me outside, that he was expecting it to happen soon. Hence the collapsing at his feet. I had never been a good actress, but that was one performance I knew I would be proud of for the rest of my life.

I kept my muscles perfectly relaxed as he scooped me up off the ground and carried me towards his car with ease. I hadn't realized just how strong he was until then. I listened as he popped open the trunk and placed me inside with excessive care.

It would have been sweet—if he weren't planning on murdering me later.

I let the low rumbling of the car soothe me as we drove. I counted each turn in my head as I felt the car rocking back and forth. When I really focused, I could have sworn I could hear music sounding from the front of the car, some pop song playing shamelessly on the radio. Either he'd turned it on so that my screams wouldn't be heard if I did wake up, or he was having the time of his life. Maybe both.

When we finally did arrive and the car engine settled, I shut my eyes tightly, trying to relax into a natural position, and waited for the trunk to open. A minute passed, and then moonlight came pouring in before I felt his hands picking me up and out of the car. He placed my head on my shoulder and his pulse fluttered against my neck.

I let my eyes open just a bit, peeking through the curtains of my eyelashes.

We were walking towards the abandoned house, the same one where I spent my days alone, lying on the floor, summoning ghosts. I'd always thought I was the only one who knew about this place, and maybe that had been true once, but ever since Connor had come into the picture, there was no saying what was really mine anymore.

We walked through the front door, which was hanging open. The top half of it had completely rotten off and he moved past it quickly. He had picked up the pace enough now that I was beginning to suspect that his pill was meant to wear off soon. Still, I did not stir.

I waited until he had sat me down on one of the rickety chairs that had been laying on its side in the kitchen. He set it up against the counter with his foot and dropped me there. When he reached behind him to grab his set of ropes, I reached under my skirt and plucked my knife from its spot on my thigh.

As he turned, I rose from my seat and lunged.

He cried out and my vision filled with the telltale red of his blood and he staggered back, a slash across the front of his chest. As I thrust again, reaching for his arm in the hopes I would be able to stand behind him and incapacitate him with my knife to his neck, he clutched the fabric of my dress and knocked me off balance, my back hitting the floor.

The element of surprise and a weapon hidden beneath my dress was all well and good, but Connor was strong. Even in his tailored suit and tie, he seemed to have full range of motion and he held me down easily. I kicked and scratched, but he did not react as my nails dug into the skin of his hands, blood blooming from where they met his veins.

He began pressing on my windpipe with his forearm. "I should have known," he said as I clawed and thrashed beneath him. "But I just assumed that no one but you could look like such a bitch even in her sleep."

I tried to get leverage and reach down for my knife, but it had already been thrown out of my reach and the edges of my vision were going black. My gaze shifted to one of the kitchen cabinets nearly an arms-length away. But just as I lifted my hand, all sense left me.

***

I woke up in the very same chair Connor had tried to tie me to before. The room around me came in splotches across my vision and I had to blink the black spots away. My wrists were tied so tightly to the wood behind me that they'd gone numb, my elbows twisted in ways they shouldn't have been able to go. All his gentleness and care had disappeared, it seemed.

Fuck. I looked up to see him sitting across from me in a matching chair, his elbows on his knees as he eyed me. I wasn't sure how long he had been sitting there, just watching. The thought sent an instant wave of nausea through my stomach, but I pushed it down.

I coughed, the world still swirling around me. "I hope that wasn't a rental."

Connor looked down at his front where his suit had been ripped open, exposing the skin of his chest. There was no binding around his wound. He didn't even seem to have cleaned it. It frustrated me that I hadn't been able to cut deep enough.

"Unless daddy bought it?" I went on, trying to seem less discombobulated than I was. "I'm sure he'll take it well. He seems nice for a mailman."

301

"I take it you figured out the letters?" he asked me, looking back up.

I tilted my head down in a soft nod, digging my nails into my fists behind me.

"I had to get you close one way or another, right?"

"Why?" I demanded through bared teeth. I caught one of the ropes on the edge of the chair where I could feel that the wood had cracked, leaving a sharp surface for me to rub the rope against. "Why me?"

He furrowed his brow, suddenly very serious. He took a breath before speaking, as if the very act pained him. "Because I love you."

I laughed. "Bullshit. You needed someone to cover this all up. You needed someone to blame for what you did to Xavier. You're a psychopath."

"You *are* to blame."

I paused. "What?"

"All this time with you playing detective, running around with your little friend, Fouzia. I bet you had her fooled." He seemed to take pleasure in the look on my face, as if he could hear my heart beginning to race from where he sat. "But you don't fool me. You're the one to blame for his death."

"What the fuck are you talking about?" I spat.

He sighed. "I saw you one day when I was passing through these woods. I was restless. The sun was setting and I had to get out of my house and do *something*. I had been so fucking bored for months. Then I found this place, this empty shell of a house, and then I found you. I recognized you, of course. From class. I know most of the student body has forgotten that you weren't exactly new in the first place, but *I* recognized you. I saw how much you'd changed since you

302

left school. And I stood there in the trees, watching you through that window while you laid on the floor. Right over there—I remember it perfectly. And then you walked out, that same knife you tried to stab me with in your hand. God, you looked so beautiful. You had that bloodthirsty look in your eye." He leaned forward, pointing to his own eye. "The kind you don't see in most people. It drove me insane. You have...no idea."

I have an inkling, I thought.

"And then I watched you kill," he continued.

"Kill?"

"A rabbit," he explained. "I don't really know why you did it. I don't really care. What caught my eye was that look on your face, that blank look as you did it, as if killing came so naturally to you. As if you were born to take lives—and some people are, you know. I think I fell in love with you then. I couldn't help it." He chuckled. "We're so similar and you don't even realize it."

"And how does that make *me* responsible for you what *you* did?"

He shrugged. "I knew if I could get the timing right, if I could put the right idea in Laura's head, the rumor would slip eventually. And then the rest of the school would see you for who you really were. A killer. Don't you get it? When I saw you that day, you made me feel like I wasn't alone." He gestured to his chest desperately. "Like I could be who I was. Drawing suspicion away from me was just a bonus. And I hated Xavier anyway. He was the perfect victim. No friends—besides that Fouzia girl, but if anything, that was an advantage for when it came time to lure him out that night—he was reserved, probably depressed, and hardly put up a fight." He laughed to himself. "That night in the empty school, after I'd gotten him to drive out there, it was really pathetic. Once he saw it was me and not his girlfriend, he didn't even think to run until he saw my knife. Can you imagine being that helpless?" He looked me up and down. "Well, I guess you can."

I kept my expression stony. He had changed so much. The entire facade had dropped, and here he was, the real unfiltered Connor on display before me. I had believed he was good, so I put him on a pedestal. Hell, I'd thought *he* was too good for *me*. And now, here he sat, a completely different person. I had just one question for him. "Had you killed before then?"

He frowned in discomfort, but I thought I spotted a slight smile curling the edges of his lips, as if he were still pretending. "I might as well tell you everything now, huh?"

"Since you're going to kill me anyway," I continued dryly. *Might as well monologue.*

He nodded gravely and I tried to pretend like my skin didn't go cold. "You remember the story I told you that one day about my brother—in the mountains?"

"That you were hunting," I answered, "and he died while you were trying to save him."

He shook his head, pressing his lips tightly together, his gaze dancing with a barely contained thrill. "It was no accident."

I stared at him.

He looked down at his hands. "I had to do it or else I would have gone insane. He just—I told you about how great he was, I'm sure you remember. He really was. *Extraordinary.* He was good at everything. *Every single* thing he tried. In comparison, I was garbage. And that's not an exaggeration. Everything he did was perfect and I was constantly suffering through the praise my parents and everyone

304

gave him, and I tried constantly to get him to do something bad. I even framed him for things I had done, though I felt so guilty about it, because I knew it was still *me* that was bad. So finally I had enough. I *had* to push him. Oh, don't give me that look, Ophelia. If I wouldn't have done it, I would have died. I was rotting from the inside out more and more every day, and as long as he existed, the worse I would get. Do you get it? It was me or him."

He was gesticulating wildly, barely paying attention to me anymore. It was as if he saw through me, completely oblivious to the cords around my wrists slowly ripping open.

"And it *worked*," he continued. "After I did it, and I gave everyone the story of how I had tried so hard to save him—breaking my leg in the process, but that was his fault. He'd fought me so hard and tried to drag me down with him. Selfish fucker, really. No matter what everyone else said." He smirked lightly, like the memory brought him comfort. Or perhaps vindication. "Anyway, I really did get better. It was like all the good things he'd done were suddenly passed onto me. My parents would say things like 'My son? Yes, he did advanced math, he won that soccer trophy, he's the most amazing kid I've ever met.' and even though they were talking about Dylan, they were suddenly talking about *me*. Because I was their only son."

He didn't seem to notice me rolling my eyes.

"And I was a million times happier, of course. I felt so powerful. All that good stuff he'd done, and I had put an end to it within minutes. All I'd had to do was make the decision, and he was *gone*. Do you know what kind of power that takes? How amazing it is to be able to take a life so easily? To be able to end something that was supposed to be so *great* with nothing but your bare hands?"

He paused. "Well, you know. Of course you know."

"I don't kill people," I stated coldly.

He grinned. "You were going to kill me. All that moral high ground and yet you were going to do exactly the same thing. I bet you wouldn't have felt *mournful*. God, that's such a fake word. No one really mourns. When I was little, I was convinced that everyone around me was faking their tears at my grandfather's funeral, just so that they'd seem normal. I didn't realize they were all really so dumb. It's all social bullshit. And once you realize that, then you can really be free of it all."

He sighed deeply in relief, looking me up and down as if I was some sort of prize he had finally won. "Isn't this great? Being able to speak so freely? Here, now you say something. Tell me a secret, something you've never told anyone else, something you're afraid to say because you'll seem *weird*, or...psychopathic, as you say."

I tilted my head. "You think because you've sat here and rambled all your bullshit that you deserve something from me?"

I saw him flex his fist, a muscle twitching in his jaw. "What would I have to do to deserve it, then?"

"Untie me."

He laughed. "You can't really think I'm *that* stupid."

"Do it."

He paused, considering it. "You know I can't."

I rolled my eyes again. "What happened to all that about power? And yet you *can't*."

"I won't," he corrected.

"That sounds more accurate."

"God, I like you."

"Go fuck yourself," I spat.

His wide grin returned, as if my words had only confirmed everything he'd thought. "I have to confess something."

"What's that?" I asked, humoring him.

"I don't really want to kill you. Not now. I want to offer you something."

"Go on."

He licked his lips, leaning forward. I thought I saw a glimmer of moisture over his eyes. "I want you to join me, Ophelia. Run away with me." He put a hand on my knee, rubbing his thumb gently over the periwinkle fabric of my dress.

So, this was his plan A.

I didn't hesitate. "No."

"But then I'll have to kill you." And plan B.

"And if I say yes, what makes you think I would even keep to my word? I'm dead either way."

"No, it doesn't have to be that way," he insisted. "Of course, I knew you'd say no at first."

"Well, that's still my answer."

Connor stared at me for a long moment, his expression shifting from desperation to something colder, harder. I could see he was trying to figure out his next move. Strangely, seeing him squirm made me understand why he liked doing the same to me.

"I'm giving you one last chance," he said finally, his voice cold. "Join me, Ophelia. We don't have to do this. I've already got my car all packed up for us to leave this goddamn town. You can finally leave your grandmother behind and you won't have to worry about anyone but yourself. Don't you see? It's *freedom*. I'm offering you *power*. You have to make sacrifices to get it. I know I did."

I chuckled. "What sacrifice have you ever made? All you do all day is hurt other people for what *you* want—"

"And what's wrong with that?" he asked, interrupting me. "When I first met you, I got the impression that you knew your worth. I know mine, too. Society—this damn school—wants to keep us insecure, because if we start doing things for ourselves, we're dangerous." He looked intensely into my eyes, a fixed intention there that I'd never seen before. "You are dangerous, Ophelia."

At least he'd gotten one thing right.

"And I have made sacrifices," he went on. "I've felt pain for the sake of the greater good."

"For your own sake," I corrected.

"*No.*" His voice was ice. "Do you remember the night we really spoke for the first time? At the diner?" He began to speak more quickly, as if he were getting excited.

"I do."

"And you remember what that dumbass Patrick did? How he took me out to the parking lot and *beat* me, him and his friends? Like I was nothing." He brought his fist to his palm, miming the motion.

"I do," I repeated, realization creeping up on me.

Connor laughed, his head falling into his hands. "I asked him to do it. Oh, it sounds so funny now. So juvenile. But no, I asked him to show up and beat me up like that—I paid him, actually—because I knew you'd come out to...defend my honor." He flushed a bit, and I got a glimpse of the boy I'd met that night at the diner. A shadow of who he'd pretended to be.

It made sense now, and I cursed myself for not having questioned why they'd done it. I supposed that in my head it simply seemed like the kind of thing Patrick would do. The mindless attack seemed right up his alley, and I—blind in what I had hoped was love—had been more preoccupied with Connor's well-being than to see through the faulty logic of it all.

"It sounds like you'd be nothing without your daddy's money," I told him.

"Wrong, again." He clicked his tongue. "Sometimes you need people so you can manipulate them. But I've always done my own dirty work. That, I'm proud of. What are you proud of, Ophelia?" It seemed that he'd taken a new liking to saying my name after each sentence.

"I'm proud that I'll never be as fucking neurotic as you—"

He struck me across my cheek, and white-hot pain shot through me. I always did have an inability to hold my tongue. Warm copper spilled into my mouth where I'd bit my cheek and I spat the blood out onto the floor.

"I'm sorry," he said softly. "I never meant to hurt you. I regretted what I did that night when I saw you with Patrick. When you were...kissing him. I was just so..." His lip curled. "I was fucking disgusted."

So it was him. I thought back to that black silhouette chasing me through the woods that night. Hunting me. I recalled the knife that had struck inches from my face, envisioning the metal's moonlit glow.

"So you didn't plan to kill me that day?" I asked.

"No." He shook his head. "No, I didn't want to kill you. I mean—I *wanted* to. But I should have controlled myself."

There it was. There was his flaw.

All these months he had been so cold, so calculating in each of his manipulations. He'd carefully made sure he was one step ahead of all of us at every turn. And yet, at his core, he was impulsive. He had admitted it himself. Perhaps that was how I'd defeat him.

He gazed at my mouth. "Why did you kiss him? Why would you run from *me* and kiss *him*?" He wasn't looking through me anymore, but really seeking answers.

I tilted my head. "Maybe I liked him better."

"Bullshit. Why did you do it?"

"Why did *you*?" I asked. "Why did you pull away at the diner if you were so fucking fascinated with me?"

He smiled. "Part of the game. If I was too eager you might have been suspicious eventually.

I curled my lip. All that shame and strife I'd suffered. "Why would I ever want to join you after everything you'd done to me?" I asked him coldly, sucking the blood from my cheek.

"I've told you already," he sighed helplessly. Almost pathetically. "Because I love you."

I tilted my head, feigning consideration. "You know what's funny?" I asked, a bitter smile on my lips.

He raised an eyebrow. "What's *funny*?"

"You really think you have the upper hand here." I leaned forward meeting his gaze with mine. "But you're wrong."

His eyes narrowed. "What are you talking about?"

I didn't answer immediately. Instead, I shifted my weight just enough to feel the rope behind me give away. My heart pounded in my chest, adrenaline flooding my veins, but I forced myself to stay calm. I couldn't afford to let the rush take over.

"You talk about power like it's something you can just take from someone else," I said slowly. "Like it's something you can hold over them. But power isn't something you get to keep if you don't know how to use it."

He scoffed. "But that's just the thing. How would you know? You don't. You've never really had power. Not here."

I smiled. "I know more than you think."

Before he could respond, I snapped the rope behind me and jumped out of the chair. My hand darted to the floor, grabbing the knife I'd dropped earlier. He was fast, but not fast enough. With desperate rage fogging my vision and my aim, I struck the knife towards the soft, vulnerable skin of his neck.

"You fucking bitch!" He cried out sharply, his face contorting with pain as he stumbled back, blood soaking through his sleeve. I had missed the neck.

Just when I thought I had got him, he proved me wrong again. He wasn't finished. With a shout, he lunged at me, grabbing a fistful of my hair and slamming me hard against the wall. My sight blurred and dizziness overwhelmed me. I felt a wave of panic rising in my chest, dulled by the sudden, spreading numbness. Before I knew it, I had sunken to the floor.

"I didn't want to do this to you, O." He panted, pinning my head against the wall with his hand, using his other to wrest the knife from my grip. "I didn't want to hurt you. I love you. I was ready to let the *world* burn for *you*."

What a fucking nutbag, I thought.

"But you left me with no choice. You forced me into this!" he cried, his words laced with unbridled anger.

"I didn't do shit." I spat back, struggling against his hold. "Let me go. Connor, let me go."

His fingers tightened against my scalp. "This is how it has to end," he whispered. "Forgive me for the cliché, but..."

He took a breath.

"If I can't have you, then no one can."

Just then, I felt the cold steel of the knife pressing against my neck. His breath was ragged and hot against my skin. I struggled against him, but he was too strong, too firm in his resolve.

Oh, fuck. Oh, shit.

He was going to kill me.

All my planning, all the classwork I'd turned in at school so that I could leave this place for good, money Nan had saved for me to do so, all the work Fouzia and I had done before I'd abandoned her because I truly believed I could best him. All that I'd done, and it was going to be screwed up because I *still* hadn't learned my lesson.

It clicked for me then, gazing into his cold, blue eyes, that perhaps he hadn't been so wrong. Maybe, in some twisted way, we were alike. It was our impulsivities that had gotten us both into this situation, after all.

Think. You're not in the woods anymore. You're not him.

I could be better.

I just needed one more second to *fucking think.*

Something caught my eye in the darkness, something shining a dim light off to the side. And that's when I saw her. Georgia Peterson in all her lifeless glory.

Warm blood began to spill down my chest as his knife pushed deeper, a tear of anguish falling down his cheek. My heart pounded like a drum, too stubborn to stop its rhythm yet.

The ghost of my mother raised her arm, slowly and intentionally, pointing her spectral finger towards Connor. Her eyes were locked on his leg.

Her message was clear, even in death.

And I remembered.

His leg. His bad leg. *Of course.* It was his one physical weakness, brought on by his own viciousness. I knew it, Patrick had known it, and my mother was trying to remind me now. My heart raced with fear as I focused on her ghost.

Then her arm moved, whipping outwards and striking an old, dusty vase off of its place on the crumbling mantle. The sound of the vase crashing into the floor rang out through the empty house and Connor flinched.

He turned to look at where the vase had fallen just as my mother faded out of sight. For that split second, I relished in how much regret he would have felt if he knew.

Friends in high places... I thought distantly before I bared my teeth and kicked out with my foot, aiming squarely for his left leg.

The heel of my shoe made contact and an agonized cry rang out in my ears. The knife clattered down to the kitchen tile, careening off the step and landing in the living room, much too far for me to reach. But I went anyway. Turning away from him, I leapt across the floor for the knife.

He grasped my ankle before my fingers could meet its handle and he yanked me backwards, my body dragging across the wood-paneled floor, old splinters piercing my stomach. I cried out, and tried to continue moving for the knife, but then he was on top of me, his face inches from mine.

"It doesn't have to be like this," he groaned, reaching out for the knife as he pinned me.

I wrenched my wrist from his grip and delivered a punch to his face. Before I could get out from under him, he returned the blow.

We fought like that for another minute, turning over again and again on the floor, clawing at each other's skin, fighting to the death. He got a hold of the knife, but I knocked it out of his hands, so it went flying to the other side of the room. He was closer. He took one look at me, and then bolted for it.

I almost ran after him, but stopped short.

Be smart, I reminded myself.

And I had been.

I ran the opposite way. I got down to my knees, and working as fast as I could, swung open one of the old kitchen cabinets and reached inside. My fingers wrapped around cold steel and wood, a smile spreading across my face.

Before that day, never had I been so glad to have had the closing shift.

I pulled out the shotgun. The very same one that had been hanging on the wall at the diner, the very same one I had pulled on Patrick and his friends that night, defending Connor.

Connor turned, the knife back in his hand, and widened his eyes when he saw me. He was leaning to the side, favoring his right leg. For a moment, he looked so weak.

And then he hardened again. "You think I don't remember that it's not loaded?" He quirked an eyebrow as if I was some bratty child, stupid enough to think that I could have outsmarted him. He began to stalk towards me with the knife.

I settled the gun on my shoulder and aimed.

"I lied."

Then I took the shot.

Chapter Thirty

It was, to say the least, a very strange thing to see the only boy you'd ever thought you could love lying on the floor, bleeding out from a shot you fired.

I knelt down beside him and watched as the light slowly left his eyes. I tried to feel something, I really did. I tried to prove him wrong. I tried to summon tears, so that he would know just before his consciousness left him that I was, and never would be like him. But my eyes remained dry

If I'd been more poetically inclined, I might have said something. We might have had a *moment*. But instead I just watched. There was nothing more he needed to know.

I thought I saw him smile just before he went slack.

It's over.

At last, it's over.

I set the shotgun down on the ground and released a breath. There would be no trial and no conviction. He was dead. He would not end any more lives. And that was enough for me.

I stood and walked over to the chair I had been tied to. I retrieved a napkin from my pocket and I wiped up the blood that I had spat onto the floor beside it. There couldn't be any evidence that I'd been here. That anyone had.

I picked up the discarded rope that he'd used to tie my wrists together and pocketed that as well. I went around the room, doing my best to clean up any possible signs of struggle. It was easy, considering the place hadn't exactly looked very picturesque before.

I then curled my hands under Connor's shoulders and dragged his body over to the kitchen cabinet. I leaned his back against it so he was sitting up, and then placed the shotgun in his lap, one end resting between his feet where he might have balanced it—had he been trying to kill himself—and the barrel pointing towards his chest where I'd shot him. The spot wasn't so far off from where he'd really died, so it looked as if the blood might have just poured across the floor overtime. And what did I care? No one was really going to look at the scene that closely. Not after what I did next.

I reached into the other pocket of my dress and pulled out a carefully folded note.

I bent down before him and plucked a similar piece of white paper tucked into his own pocket, the edges stained with blood. When I opened it, I found a very nicely written suicide letter, signed by my name.

Connor did have good ideas, I had to give him that. His only mistake had been his need to write them down.

Of course, I'd known about his plan to make it look as if I'd killed myself tonight—given I were to reject his offer. After reading his journal, I had been so impressed by it that I'd actually thought to take the idea for myself. Call it plagiarism, I didn't care.

And so, using a page of school notes that I'd stolen from his room, I saw fit to make my own letter. A rough imitation of his scrawl.

I took the letter I'd written for him and placed it gently beside his body. One day, whether it be in a week or a month, someone would find him lying here. Maybe they would send out a search party, and a volunteer mom would walk in the front door only to find his rotting body laying here with the shotgun between his legs. The police would then find the suicide note beside him, signed in his name, and the case would be closed before it even opened.

As for the gun, it had no serial number nor any unique aspects. I'd made sure it wasn't registered anywhere, and would have no ties to the diner or me. None verifiable, at least.

The only loose end was Laura, but something told me that she would keep her mouth shut. She'd gotten her money, and there would always be other boys. And if she did eventually decide to tell the police about what she'd written for him, my suicide note included, I would already be long gone.

Before I left, I checked his car to make sure that there was nothing else he'd left inside that would give anyone a notion of what his plan had been. Covering up his murder required covering up my own kidnapping. I took all the ropes and the weapons he had in the car, and then I left it for good.

Maybe one day I would realize he had been right all along. Maybe I would regret having not gone with him. A couple months ago, I would have taken his offer. I would have delighted at the opportunity to escape with someone as vicious as I was, to no longer have to restrain myself. But now?

Now, I had a concert to attend.

***

Fouzia's voice was audible before I walked into the gym. And once I was inside, it seemed to swallow me, ringing out like a bell. She rose above the crowd of students and teachers, the microphone held to her face as heaven spilled from her mouth.

For some reason, even after she'd told me that she was going to sing, it had never crossed my mind that she was *this good*.

Limping, I moved towards her siren-like sound and grabbed a chair sitting at the side of the gym. I dragged it over to the back of the crowd, where I could see her clearly, and then sunk onto it. My muscles relaxed, giving way to exhaustion.

I was well aware of how ridiculous I must have looked. I could feel a black eye blooming around my vision and every inch of my body ached with the results of my fight with Connor. Peeking beneath the skirt of my dress there was an abundance of cuts and bruises across my legs. I pulled my jacket tighter around me, covering the dried blood that still stuck to my chest and neck.

When I glanced up, I saw that one of the girls in front of me, wearing a sparkly black dress, was looking over her shoulder at me, making an odd face.

I followed her gaze to see a small splotch of bright red blood along the edge of my shoe. I bent down and wiped it off with my hand, then gave a small grin to the girl. She averted her eyes, noticeably paler than before.

Fouzia sang about uncertainty and the passage of time in her sparkling purple makeup that matched her mulberry dress. I thought it was fitting for the occasion, with graduation right around the corner for most of the students around me. I sat there calmly for the rest of her time, listening closely, enjoying the moment.

When she finished, I lifted my hand to my face to find that my cheeks were wet with tears.

Applause rang out through the gym, deafening but deserved. She stepped off the stage, her face aglow with pride. I had never seen her look so beautiful, her eyes glimmering like diamonds.

And then she spotted me, standing in the back, waiting for her. She approached me, her glow dimming.

"Ophelia." She said my name. Not in the way Connor had said it—like he was trying to prove a point, like he was desperate to do so. Fouzia said it softly, intentionally, she said it because she wanted to, not because she needed to. She somehow managed to make those few syllables as beautiful and melodic as her song. I wanted to melt away.

"You were amazing," I said. I was still crying, but I didn't care if she saw me do so. I didn't care if it seemed weak. There were many worse things I could be.

She came to stand in front of me, looking me up and down, taking me in. Something seemed to click into place in her mind. "You didn't."

I nodded gently.

"It's..." She struggled to find her words for a moment. "It's over?"

"It's done."

I'm not sure what exactly I had expected her to do here. I'd had images in my mind of her spitting at my feet, screaming at me in front of all the other students, making me swear that I would never show my face here again. I'd thought of how disappointed she would be with me when she found out. I'd considered trying to hide what I'd done. I'd dreaded this moment.

But she did not scream. She did not shun me. She did not shake her head with disappointment, and she did not leave. She grabbed me by the shoulders and pulled me against her, embracing me with her tight, trembling arms.

Her voice was no more than a whisper beside my ear. "Thank you."

She pulled away.

"I'm leaving now, Fou," I told her. "I came to hear your song and now I've got to go."

"Where?" She furrowed her brow.

"To the city. I've sorted everything out here and I'm going to go live my life. Really live it."

She looked me in the eyes and smiled. "You don't really know what you're going to do, do you?"

"Not a fucking clue."

She laughed. "If you wait, I'll come with you."

I was taken aback. "Really?"

She nodded.

"How long do you need?" I asked.

"If you can wait until morning...I've done everything I need to graduate already. If I just mail a couple letters, I'll be ready to go."

We ran out across the lawn like criminals into the night. Fouzia had to pick up the skirt of her dress so that it wasn't ruined by the damp grass as we ran, and I bundled up the back of it in my arms as she stepped into the cab. I closed the door behind her and ran around to the other side so I could fold the seat and stick my bike in. Then we sat beside each other with our hands locked as we drove back to her house.

When morning came, we called another taxi. Fouzia's parents tried to stop her. Her father yelled and her mother just wrung her hands, but Fouzia had turned eighteen in January. I had money to get the both of us out, our ride was waiting, and there was nothing they could do.

Before we left, we tore down the papers pinned to the board in her garage, erased all the chalk marks. It all came crashing down in a beautiful pile of garbage.

And so, with our suitcases and trunks filled with everything each of us owned, we drove away from Hinton.

When I glanced out the window of the cab, ghosts lined the streets, crowds of silent spirits standing on the sidewalks, watching me as I sailed away. I spotted my mother among them.

Unlike so many other times, I did not avert my gaze from them. I savored the sight. Somehow, I knew it would be the last I would see of any of my ghosts for a while.

I turned to Fouzia and told her everything.

About the Authors

Augusta Owens is an American living in Spain. She wrote her first book during the Covid lockdowns, at the age of thirteen. Her interests include singing, songwriting, all things art-related, and ghosts—obviously. This is her third published novel.

Douae Barghout is a young author of Berber Moroccan origin, also living in Spain. She enjoys learning about culture and languages, and her many hobbies eventually led her to discover a passion for writing. This is her first novel.

ALSO BY AUGUSTA OWENS

When her home is attacked by two strange girls, Amelia and her best friend, Sam, find themselves thrown into a new reality where witch-craft—and witches—are real.

Available wherever books are sold!

Want more?

@pepperbackpress

www.ingramcontent.com/pod-product-compliance
Lightning Source LLC
Chambersburg PA
CBHW061631190726
48289CB00006B/1562